In the Matter of *Isabel*

Paul A. Mendelson

The Book Guild Ltd

First published in Great Britain in 2017 by
The Book Guild Ltd
9 Priory Business Park
Wistow Road, Kibworth
Leicestershire, LE8 0RX
Freephone: 0800 999 2982
www.bookguild.co.uk
Email: info@bookguild.co.uk
Twitter: @bookguild

Typeset in Minion Pro

Printed and bound in Great Britain by CPI Group (UK) Ltd, Croydon, CR0 4YY

ISBN 978 1911320 876

British Library Cataloguing in Publication Data.
A catalogue record for this book is available from the British Library.

To my wonderful daughters, Zoë and Tammy, who are everything a father could wish for.

To my grandchildren Noah, Woody, Nancy and Arlo, for whom I wish everything.

And to the special person who was there when the story began and has always been there. Words can't begin...

AUTHOR'S NOTE

It's a long time since I practised law and handled (or mis-handled) the case that very loosely inspired this tale.

If I have taken certain liberties with the legal process, in the interests of storytelling, I hope any lawyers reading this will forgive me.

I have certainly taken liberties with the facts. Just in case any lawyers won't forgive me.

12 YEARS AGO

Ignorance of the lawyer is no excuse

When Evan Griffiths chose to slither into my poky office and show me his smile, bad news was never far behind. This much I remember. But I'm still not sure, all these years later, why the Welsh lizard was so disagreeable. I was hardly a threat. My colleague Leila used to say 'He's just being Evan' and I couldn't really argue with that. But he was being particularly Evan that morning.

"Hoy, Arnie Becker – boss wants to see you. Now!"

"Oh shit, the Dawlish thingy!" I swiftly grabbed a mayonnaise-smeared folder from the pile – probably not even the right client. Hence the LA Law jibe, which of course was way out of date even then. Tosser. "Evan, why are you the messenger?"

I knew why. He'd been having a smirkathon outside the boss's office, with his little friend Miss Collins, when the summons arrived.

"He's probably making a hostile bid for Apple and he wants your input, Rick."

Ha bloody ha.

It was getting pretty impossible to see Barney Cracknell these days and my small department – okay, me – was hardly his main concern. (I reckon it simply looked good on the Darcy, Cracknell website, which was more than he did.) But now that the man himself was actually summoning me, albeit for a bollocking, I could finally give him my long-simmering ultimatum. And probably lose my job.

I almost felled the unnecessary Evan on my way out of the office. And for once I didn't let scary Miss Collins stop me at the gates with her two heads and her bouncer's scowl. I was on a roll as I stormed determinedly in to plead my case – or as near to storm as I could manage with a door that solid.

"Barney, just one chance! Please? I've had it up to here with miserable, weepy... oh!"

That was when I saw her. And the past few months suddenly melted away.

12 YEARS AND
A FEW MONTHS AGO

Res ipsa something...

ONE

"I shouldn't be here," I told the back of his neck.

The prison guard just nodded, his new boots creaking as he walked us solemnly through the gate. *Yeah, yeah, heard it all before, sunshine.*

I remember the neck was boily. With everything that went on that extraordinary summer, with all I'm finally trying to get straight in my head after so many years, why am I recalling the pustular neck and noisy footwear of a jaded prison guard?

"It was my boss's fault," I moaned. "He got me into this."

More nods. Like it's always someone else's fault. His boots were making more conversation than he was.

"Still, won't be for long," I persisted. You can imagine the response that got.

Every cell I passed that miserable day was occupied. No room at the prison. I suppose technically it wasn't a proper prison, not in the Alcatraz/Parkhurst sense, but below-stairs at the Old Bailey was prison enough for me. Cramped and winding corridors, smelling of fear and pre-trial ablution, way down in the chilly, clanky part of the famous courthouse the tourist never sees.

I mention tourists because London was heaving with them that sweltering, heady summer. The summer of Isabel Velazco.

You had to battle your way through irrepressibly perky guides telling today's batch of foreigners in hi-viz tour hats, with cameras soldered to their faces, that old lady Justice on the top of the courthouse, the one with all the bling, isn't as blindfolded as you thought. And that she's witnessed some of the most horrid and evil criminals known to man. Or woman. Ever.

Why would you come to a great city like London and want to see a law court? I was a lawyer – okay, trainee-lawyer – and even I didn't want to be there. I was set on being in the sexy, corporate part of Darcy, Cracknell, Solicitors-at-Law (come on, we all were), not at the arse-end defending hopeless criminals.

That's what I had signed up for. City stuff. It's what the pricey, but so-smart, Top Man suit (thanks to a loan from my dad) and the hot-off-the-pig, leather briefcase (a gift from my mum) were all about. Plus the new Apple Mac (don't ask!). But Barney Cracknell, my unimaginative boss, apparently saw it differently.

I was already talking to Barney in my head that morning, giving him the sort of wittily merciless hard time you can only inflict when recipients are way out of range. Like when you're dragging yourself down a dingy walkway, past London's premier collection of the 'stitched-up, shafted and falsely-accused', to pay a final visit to your client. Before the fun starts for real.

Unfortunately for our Mr Flax he looked far too much like everyone's idea of a villain. Even in his tested and much-tried blue suit, with his face shaved to the bone and his over-gelled hair parted like the Red Sea. Each time I saw the man I couldn't help thinking he had probably worn his career-path imprinted on his face from the moment he was born. He might as well have had business cards that read Anthony Flax, GBH.

And we were expected to defend him. Well, not me personally – the barrister did the heavy-lifting – but she clearly wasn't here yet. Unless he had eaten her.

He stared at me like he wanted to kill me too.

"Morning, Mr Flax," I said pleasantly, "How you doing? Big day at last, eh?"

It's not easy making small talk with someone who's about to go down. You can't just chat about the weather, it only makes them feel worse.

"Where's my brief?" he asked.

I tried not to stare at his hands, although when people have words tattooed onto every finger, I'm reasonably sure they're expecting you to read them.

"Er… any minute," I guessed. "Could be stuck in traffic. It's murder out there."

I probably shouldn't have said that. I tried to check if I had received a message on my new Nokia camera-phone. (Which I was terrified he would steal.) No signal.

"*Jesus*, don't you hate this place?"

Probably shouldn't have said that either. I do remember words. Conversations. Not word for word, but pretty close. This and boily necks. But that's the thing about lawyering I didn't always take on board back then. One of the things. You have to think about every little word you say, just in case it comes out wrong. You're dealing with very sensitive people. Doctors probably feel the same way. And hostage negotiators.

If I had thought harder, I might have found it more prudent just to stick to the facts of the case. I know I didn't go to one of the top universities – regrettably, not even close – but I'm not stupid. Back then, however, I was more concerned about getting my own life on track than Mr Flax's. I had been banged-up in the firm's Criminal Department for months now, in fact ever since I started at Cracknell's, and I was getting stir-crazy. This wasn't what I had signed up for and I just wanted the case to be closed. The man was guilty as hell. It was written all over his face.

"Mr Flax," I began, "I've been sifting through all the evidence very thoroughly. Working really hard. Y'know, until late." Did I actually *say* that? "Even on weekends." Which wasn't even true. "And to be honest, counsel and I agree that it would probably go a lot better for you if you just pleaded guilty. Because of the CCTV footage. And the blood…"

I think it was then that he grabbed me by the throat. I recall his hands smelling strongly of a rather nice soap, which surprised me. As did his speaking voice, which was unusually soft and gentle for such a large man and deeply unsettling.

"Pardon?" he asked, as he pulled me towards him, although I think he heard. I felt I probably owed him an explanation, if he could kindly ease his grip on me the tiniest bit.

"You know what, Mr Flax," I squeezed out, "this isn't really my field. I'm more of a corporate lawyer, to be honest. It was my best subject. Mergers, acquisitions…"

In my own spotty defence, I had just turned twenty-three. Looking back on that summer, trying as forensically as I can to isolate the Rick Davenport that I was from the Rick Davenport I dearly wish I had been, there's a lot that makes me squirm. (And probably not just me.) But, as they say, that's the trouble with hindsight. Which is why I can only tell the full story now. After the event.

Why I feel impelled to do so is another matter.

My client took it as well as could be expected. "And here's me sold all my shares."

I heard a loud, electronic buzz at the exact moment that he flung me back into my chair, like a rejected ventriloquist's dummy, and I skittered speechlessly towards the wall.

I don't recall the name of my barrister, but she wasn't much older than me and sternly attractive, cleverly managing in her basic black to look both sombre and summery. Her face said well-bred and great genes the same way Mr Flax's said not a chance.

"I am so sorry I'm late, Mr Flax," she apologised between breaths, as the door slowly locked itself once more. She stared quizzically at me and my mortifying struggle to stay upright. Dignity would have gone out of the window, except there wasn't one. "Is everything… okay?"

"Ask Richard Branson here."

This was probably the moment when Mr Flax decided he was going to sack us and conduct his own defence. They've seen it on TV and apparently pleading guilty to a crime everyone knows you've committed, including your mum, goes against one of the Kray commandments.

In what seemed like seconds I was back on the overcrowded street, standing next to yet another excessively chirpy tour-guide. The grumpy barrister was slamming her papers, still bound with pink-ribbon, hard into my chest and stomping off back to her chambers round the corner to badmouth me to Tarquin or Piers or Davina. And most probably Barney Cracknell too.

Shit!

Tourists were all snapping away at me now. Like they'd just witnessed their very own courtroom drama. Of course their guide wasn't moving them on, but simply looking hugely grateful that I had brought a genuine glimpse of legal London to her South Korean 10am run. I decided to help her out.

"They might like to know," I whispered, "that whenever the late Lord Chief Justice Goddard passed a death sentence, he'd climax. Right there on the bench. Fact. They don't tell you that in the *Rough Guide*."

She started to giggle, which cheered me up a bit, considering I was about to phone fearsome Miss Collins – currently policing our offices on the Edgware Road – and demand an immediate appointment with the man himself. No more excuses. No fob-offs. No windows.

If he could spare the time.

TWO

"Darcy Crack-nelllll, kelp yoooo?"

I used to love the way she said that. I still replay it in my head some days.

Dimpy was our receptionist, around my age, chubbily pretty and my best friend at the firm. (I can't ever say that last word without thinking of the Tom Cruise movie. I suppose I'm of the generation of lawyers who count John Grisham as their major influencer – although I probably shouldn't have led with that at my interviews.) Her mum made the best vegetarian pakoras I ever tasted.

"Darcy, Crack-nelllll *and* Davenport, kelp yoooo?" I sang, as I steamed into our compact but reasonably plush reception, causing the morning's glum assortment of clients to look up from ancient, third-hand Hellos they were reading.

"Yeah, that'll happen, Rick."

I couldn't stop to chat. I had to dump a now sadly redundant Flax file in my office, force down the hot and leaky tuna-melt ciabatta I'd grabbed on the way in and make that meeting. The one that would change my life forever. Possibly.

I said 'office' just now, but I've seen Wendy-houses that are more spacious. When you receive sympathetic looks from people who are about to spend their next few years in Wormwood

Scrubs, you know you aren't exactly the high-flyer you lead people to believe. (Including your own long-term girlfriend. *Mea culpa.*)

Two things happened simultaneously: the skinny Welshman slid in to smirk, waving a thick document in my face, and Sophie called me on my mobile.

"Jackson Holdings. Big boys' law."

"Wanker."

That wasn't Sophie – she was asking me if I'd been to see Barney yet and telling me once again that it was time he did for me exactly what he'd promised. (Or what I had told her he'd promised. *Mea maxima culpa.*)

I answered both with a single, but not unimpressive, half-truth. "Love to chat but Barney's just called me in for a heavy meeting."

That shut smarmy Evan from Carmarthen up. I'm sorry, but I didn't like him. He was a year older than me and a head taller, thin as a toothpick, with a throbbing adam's apple like a snake had just swallowed a chicken, but he was Barney's golden boy and a seriously sharp lawyer, so looking back it probably wasn't the Welsh bit.

Naturally, Sophie was sweeter. She wished me a touchingly confident good luck then I heard her fingers resume their familiar keyboard tap. We swiftly arranged exactly when and where we'd meet up that evening, to see yet more flats. And, of course, 'celebrate'. She was more efficient than I would ever be. And she could type while she was talking.

Fortunately Leila, my only other friend in the firm (I wasn't unpopular, it just wasn't a very big firm), was coming out of our conference room with a client, as I shot past. Leila was a smart, black lawyer in her thirties, startlingly deep-voiced, with a genuine warmth that came off her like a scent.

She specialised in commercial property, which was probably as boring as it sounds, but she was so far from that, once you got to know her. She had a dangerous sense of humour and a dirty laugh that rumbled up from her boots and she had been kind to me from the start. Right now she was nodding vigorously towards the half-eaten ciabatta that still oozed cheesily from my hand, yet making it look like she was acknowledging every word her client said.

Shit!

I chewed and swallowed and wiped and thanked in one seamless routine as I headed towards Joan Collins.

That really was her name and probably always would be. Its careful owner was Barney's long-time personal assistant, pit-bullishly loyal and protective, the type you'd think a boss's wife might choose in order to make certain he wouldn't stay late at the office. I know this sounds sexist and cruel, and I do appreciate that she had probably endured a truly sad and lonely life, looking after an ailing mother whilst quietly nursing a never-to-be-requited love for her oblivious boss. But none of that was my fault and I loathed her.

"He's got a lunch." She showed me his diary.

"That's okay. So've I." I showed her the inside of my mouth. How to win friends…

I steamed into Barney's office, trying to appear a lot more confident than I felt. If Barney had even bothered to look.

The room could have eaten mine as a starter. It was a cavern of dark, panelled wood with shelves heaving with law-books he had probably bought in a job-lot, because I never caught him opening one, and which may well have been glued together over a secret door that led straight out to this year's Jag. There were photos too, of the man himself with minor celebrities, whose cases he must have handled and clearly, from the smug smiles on their faces, won.

And a fuck-you desk. Not small and bowing like mine, with papers everywhere. And not millennium-sale-at-Ikea like mine either. No self assembled this one – unless the self was a master-carpenter commissioned to tailor it around a thick-thighed, pot-bellied solicitor, who dressed to the left of his solid brass drawer-handle.

He didn't change his posture a smitch as I came in. Favouring me with a view of his huge, humpty-dumpty shaped head, with its soft, baby-like strands of blond hair, he continued to read the document clamped in his hand. It was a curiously prissy, manicured hand, with its porky pinky sporting a diamond-centred gold ring. Taste no object, as my best friend Oliver Rosen would say.

I waited, which is what you were supposed to do, until the great man spoke.

"Know the secret of being a good solicitor?" I said nothing – I wasn't meant to. "Course you don't, you little pisser." Told you. "Probably never will. It's making the client feel you're here just for him."

"Like a high-class hooker... in a way." Into thin air.

"Opened this an hour ago," he said, waving the document. I could see the yellow streaks from his highlighter, barely dry. "Client'll think I've read nothing else all week. Do that and you're fired."

O-kay. Now or never.

"I want a move, Barney."

You could call him Barney. It made him feel we were working in a benevolent dictatorship and were all one big, happy family. Although, thinking back, I probably should have said 'please'. But his response threw me.

"Firms?"

Shit. Again.

"NO!!" I explained, the panic rising. "I'm a corporate lawyer, Barney!" Now he looked up. "Trainee," I amended. "It's all I ever wanted to do. It's my... skill-set." I pointed to his solid door and the great, gleaming financial world that thrummed beyond. For which, admittedly, an equally solid aptitude was still waiting to be revealed. "Evan's got—"

"Evan's got an upper-second from Cambridge." True. "You've got cuff-links." Also true. Gold ones, from my dad's late father. The only thing he left me, aside from alone outside The Grapes in Hackney, when he went in to get 'bladdered' with his mates.

I should point out that Barney wasn't born with that silver spoon either and he made his own way up the legal ladder by the sheer force of his unpleasant personality. I was sure I had what it takes to do the same.

"Ever been to The Ivy?" Where did that come from? "Tomorrow."

"The Ivy?" I echoed. "The *restaurant* The Ivy? Barney – you're taking me to The Ivy tomorrow?" I couldn't believe it.

"No, I'm off to The Ivy now. And you move tomorrow. It was a *non sequitur.*" I shook my head. "I listen to my people." Even if he never actually remembered their names.

He rose from his desk with a grunt, like a pin-striped, albino hippo. But I didn't care – I was moving tomorrow. Bye bye Bailey. So long GBH. Thank you, Mr Cracknell.

"Hope your Family Law's better than your criminal," he muttered.

The air froze.

Family Law? The Kleenex Files! What the f—?

"What the f— sorry, Barney, I'm a bit confused."

"My guy's leaving," he continued, "which is a shame, because he's a real bastard. But you're not getting his office – or his salary."

"*Family!*" I think I yelped it. "Barney – me? Family?"

Now he was looking at me. But not in a benevolently dictatorial way. "Listen, sunshine, I gave you this job as a favour to Cyril Rosen." My best-mate's dad, how could I forget? "But it ain't like he saved my life in the war."

With that he was off to his posh trough, pausing only to warn me that if I screwed-up one more time, I was out of there. My sombre-yet-summery barrister had obviously made her report.

As the door opened I caught Evan and Joan Collins (no

relation) sharing a nourishing lunchtime gloat. Bad news travelled fast.

I felt my sharp new suit begin to sag.

THREE

I could hear the accordion before my old MG had even turned the corner. Summer in Hackney. Windows wide-open, sounds of *Emmerdale* and domestics and life all competing for bandwidth. Along with my beloved car possibly coughing out her last, sad breaths.

She was green, she was beautiful and she was costing me a bloody fortune. I only mention the MG because she's a player in the story. To be honest, I wasn't particularly interested in cars. But I was interested in how much more interesting I could seem with an interesting car.

As for the accordion, it isn't hard to replay that particular sound memory – I had heard it since before I was born.

My mother is a teacher and I could tell immediately that this was one of her pupils, but don't ask me which one; there've been hundreds over the years. All ages and sizes, all gaining a working proficiency in what had to be the saddest instrument known to man. But it must have been music to my dad's ears. He was totally besotted with Mum. So much so that he once let her teach him to play, even though – as our neighbours will attest – he didn't have a musical bone in his body. Ron and Wendy Davenport, late bloomers, still squeezing.

Dad was a genuine Hackney Cabbie and he was under his

precious motor as I quit the ailing MG. But of course I couldn't see him, so when he just popped up, all five-foot-four of him, brandishing the thick Swiss Army knife he seemed to use for every eventuality, he scared the crap out of me.

"*Jesus,* dad!"

"You need that sorted, son. I'll do it."

I'd take a lift from my father anytime but I'd never let him near the MiG. (I know that's a Russian fighter, but it sounded good to me back then. A lot of things sounded good to me back then.)

"No thanks. I'll get it done." I insisted. "Won't be cheap though."

"You can afford it now, Mr Mergers and Acquisitions." God help me, I didn't say a word. "Ooh, Rick," he segued delightedly, "I found a whole new way of getting from Liverpool Street Station right through to Dalston Kingsland. Fact."

I hadn't bothered to tell my mum and dad that on the very first day I arrived at Cracknell's, Barney had dumped me into Criminal. There seemed absolutely no need to mention it, as I was convinced it was only temporary and they had already bought me the briefcase. As things turned out it was indeed only temporary, so in a cruel and devastating way I was right.

I recognised the tune as soon as we walked through the door and into accordion hell. It was, bizarrely, 'The House of the Rising Sun', which I suspect my mum thought was about an east-facing Louisiana bungalow as she was fearlessly singing along.

"'*And it's been the ruin…*' – Samantha, *fingering!*"

I imagine Samantha-fingering looked like they all did. Earnest, diligent, a little pigtailed head nodding almost to the beat, equipped with everything but the gift.

"'*of many a poor boy…*'"

It wasn't exactly a private lesson. Samantha may have been the only accordionist, but there were toddlers everywhere – on the floor, in crusty high-chairs and flaking playpens, dribbling and crying and pooing, like a Primark-clad infestation. My mother was also a childminder. I would have said in her spare time, but my sixty-one-year old mum didn't have any spare time.

Or space.

"Hi love, oh be careful of Caris."

I wasn't sure whether Caris was a child, a treasured doll or an STD, but I froze where I was on the shagged-out carpet, just in case.

Not that I would have been that bothered if I had squashed a kid. When I tell people I'm an 'only', it feels like only half the truth. I had shared most of my waking moments, from as far back as I could remember, with other people's see-you-later-dollface children and I was afraid there might be an awkward conversation to be had with Sophie some day, assuming Sophie was thinking of being the mother of my kids. Which I had a feeling she was, work permitting.

I rarely more than glanced at my mum. She was just there. Though never a snazzy dresser – floral usually did it for her – I do recall that her hair was newly-crisped-and-curled into exactly the same style every week, sitting atop her round, pale face like a bag of brandy-snaps spilled over a large scoop of vanilla. This was her one bit of vanity, aside from the accordion diplomas covering the cracks in the walls.

I knew Wendy Davenport must be a warm person, because everybody would warm to her, but at the time I just found her and my father intensely irritating.

As for parental pride, I couldn't ever be with her or my dad without getting the full Klieg. They even had my law-degree framed above the mantelpiece, next to the blown-up A-Z page with our street on it. (In this dawning age of satnavs and Googlemaps, my dad was a resolute A-Z man). Thankfully nobody close to them had been to university, so most thought a 'third' was as good as it gets.

Linda certainly did. She was Mum's hairdresser and it was as if somebody had taken a look at our overpopulated living-room and decided that what that tiny, unused corner near the window really needed was a big and busty, good-humoured woman with a portable dryer and a constantly morphing head of hair.

"Love the hair, Linda," I lied.

"Oh thanks, Ricky. I did it myself," she beamed. "You made partner yet?"

"Only a matter of time, girl."

That wasn't me, obviously. I wasn't that crass. But my dad was that crass. So far as I could tell, my parents were nauseatingly content, even though they were forever stretched and struggling, yet they made that basic equation of happiness with wealth which seemed a requisite part of wanting better for your children. Who was I to disappoint them?

"I bet your Sophie's proud, eh?"

I didn't feel like answering, not about that, even though Linda was a lovely person and a criminal hairdresser, who didn't deserve to be ignored. So I looked out onto our small back-garden, a two-finger job from those of us in sixties social-housing to our more prosperous neighbours in their rapidly-appreciating (but garden-less) Victorian flats. I was hoping for just a touch of newly-mown, grass-green solace.

What I got was Gerald.

Gerald was ten years old and everyone figured that ten would be a magic number in his life. Ten weeks for shoplifting, ten months for assault, ten years for murder. It was like looking at my Mr Flax as a child. But without the charm. The boy was out there in plain sight, kicking the heads off Mum's precious flowers with his soccer-boot.

"She's had my Gerald all day," explained Linda.

"They ban him from school again?"

"Yeah. Bless."

I had no idea that day how involved Gerald would become in my life and that of Isabel Velazco. (Fortunately, neither had she.) I just knew that I had to make my escape before Hackney's last genuine urchin saw me and latched on like an unwanted pup.

"Your dad's doing us a carbonara tonight," enthused my mum.

I turned from the window and banged straight into Threadbear. He was a gigantic teddybear, twice the size of an average toddler, who had seen better days and a drawerful of eyes, but whom generations of kids throughout East London had adored to furry pieces. (He gets involved too. It's a family affair.) I kicked him, not too gently, into a tower of Lego.

"Sounds lovely, Mum, but no time for food." I threw her one of my endearing parent-smiles. "I told Sophie I'd meet her – she's booked us in to see some more flats."

My parents exchanged looks of quiet disappointment, which I put down to supper-rejection, but I now reckon was because it had finally dawned on them that kids don't stay home forever. Unless they're really sad.

I couldn't resist my exit line – for Linda's sake. "Then I'll practise my fingering."

The whoop followed me as I fled the room.

FOUR

Isabel was probably booking her flight around that time. Or maybe she was already on the plane. It's harder to remember the stuff you never knew.

If she was on the plane, I'm imagining two things quite clearly. Okay three things, because it's her legs I can picture, those long, tanned, muscular legs compacted into her economical airline seat for that incredibly long flight. Quite possibly behind some huge, sagging bottom – three times the size of her own – using the recline facility for all its inconsiderate, long-haul worth. Bastard.

The other thing in my mind is a small, furry giraffe, a bit faded and fondled, that she was carrying with her when she arrived. I can see it just flopping out of the scarred and bulging leather handbag that would be under her feet, giving her even less legroom. Or maybe 'Rafa' was in her hand, constantly winding through her fingers like a fluffy rosary, offering her some snatched-at comfort and a tiny bit of hope, now that she was finally on her way.

But what the hell do I know? I was in a heaving Hoxton wine bar that evening, celebrating my elevation to dizzy and mythical corporate heights with Sophie and some of her pals from the events company where she worked and thrived.

We had seen yet another flat that wasn't suitable, at least not to me. But Sophie had that special gift of making people feel she was genuinely interested in what they were saying – or selling – whereas I couldn't even make people in whom I was genuinely interested feel that way.

Yet perhaps my resolute ambivalence that evening was because, as I kept explaining to her, I was still on trial at work and the expected rise wouldn't come through until I had proven my worth. As I inevitably would. (The trial bit was true enough.)

She was very sweet and patient. It wasn't about the money with Sophie – she simply wanted me to have what I wanted. Which, I confess, was the money.

She was being so decent that I couldn't help wondering why I hadn't just told her the truth. I don't think I could have taken the unbidden waves of disappointment rippling over that pretty, summer-freckled face, nor her girls' minor private-school, chin-up consolation. It had been hard enough fessing-up when I was dumped that first grim day into Criminal. (I do realise that running a West End family-law department wasn't the exact equivalent of shelf-stacking at Asda, but neither was it my field of dreams.)

I watched her through the fashionably-underpowered lighting, over my half-empty (half full? No, half-empty) pint. Sophie gave me all the light I needed, especially when she was with her flashy workmates and showing me off, which she seemed genuinely to enjoy, although I'm still not totally sure why. I only know that it was mutual – there was nothing like a great-looking, natural blonde with a lovely body and terrific Home Counties teeth, (just enough overbite to be sexy rather than neglected) to make you feel good about yourself. Which is something I felt far less often than I might have wished in those days, but I suspect wasn't that uncommon for guys of twenty-three. Was it?

"Ching ching."

One of her posh pals from Maine Events, rubbing his fingers together like a demented locust to mark my financial elevation. I just wanted to smack him. But I took it like a businessman. And tried not to think that tomorrow's business would be divorce, divorce, divorce.

Then I saw Oliver.

Oliver Rosen – son of the aforementioned Cyril – was my oldest friend. And, aside from me, probably the most pivotal grown-up in this story. Which surprised us both, as we had never considered ourselves to be pivotal to anything. Or grown-up.

Oliver and I had been at school together, the only difference being that his parents had a choice, and for reasons that still baffle me, but are something to do with socialism, they selected our area's gang-ridden comprehensive. Where bullying was a core subject and my podgy friend was quite often coursework.

We'd both had ambitions to become lawyers (well, I probably did because he did) but Oliver had chosen the predictable route of joining his father's suburban practise. It was through him that I'd met Sophie. She and Oliver had shared a house at their uni, which was a whole lot better than my uni. I sometimes think that he wished he hadn't introduced us, because in doing so he relegated himself to 483rd most likely person she would sleep with, down from his hopeful 482nd seeding.

I'm not saying Oliver wasn't fanciable and wouldn't have made a wonderful partner to someone. I'm just saying that back then I couldn't quite picture who that person might be. You tend to imagine your pals' likely soul-mates as basically them in a wig (okay, I do) and I was sure that somewhere out there was a chubby, dishevelled Jewish girl with appalling dress sense and colossal sexual frustration, but possessed of a fine brain and an enormous heart. We just hadn't found her yet.

I needed to talk to Ollie but his eyes were currently at a size that couldn't solely be accounted for by his industrial-strength glasses. He was focussing them, as ever, on badly-lit but attractive young women who sadly wouldn't fancy him poached. I managed to step into his line of vision just as Sophie grabbed my arm again.

"What do you think of our City whiz-kid, Ollie?"

Who says whiz-kid? Only Sophie, which is sort of cute and embarrassing at the same time.

"I never thought Barney would let him anywhere near it," said Oliver, which was sort of true and embarrassing at the same time.

Yet he does know my Mr Cracknell. Not intimately, but as Barney insisted on reminding me, it was Oliver's dad who finally managed to find me a job with the great man – a suburban associate of his – when all other avenues weren't just closed but cordoned off, evacuated and condemned.

"My dad *also* never thought in a million years…"

"Yes, okay Ollie."

Oliver's voice gains volume when he drinks, with the tact-level diminishing in the same increments. He keeps telling me that Jews don't really drink – but he only mentions it with a glass in his hand. And only in pubs, restaurants and the odd 'simcha', which means party or celebration, that he blags me into as his best 'goy' friend.

"Well, your dad was wrong," said Sophie, stroking her old friend's cheek with such affection that it went red instantly and I could only guess where else she had sent his blood flowing. "Gotta just say hello to someone, Ricko. Then maybe we should be going, yes?"

With that tease of more celebrations, she was off. As soon as she was out of earshot, I told him.

"He gave me fucking Family, Ollie!"

It took a while for the bad news to sink in. "I do 'fucking Family'!" he said.

"You *like* people, Oliver!" Dear God, wasn't it obvious?

26

"You lied to Sophie!" What could I say, other than 'Keep your voice down'? "*And* to me!" he persisted, as if this were worse.

"I will tell her," I said, quietly. "Course I will. It just has to be the right time." Even quieter. "You know she earns more than me? Not that it…"

I looked around the crowded wine bar. The suits, the wads, the laughter. Winding themselves down as they wound each other up. It felt like they'd all gathered there just to rub it in. My smile was beginning to hurt.

"Barney's never going to transfer me, is he?" I said, suddenly plummeting to that place where dreams go to die. "I should move to one of the big City firms." I rally fast.

Oliver stared at me, eyebrows raised. He didn't need to say anything. "Took you two years to get the Cracknell gig. And that was only because of my dad."

He really didn't need to say anything.

"How do you stand it, Ollie?" I asked, with genuine interest. "Family."

"You haven't started yet." He tried to smile reassuringly, as I drained my glass. "Rick, you may like it, you never know."

I did know. Without being overly pessimistic, tomorrow marked the beginning of the end of my life. And, as I recall, I had to try extra hard with Sophie that night, just to prove to her – and to myself – that things weren't so bad.

I didn't fake the orgasm. Just the bits on either side.

FIVE

If you want to be put off marriage for life, spend a week in the office of a family lawyer.

There I was, barely out of college and professionally unqualified, sitting at my shabby desk in my equally embarrassing workspace, a few musty inches from people who were invariably a good deal older than me and possibly even more depressed. Trying gamely to steer them back to the legal stuff (about which I knew nothing) and away from what sort of bastard their spouses had been and how they'd already known as they'd walked down the aisle that they were making the biggest mistake of their lives. And the pig/swine/cow/bitch is going to give me everything they've got/not getting a penny/should step on a mine.

As the days crawled by, the clients blended into one black hole of abject misery. Theirs and Rick Davenport's. But there are a couple I do still remember and should probably name-check, because they kept impinging cluelessly on the Isabel case.

The first one, Mrs Armitage, was hitting the Kleenex at her introductory appointment. She must have been in her mid-forties, which for me just put her in sub-group 'old'. The drab woolly cardigans, even on the hottest summer days, didn't help.

I remember that she began with halting apologies for

coming in during my lunch-hour, which she probably intuited because it was one o'clock and because I was eating a ham and cheese panini. I suppose it was a bit insensitive, but I was always ravenous by this time. I wouldn't have done it had it been Ramadan or Yom Kippur. I'm not a total moron.

"So you began to grow suspicious when your husband would come home very late at night." I was reading aloud what I had just written, which helps to get them back on track when they're sobbing for Britain.

"He said he'd been working overtime," she moaned, clutching her bag with both hands.

"And you didn't believe him."

She tapped my yellow pad really hard. "He's a milkman, Mr Davenport."

Law is about joining the dots. But it can be more difficult when you're a rookie and also when you don't give a toss.

The angry Irishman – a ruddy-faced crag of a fellow with equally angry red hair – was more straightforward. "I want you to screw her, Mr Davenport." He leaned over my desk until his face was barely millimetres from mine. Even his nose-hairs were angry. "I want you to screw her like she fucking screwed me."

There's no real answer to this, but I soon discovered there was one stock response that would unfailingly send clients out of my dismal office and onto the considerably higher-ply carpeting in a far better state of mind than when they had entered.

"I'm putting your case right on the top of my pile, Mr Ryan. 'Screw Mrs Ryan'. See, right on top."

If you had shot one of those speeded-up films of *Rick's Day in the Office*, it would have looked like that game you play with kids when you lay your hand on top of one of theirs, then they slip their other hand on top of yours and so forth until it all ends in a slapfest. My mum plays it with all her kids and they never fail to laugh hysterically.

I was hysterical too. But I wasn't laughing.

***

Three weeks later, just when I was ready to slit my wrists with a decree absolute, Isabel Velazco walked into my life. And onto the top of my pile.

SIX

"Ah, Mr Davenport. This is Ms Velazco." Insert scuzzy Cracknell client-smile. "Or should I say, '*Señorita*?'"

She leaned slowly round in her chair. The patent surprise on her face was instantly mirrored and magnified by the eye-widening, lip-clamping shock screaming silently out from mine.

Isabel Velazco was a creature – a being – for whom not a single moment of my twenty-three year Hackney existence could possibly have prepared me. She was less a person at that moment than an event and like nothing I had ever experienced, nor had the temerity to hope that I might. I've had time to think on this since and adjectives just don't hack it.

Imagine, say, being at one of those local authority life-drawing classes, the sort in which my mum used occasionally to enrol, and suddenly the Mona Lisa lady sweeps in and takes her coat off. Or, if we're talking bodies, the Venus de Milo, although admittedly this would be a bit more difficult.

I can remember exactly what she was wearing. It was something orange. A bright orange two-piece suit made of a sort of shiny material. Probably not expensive, given what I soon discovered to be her circumstances, but she made it look like she had just nipped off her catwalk for an hour or two to make a lawyer's appointment. Alright, she wasn't as tall and skinny as a model, which was actually fine with me. And she was perhaps too old – I reckoned definitely mid-thirties – but she had clearly worn well.

I was probably staring. I know I was staring. Who wouldn't? But my first impression, once the glorious shock had subsided, was how come someone with a demeanour so cold could look so hot? Perhaps not cold so much as sad, distant, almost bereft. Yet curiously there was a simmering anger too in that beautifully unusual, finely-sculpted face, a face crafted by someone who clearly knew what he was doing and wasn't going for just your standard supermodel-stunning. With eyes so fiery they almost matched her outfit. If this makes her sound like a tigress, then perhaps it isn't so far off the mark.

Unfortunately the woman was looking at me like I was Barney Cracknell's schoolboy son and it was Bring Your Kids To Work Day.

"Mr Davenport here is the rising star of our Family Law department."

Even though it was total cobblers – Barney had no idea what I was up to and neither, of course, had I – it made sense to go along with the unexpected big-up. So I put on my professionally-concerned face, the one I had perfected over the past few tedious weeks.

"Divorce, is it?" I asked, solicitously.

She uttered only three words in response, and these in such a quiet, wistful tone that they barely carried, but I found them the most exotic sounds I had ever heard.

"No. Not divorce."

Now I understood why Barney had said 'señorita'. She was Italian. Or Spanish. Or something. Which accounted for the naturally rich, glowing tan that began on her face and glided all the way down her slender arms and those gorgeous, muscular legs. And definitely didn't come out of a spray-can.

Barney was standing now and gently encouraging our new client to join him in the process.

As she unfolded I could see that she stood taller than she actually was, if this makes sense. It's all about posture, I suppose. And of course some seriously raunchy high-heels. Her fashionably cut, shimmering hair, which brushed across her face as she turned, was – well at least to me – unexpectedly fair. Not blonde but certainly not as dark as I might have expected, with a delicate trace of red. Perhaps it was dyed, who knows? Yet it seemed totally right, as if her miraculous face, tan and all, could lead you only in that direction.

For some reason Barney, looking so pasty in her orbit, was keen to get rid of her, while my goal had suddenly become to stay with her for as long as humanly possible. I had totally forgotten why I had originally stormed in.

"I'll let Mr Davenport go through the nuts and bolts," said my smarmy boss, giving her his full end-of-session beam. He concluded with the trademark clammy hand on her back. "But rest assured, señorita, every case receives my personal attention. You won't find this service in Rio."

Ah. Rio.

"Buenos Aires," she corrected.

Ah. Buenos. Where exactly was…?

Barney just shrugged. "Safe hands, señorita."

He drew me aside, as she walked uncertainly towards Miss Collins' desk. "Don't waste any time on it," he warned, quietly. "Legs but no assets."

As the door clicked shut, we found ourselves beside his grimacing and considerably homelier PA (which was probably why she was grimacing), neither of us having the vaguest clue as to what to do next. I felt like Guy Fawkes Night had just begun in my lower bowel, but if there was ever a time to be coolly authoritative…

"We'll take that coffee now, Joan," I said to the confused

woman and walked my best-ever client towards reception.

'So. Buenos Aires, eh?" I began. Just to get the ball rolling.

"It's in Argentina."

Thank you.

"Yes, I know," I said. I had thought it was somewhere in that direction.

I had never even met a South American, let alone acted for one. This was just getting better and better and I remember wishing above anything that there was someone around to whom I could show and tell.

We were on our way to my office, passing an unashamedly fascinated Dimpy, when I saw Evan standing there. Leering. Even though it wasn't a million miles from what I was doing, it still pissed me off. But I suddenly panicked, as reality flooded back in.

My office!

It was absolutely no place for someone like this. It was somewhere a squirrel would be ashamed to hide his nuts and could shatter my 'rising-star' cred before I had even got started. So I swiftly steered my vision in orange back towards reception.

"Dimpy, is the conference room free?"

"It is at the moment, 'Mister' Davenport." Bless her.

"Fine. Absolutely no calls. This way, señorita."

I could feel my colleagues' eyes like skewers, as I flung open the doors to the small but pukka meeting-room. More dark, shiny wood, especially on the long and I had to assume expensive table. With fading old prints framed on the walls and fresh yellow writing-pads next to the plates of good biscuits.

Then I heard that soft, throaty voice again. "Please, Mr Davenport, not señorita."

I responded loudly. "And you can call me RICHARD". And closed the door.

***

It's quite a stretch making someone feel at ease in a room you've never actually set foot in yourself. But I believe I did all the right things, pulling a chair out for her, trying my best to open a window, pushing the good-biscuit plate her way.

"What's Buenos like this time of year?" I asked. "Bet it's even hotter than…"

"I want my little boy back."

Excuse me?

Even as I tried to fathom what she had just said, I somehow sensed, with the fragments of my brain still thankfully working, that this was seriously uncharted territory. And potentially quite scary. But I couldn't just sit there, so I grabbed a yellow-pad, took out the shiny new Parker that hairdresser Linda had given me – and that her tyke Gerald had probably 'sourced' – and got down to business.

"Right. Full name? Your full name." Davenport on the case.

"Isabel Maria de Alences Velazco." Bloody hell. "V-E-L-A-Z-C-O." Thank you.

"My son is Sebastian. Sebastian Menzies. M-E-N-Z-I-E-S."

"That's an English name."

'My ex-husband would say Scottish."

Now I understood. "That's how come you speak so well."

"No. English we learn at school."

"Yeah? With us it's French. Or Spanish, actually." I was getting into the rhythm. "Spanish is becoming very—"

"I meet my husband – Laurence – in Buenos Aires. He is there for his work."

She stopped suddenly and I realised that I was simply staring at her moving lips – which weren't her worst feature – when I should have been writing all this down. So I wrote all this down.

"We marry and we come to live in London."

"London. Ah, you live here now?"

"No, I live in Argentina. Please. Shut up. Our son, he is born here. He is just nine years old. The marriage it went wrong – this happens – so we divorce. You are not married?" She didn't wait for a response. "Of course not. Three years ago I take Sebastian back with me. To 'Buenos'. Laurence agree to this. HE AGREE! He is all the day and the night with his work, his companies. He has no time for his little boy."

I thought I might have heard of this Laurence Menzies. But I didn't have long to mull on it, as moments later her chair was clattering noisily onto its side and our best chocolate biscuits were sliding at some speed along the polished wood and onto the floor. She was up and leaning over the table with a scary look on her face. She didn't pick up the biscuits.

"*Che*! I cannot sit like this! Like a goddam dinner-party!"

I'm almost sure that she didn't raise her voice, yet it felt like an earthquake. I don't think I had ever seen a grown woman angry. Sophie would get pissed-off when a boss would patronise her and my mum would be fed up with my dad when he decided to do an early airport run and woke her up. But anger of this intensity – never. I found it quite disturbing and my body reacted with an involuntary jolt.

It was pretty clear that the anger hadn't bubbled up from nowhere. It must have been simmering in Barney's office and probably for the past however many weeks it was since she had last seen her son. Perhaps even watching me walk into the office had kicked it off – she was doubtless expecting Barney himself to take her case. Or maybe she was just being South American, it was hard to know.

She looked at me apologetically. "I am sorry," she said.

I just shrugged. Happens all the time.

"Last year," she continued, more calmly, "he came to Argentina. My ex-husband. To see Sebastian. Good – the man is his father. So this time he ask me to send him here. A few weeks at Christmas in his new house. He has a new wife also. A younger, *English* wife."

I was just processing how 'English' could sound like the worst thing you could call someone, when I noticed her examining the

36

framed prints on the wall. She moved like silk, those legs that went on forever gliding across the floor on stylish but far from ridiculous heels. The prints were of old buildings and a river with some boats on it. By squinting I could just read the word 'Cambridge'. Barney must have bought them for show, as I was almost certain he had never studied there.

"So I send Sebastian for a long vacation. It is good for me also. My mother, she was very sick. And I am only child."

"Oh, me too!" I said. Like she cared.

"He never c…" Her voice drifted off, so I couldn't hear.

"Sorry? I didn't quite…"

"*My little boy. He never came back!*"

"Oh." This was getting bloody complicated. "So… your husband held onto him."

She didn't respond.

The door opened – it was Dimpy needing the conference room. Evan had apparently booked it a week ago. Typical.

She took a swift look at my new client, who was now leaning against the window with her head down, long, manicured fingers pressed against an impossibly high-boned cheek, quietly sobbing and spent. It was as if someone had switched her off. Dimpy's sweet face seemed to dissolve into mush as she turned to stare quizzically at me. Like it was my fault.

"It's the effect I have on women," I said quietly, to lighten the mood.

Dimpy just shook her head and retreated.

I picked up my pad, coughing authoritatively. It was time for me to set in play a whole new style of lawyer-client consultation, one that I had made up on the spot and which was to become our own special M.O., as my old criminal colleagues would say. At least the posier ones did.

After all, what did the sobbing señorita know about English legal custom – she was from a different hemisphere.

I think.

SEVEN

"You bring all your clients to the park?"

I skimmed another stone across a gleaming Regents Park's boating lake, luckily just missing an afternoon rower in a small boat. I didn't answer directly.

"I come here a lot, Ms… Velcro. Especially when I've a tricky legal problem to solve." I paused, thoughtfully. "Maybe it reminds me – you know – of Cambridge."

She looked at me and I realised I had stopped breathing.

"You were at the university?"

She seemed impressed. I'd be impressed too. I exhaled a bit exuberantly, put on my RayBans and continued digging my hole.

"Cantab? Oh yes," I said, with an air of nostalgia. "A good while back. Before I became a qualified solicitor." (Just in case she still thought I was twelve. Or just a trainee. Or anything I really was.) "Thank God a double-first in Family Law still counts for something."

I'm not a pathological liar – at least I don't think I am – but having told a van-load of porkies to my parents and Sophie for the past few weeks, the stuff kept cascading out of me. It must be the same when a one-time murderer becomes a multiple. Once you've taken that important baby-step.

"I am dancer."

Where did that suddenly come from?

She must have caught me staring at her legs. Or maybe she simply wanted to move things on by providing more background information. I took my notepad out anyway, just in case.

"Uh huh. What sort of dancing do you do? Ballet...?"

"Si. And Modern, Latin, all the sorts. I choreograph, I do the teaching. *Che!* If I still have job."

I thought the way she talked was so unbelievably sexy, putting in definite and less definite articles when they weren't necessary, omitting them when they definitely were, and saying *Che!* a lot. I assumed at the time that this was short for Che Guevara, the guy on the T-shirts – I supposed like some of us shout *Gordon Bennett!* – but it's actually just something that Argentinians say all the time, apparently, although I won't put in every one of them.

Yet even I realised we couldn't bang on about dancing forever.

"Would you like to hear what my own game plan is?" I ventured.

"No."

Moving on.

"It's called custody, what you want," I informed her authoritatively.

"And is called kidnap, what he did. *Bastardo!*"

She was off again, staring at me with those unblinking tiger-eyes, raising her husky voice. "I phone to my little boy. I write him. Of course. Then one day Laurence, he tell me Sebastian will not talk with me. With his own *mami!* He say his son he is so happy to be back in England. In school in England. I do not send him for school – I send him for fucking Christmas!"

People nearby were staring. A few mums with kids were keeping their distance, as the crazy, foreign woman began to rummage dementedly in her handbag. Even though, this being

London, they were most probably foreign women themselves.

This was the first time I met the furry ex-giraffe, but I had seen too many worn-out, charity-shop toys back home to take much interest. Yet the letter she pulled out from beneath the ratty little toy did interest me. But not in a good way.

"My husband's lawyers. It is he who take *me* to court! To 'settle' the matter once for always. Bastardo!"

I knew the firm by reputation. They made Barney look like the Dalai Lama. I had hardly finished reading the letter – some bewildering technical jargon about 'residency transfer application' and 'unsuitability' – when she was ferreting into her bag again and waving a small pair of denim jeans in my face. It was like Mary Poppins.

"I buy the one size bigger," she told me, looking quite uncertain. "It is okay, yes?"

How the hell would I know? But of course I nodded comfortingly, the kiddy-jean expert, which seemed to please her. She kept stroking the garment, as if it was a small animal.

"*It has been five months!*" she said.

My face lost its comforting look. Five months? Jesus!

"You do NOT look at me like this! You do not!" The tears were back in her eyes again. "Laurence he say he is sending Sebastian home, of course he is, then no, then is the silence. I have to find money... so much money. You do not know. To come here, to pay for my mother's treatment, to stay here for many weeks until— To pay for *you*." I wish. "And still he does not let me see him. I am not rich, Mr Davenport, my family they have nothing. But from my husband I *ask* for nothing! This is deal we make. I ask only for my son to be home with me."

This surprised me. In my vastly limited experience most clients wanted all they could get. I noticed more mums with kids were passing, making the most of the sunshine. My client couldn't stop staring at them and I think it was starting to freak them out.

"Is your mother still…?"

"Mm? Si. Dead." Oh. Okay. "I do not leave UK until I have my little boy. You hear this, Mr double-the-first of Cambridge? *I DO NOT LEAVE WITHOUT HIM!*"

By now there were mothers and children everywhere. Maybe it wasn't the best place to have brought a custody client who had just had her child snatched.

My phone buzzed – a text from Dimpy: 'WHERE THE FUCK ARE YOU?'

"I'm so sorry," I shrugged to my sighing lady. "I have to go to court. Another custody battle, I'm afraid." The stuff was just pouring out.

She nodded sadly, looking at all the kids. "How many custody cases have you won, Mr Davenport?"

I offered my most reassuring smile. "Let's just say I haven't lost one yet." Which was the truest thing I'd said all day. "Right! We start work on this tomorrow. First thing, Ms Vel… Venez…" Okay, Ricardo – go for it. "Isabel."

"Where do you take me? Legoland?"

EIGHT

"You jammy sod!"

Oliver's office was a lot bigger than mine and a hell of a lot fancier. But he didn't have a hot new client.

"Oh," I added, "and she's a dancer."

"Unfair! On tables? No – poles!" He had covered the phone while he was saying this. He's very professional. "You'll get the keys tomorrow, Mr Banks."

In seconds he was prancing around the office, doing what he had to assume was a sexy dance, but came over like the bar mitzvah boy's embarrassing dad.

"All I get are schleppers!" he moaned, running his hands through what was left of his hair.

"She needs me, Oliver." I rubbed it in. "She's flown thousands of miles and the Rickster, he is all she has got."

Oliver just smiled. "So suddenly Family ain't so bad?"

"No," I assured him, "it's still drek." (That's Yiddish; I pick things up) "I'm hardwired to be a corporate man, Ol. You know that. But until Barney sees the light…"

Oliver was already hanging out the window and yelling to the street. *"Rick's got himself a MILF!"* He turned back to me. "So, what have you told this hottie?"

Of course he meant about the law on custody, but it was

because I didn't know anything about the law on custody that I had beetled over to see him as soon as I'd left Isabel.

"That I'm an ace family lawyer – with a double-first from Cambridge."

He stared at me. "You couldn't even find it on a map."

***

Whenever we talked about women, which was pretty often, Oliver would be overtaken by this yearning to go out and look at some. So, inevitably, we were in a crowded bar that evening, the first of several. He kept pointing females out to me, talking in hushed tones like David Attenborough when he doesn't want to frighten off something extraordinary.

I needed to keep him focussed.

"So what do I do?" We both knew I couldn't ask Barney and sink even further down his Christmas list. "*Please*, Ol! You do this sort of stuff all the time."

A waitress happened to give me a passing smile and Oliver was immediately on my case. "Why'd she smile at you? Is it a Gentile thing?" Ollie! "Okay, *contact*."

Suddenly he looked very earnest. It was revelatory to see him switch into lawyer-mode and I felt a genuine pride.

"Contact?"

"Legal term, Ricky. Don't get excited. You just want to make sure mum gets *immediate* contact with her kid. It's no big deal," he said, "you call the dad's solicitors. Oh and that firm he's got himself – it's full of piranhas. But they'll know they pretty much have to give you weekends, right up to the hearing. Standard practice."

That sounded fine. Contact. Loved the word. Then he had to go and spoil it. "Have you told Sophie yet? About you're not being in Corp—"

"I will, Oliver!" *Jesus*! "I'm just waiting for the right time.

43

And Barney has to give me a crack at the real stuff soon. Family doesn't even pay his lunch-bills." I fetched up what little I knew about custody cases. "Mums always win these things, don't they?"

He looked at me in that patronising way people do when they're party to some arcane wisdom you yourself don't possess. And they don't have a really hot client.

"You wish," he said, draining his pint, which should have been his limit for the night or the week. "Rick, the kid's English, yes?" He began to count on his fingers, or at least those that weren't already burrowing into his bowl of designer-crisps. "*One*: poor little bugger was born here... *Two*: lived here for years... *Three*: he's already been back here, what, FIVE MONTHS? With his *Four*: British dad. Who happens to be *Five*: rich and *Six*: remarried – to a woman who's *Seven:* English!" He was starting to annoy me now. "Join the frigging dots and win a Volvo!"

He looked almost upset about it, which I found odd at the time. He didn't even know my client.

My first thought was that *One*: he was definitely right, followed immediately by *Two*: I am *not* telling Isabel any of this. At least not yet, when things were starting to go so well. But Oliver's new question threw me.

'The kid's plane ticket. It wasn't just a one-way, was it?"

Before I could answer – not that it was something I had thought for a moment to ask – he was off again, but I could tell that this time he was trying to impress the two young women who had just parked themselves on stools next to him.

"*Best interests of the child*," he declared. "Fundamental principle of English law. It's all that counts when we lawyers are talking custody. Or anything kiddy. Absolutely all that counts." If I had been those girls, I would be on the cusp of being impressed. "Hey, maybe your Argentinian totty *wanted* him out the picture. Maybe there was a guy. Two guys! *A three-way!*"

The girls went back to their drinks.

"But now she's changed her mind" he ploughed on. "Need I cite Kramer v Kramer? Christ, I really want a hot client, Rick!"

I wasn't going to get any more sense out of him that evening. But it didn't matter. I suddenly felt more alive than I had done in months.

There was someone I needed to see.

NINE

You had only to ring Sophie's doorbell to understand why she was desperate for a new place to live. It seemed that whatever time of day or night I turned up, Kim, her flatmate, would answer. There was a protective quality about Kim, like a shaggy, 6'1" guard dog.

"Oh, it's you, Rick."

"I'm fine thanks, Kim. Yourself?"

Here it comes. She shoved a huge hand into her hair and I wondered if it would ever emerge.

"You know I'm very tall, right? Well, my counsellor says I've been in conflict all my life, because my tiny name and my height have been battling it out. So, no more Kim!" O-kay…? "Cypress," she continued, serenely. "Like the tree. Not the country. It's a tall name."

Thankfully Sophie's bedroom-door opened and she peered out. She was wearing a weary smile and a flimsy dressing-gown that wouldn't be on long.

"I thought I heard something. Thanks, Kim," she said.

"It's fucking Cypress!"

Sophie didn't even have time to give the ritual 'I *have* to get out of here', before I was on her soft, warm lips and steering her towards the bed, unwrapping as I went. The fluffy toys cuddling her pillows didn't stand a chance.

I noticed briefly on the way down that her laptop was backlighting us from her desk. She was obviously working her way through some company document. And a duty-free Toblerone. I also couldn't help sensing that she seemed more astonished than elated by my ardour. Which made me realise just how off my game I must have been these past few months.

"Have you just taken something?" she asked, suddenly. "Oh my God, you've lost your job; you're overcompensating!"

Everyone's a therapist. "No!" I protested. "I got a very interesting client, Soph! I feel good about myself, for once. Okay?"

"Gosh, that's flattering for me. So who do I have to thank for tonight's event?"

"... Velazco. Holdings. You wouldn't have heard of them." I tried to get back to the business at both hands.

"Velazco...?" she pondered, futilely. "Nope. But I'll look them up." She deftly freed herself from my manoeuvrings and skipped over to her desk, her newly-unbuttoned pyjama-top twirling. "I'll do it now."

"*Sophie!*"

"Hey, if they do conferences…" Good luck with that. "Well, I hope you got that raise to go with it," she called back, Googling excitedly. "Cos I found some more flats."

I really didn't want to talk rental property that night. I looked around the room, which was a bit bigger than my own, a lot more flowery and roughly eight times as tidy. I mused briefly that if hers could smell so girly, God knows what mine smelled like.

"Great! Saturday. We'll spend all day Saturday," I muttered. "Hunting down flats. Be great."

She turned to me, suddenly serious. Even Kim's banging on her flimsy wall, which she did whenever Sophie's bed began to creak, didn't deflect her. "You do want to do this, don't you, Ricko?" she asked softly, aiming the kingfisher-blue eyes I loved straight at me. "Y'know – live together?"

"Eh…? Of course. Of course I do, Soph."

And I did. More than anything. So why was I checking myself out in her wardrobe mirror, my best lawyer-suit trousers crinkled around my ankles?

And why was I asking her, "Do you think I could pass for twenty-seven?"

***

A good solicitor will always have a pile of cases on his desk, either pending or in the throes of being dealt with. As for me, the pile spilled over my desk and onto the windowsills and even the floor. I'm not saying that this is because I was an ace lawyer – it was more that I was a slow and unmotivated one. And that I had a crap little office.

But that morning I woke up like Spiderman the day after he made his big career move. And I was about to spin webs.

I had already arranged regular weekend contact for Isabel and Sebastian by the time Dimpy buzzed to tell me that Mrs Armitage was making her first call of the day. Oliver had been spot-on, all it took was a brief and mildly scary conversation with the real lawyer on the other side. Who – because he assumed I was also a real lawyer – had been expecting my call. I had surprised myself by sounding almost like I knew what I was talking about and not raising my pitch to dog-whistle level, which I can sometimes do under stress.

I grabbed my briefcase and rushed off towards reception and Dimpy.

"Tell Mrs A she's—"

"Top of the pile." She knew me so well. "Where are you off to now?"

I spotted Barney as he emerged from the conference room, a client by his side and biscuit crumbs on one of his chins.

"Court," I said loudly. "Just off to court."

I could feel the porcine Cracknell stare, but I wasn't bothered. I was emerging into the West End sunshine and I was about to make a captivating older woman extremely grateful.

TEN

I once heard somebody say that if street-entertainers were any good, they wouldn't be in the street. But I can't imagine many venues where people would pay serious money to see a man with a broad Glasgow accent and a yellow kilt juggle plastic chickens.

So perhaps the Piazza in Covent Garden that sultry summer morning was the best place for him. The tourists certainly thought so. I was a bit early for my client-meeting, so I was able to stand way at the back of the crowd and watch him engage in some audience participation.

"So go on, ask me – am I feeling plucky?"

The audience dutifully answered back. "ARE YOU FEELING PLUCKY?"

Apparently he was. Gazing around the rapt faces, I noticed that Isabel had also arrived ahead of time and was taking in the pluckiness. She looked totally confident yet at the same time utterly lost. I could only assume that, unlike me, confidence was her default state and the more recent overlay of despair was what she had contracted us to dispel. (And thanks to a serial villain called Anthony Flax, 'us' turned out to be yours truly. Owe you one, Tony.)

She was wearing a lightweight pair of trousers that morning, which was a shame, and a buttercup yellow blouse with the top couple of buttons undone. I was pretty sure this last effect was in deference to the weather and not in anticipation of our meeting, but I didn't care either way. Señorita Velazco looked sensational. With my jacket casually slung over my shoulder and the sleeves of my crisp Turnbull and Asser shirt (£1.25 from the Barnardo's shop in Shoreditch) neatly rolled up, I reckoned I looked pretty sharp myself.

My new client turned and caught me staring directly at her, which even I realised was happening a bit too often and that I'd have to cool it for a while. She walked purposefully over to me, through the crowd.

"In Buenos Aires we use sticks of fire. Try to feel plucky then."

The juggler dropped a chicken. It was as if he had heard. I was up for a good stroll, perhaps across Waterloo Bridge to the South Bank – I felt far too energised to stay still.

"We just sit this time, okay, Mr Davenport?"

So we found an open-air, self-service café just out of range of poultry. I would have killed for a pastry but desisted because Isabel told me she had eaten. I imagined a dancer has to take care of her figure.

"So, how do you like it here?" I asked, as we shuffled along. It's always best to start with some small talk; you can't dive straight into work.

"I am not on fucking vacation."

Okay. Small talk over.

I paid and followed her to the quietest table she could find, which at that time of day wasn't that quiet. Looking back, Covent Garden was probably another less-than-ideal venue for a discussion about child-custody, but I blame my dad. Cabbies are always keen to give visiting foreigners the finest impression of our city and transport them, at their own expense, to the favoured sites. I suppose it's in the blood.

"Totally understand," I said, taking out my trusty pad and

steering my extra hot Americano (the coffee, not the client) well out of the danger zone. "First, I have to know all about your life in Buenos. With bastardo."

"Sebastian."

I nodded. She suddenly leaned across the table towards me and I mobilised every sinew in my face for the crucial mission of not staring down her blouse.

"I must see him, Mr Davenport. Please. I *must* see my little boy!"

Intense. But I was ready for it – I had been preparing all the way here. I began by doing that whistle through my teeth, the one that plumbers do when they discover what the last guy did with your overflow.

"Ah," I said. "You're talking about 'contact'. That's what we family solicitors call it. *Contact.*" Now she was all ears, chewing the word over like the cake she wasn't eating. "I won't lie to you. It's tough, Isabel. I can call you Isabel?" She nodded, eager to proceed. "Okay, I'm Rick. To my friends."

I smiled warmly but it wasn't returned, so I went back to serious. "You see, Isabel – first we have to file a claim. Yes? And then we're obliged to… lodge an *affidavit.* Then there's *habeas corpus* – excuse all the Latin – *noli prosequi, mens rea,* naturally… maybe even – I'm afraid – a *res ipsa loquitur.*"

I had lost her – yet I had her.

It's amazing how, when you're any sort of a professional, you can bedazzle people with bollocks. Isabel started to blink quite rapidly, biting her fulsome lower lip with those extraordinarily white teeth. Her slender hands, bronzed by a different sun, cradled the unsipped espresso. She just needed to hold on to something, I reckoned. I decided that a gentle tap on those lovely hands, purely for reassurance, would not be inappropriate at this juncture. And might even…

"Jee-zus, the prices in this fucking city!"

My hand shot back into my lap like a rabbit into its hole.

The woman was American, around the same age as my client but twice as wide, with one of those voices they seem to pack for overseas holidays, because they feel they're competing with history. (I've never been to America – they may be just as loud over there, but they have a lot more space.)

"Is this him?" she continued. "Shoot, we could be his mom." She kept staring at me, in what seemed like disbelief. "Joanne – her loyal friend."

Isabel didn't seem in the least surprised to see her. "Joanne is in my dance class, when I live here," she explained, with an affectionate smile. "Now she is my landlord – landlady. Yes?" She turned sadly to her pal. "He say it is difficult – the weekend."

"He does? Izzie, go fetch me a Danish."

I was praying this woman wasn't a lawyer or I was in such deep shit. Isabel trotted dutifully off and the big woman, who had clearly been primed to turn up and give me the once-over, landed on the chair next to me. I felt the air being sucked out of the piazza. Anyone who could give Isabel Velazco orders had my attention.

"Listen, fella," she growled, without preamble, "I know from lawyers. You have the scruples of linguine." It was like she was talking a foreign language, yet still somehow fascinating. "And you got this great fucking heap of cases on your desk." I felt the urge to say 'fucking pile' but it seemed important not to break the flow. "And guess what, the folks with no dough stay right there, kissing mahogany."

How did she know this?

"I got a divorce last year," she explained. "Guy was an asshole."

"How long were you married to him?" She just stared at me. "Oh, the lawyer."

"Someone told me your firm was nasty." This explained things, although she was probably thinking of my predecessor. "We need nasty. That little boy is her life, *capisce*? Her *life*. Do-you-get-this?"

She seemed to be expecting a response, so I nodded, although to be honest I wasn't absorbing it to the full. Sometimes delivery can actually obscure the message, especially when you're rattled down to your Church brogues. (Oxfam, Bethnal Green. £2.49)

"Do right by her, kiddo." I thought she had finished now, but… "Keep your eye on her case not her tits or I'll have your undescended testicles with my breakfast toasties. Okay?"

To my profound delight Isabel came back at this point. My new client was volatile, but this woman was giving me hives. Fortunately Joanne grabbed the Danish from her friend and stood up.

"I got a recall for a commercial. Fat mom waving vitaminised kids off to school."

She was an actress! No wonder she and my dancer were such buddies. I had never met an actress before, but I really didn't want to meet this one again. She kissed my client and gave her a huge hug, like she was squeezing the last dregs out of a plastic ketchup bottle. But she never took her eyes off my face.

"Do not give an inch. I COULD JUGGLE BETTER WITH ONE HAND UP MY BUTT!" That was to chicken-guy, obviously, but it registered with everyone in the shockwave zone.

We watched her go. Well, I watched Isabel watch her go, but I was thinking fast. I had a plan. I can't say it was the most honourable thing I'd ever conceived, yet I seemed somehow programmed to do it anyway. I just wished I didn't feel so shaky.

"Joanne is big person," enthused Isabel. "I love her so much."

"Yeah. I can see that. The big bit, I mean." Standing up. "Time to go, Isabel."

She looked at me as I beckoned her to follow.

"*Deo!* Where do you take me now?"

ELEVEN

The first thing that strikes you about Somerset House is its whiteness. At least that's what had struck me the first time I saw it, especially with the sun lending a painterly hand. Followed swiftly, I suppose, by its size. Built around a massive courtyard, it's a seriously impressive old building, with fountains and terraces, on the south side of the Strand near the river. Not far from the Royal Courts of Justice, actually. Our ultimate destination. Apparently it dates from around the end of the eighteenth century, but it still looked remarkably clean.

Of course I didn't know any of this (and I had thought 'neoclassical' was to do with that music), until I visited it with my school, just before GCSEs, to inspire us with the awe that was considered lacking in our impoverished lives. I had instantly forgotten the bulk of it, until today's return visit.

There was one thing, however, I did remember. Somerset House had once been the Registry of Births, Marriages and Deaths. For some reason, perhaps because it sounded vaguely legal, this had stuck in my mind.

Somerset House isn't a registry of anything any more. It's a world centre for art and culture. So naturally I had kept it at a healthy distance since that school trip.

That day, as every day, it boasted The Courtauld Institute

and some other arty stuff. Yet, so far as Isabel Velazco was concerned, this building held within its implacable walls the key to seeing her little boy again after so many months apart.

Because that's what I had told her.

I carefully explained, as we walked into the famous courtyard, already peppered with groups of tourists yet still looking vaguely governmental, that it could take a fair bit of time. Battling with the other side, making deals, banging heads. Lawyer stuff. So she might as well sit somewhere comfortable with a coffee and a magazine and I would come find her once it was settled. If indeed it could be, I cautioned, adding a responsible note.

She chose a pretty outdoor café on site, overlooking the Thames. But before I left to do the serious business, there was something I knew I had to ask.

"The plane ticket. It *was* a return, wasn't it?"

She didn't answer. I supposed all her thoughts were on the tough meeting I was apparently about to have, so I didn't push it. Perhaps I should have done.

***

There's a lot of waiting you do when you're a lawyer. Waiting for documents to arrive, waiting to go into court, waiting for a judgment. But that particular working-day I was simply sitting on an uncomfortable, wooden bench beside a painting that did nothing for me, on a secluded landing well away from my client, reading the *Financial Times* (you have to keep abreast) and waiting for something that wasn't going to happen.

Because it had already happened, much earlier in the day, in the course of one simple phone call.

I began to worry at one point that someone might see me, before I reassured myself that no one I had ever met would come anywhere near this place. I also started to wonder where exactly

I was going with all this, but – if I'm going to be as honest as intended – I don't recall letting it distract me for long.

I could tell that Isabel had drunk a hell of a lot of coffee by the time I returned. She was pacing the walkway by the river, backwards and forwards, stamping her elegant feet as if she was practising a Flamenco or whatever it was they did in her country. And smoking. I don't smoke and I don't usually warm to people who do, but this woman had a way of smoking that made you feel it was the sexiest thing anyone could ever turn their mind to and that people who didn't smoke were somehow less-evolved human beings. Mind you, if she had gone in for a frenzied bout of nose-picking, I would probably have been turned on by it.

I had no idea what it looked like to have gone through a tough meeting with a mean bunch of family-lawyers, as I had thankfully never experienced it, but I assumed that a tie roughly loosened and hair a bit dishevelled wouldn't be far off the mark. Although I did half-suspect that it just made me look slobby. My words, however, were spot on.

"Isabel…"

She turned towards my voice, the dance-moves stopping, the cigarette dangling precariously from her hand. Her frantic, feline eyes immediately locked onto mine.

"Friday." I let it out slowly, like a man thoroughly spent. "Five o'clock." Sigh of a job well done. Finally, just so there was no room for doubt. "Sebastian."

Now it would come. The gratitude. The tears. And, who knows, perhaps the embrace. We're human – it's personal – and let's not forget, she wasn't English.

Isabel said nothing – clearly too overwhelmed for words. Then it began, the moisture. As she spat right there onto the ground, her small fists clenched as if she was going to deck the very next person who came anywhere within reach. Her eyes were like hot coals.

"He make me *fight* to see my son?"

57

Not quite the reaction I was expecting, but I could work with it. Before I could respond, however, she was gone, striding off on those wonderfully powerful legs towards the river. If she had been walking through grass, the earth would already be scorched.

I followed her, watching in confused fascination as she flung her wiry, buttercup arms about her, having an angry conversation with herself. I had been there many times but perhaps not so flamboyantly.

Visitors around us were beginning – as ever – to stare. I hoped that Isabel wouldn't think they all looked unusually jolly for people who were going off to family court or to register a death.

"IT'S HIS SOLICITORS, Isabel!" I called. "They play hardball."

I had never heard anyone in my profession use that phrase, or even in my country, but I knew it sounded terrific even as I said it. I finally managed to catch up with her and take her arm very loosely. She didn't flinch or move away, which was good, but I stepped back once I had her full attention. She was still seriously pissed-off.

"But listen – listen to me, Isabel. Please." She listened, through the flames. "I've secured you *every* weekend until the hearing."

All I received for this landmark ruling was a shrug. Which made me feel curiously insulted, even though of course I had been involved in no such lawyerly-skirmish. Yet it only made me want to push on.

"Hey, I have never *ever* known that before. I doubt any of my Family Law colleagues have *ever* known it either… *Every* single weekend." And then, to nail it. "Phew!"

At this point she did look at me with a sort of sad smile and say 'thank you', which was a relief. But then I felt her hand on my own arm. It was incredibly gentle yet the sensations were intense and the heat parachuting through my body was both overwhelming and vaguely embarrassing. I stared at the elegantly strong fingers, then up at her face, which was now suddenly so much softer. The anger in her eyes had subsided and in its place was just this crunching, teary vulnerability. They talk about eyes pleading – hers were almost kneeling in supplication. It was quite magical, yet at the same time really scary.

"I – I do not think I can do this on my own, Richard," she whispered.

I was so elated she had called me by my first name, longer version, even though I don't usually like it, that it took some seconds for the full portent of her words to register.

"Oh no," I said, shaking my head in a way I don't recall usually doing. I'm not a head-shaker. "No. Sorry, Isabel. Not possible, I'm afraid." She was still looking at me. "Lawyers… don't do that."

TWELVE

I'm sure my mum and dad weren't actively trying to get up my nose that summer. But that's probably because they didn't need to try.

I'm thinking right now of the afternoon I came home from Somerset House, sweaty and stirred-up, mulling on the unforeseen proposal my new client had just slung at me. I was on the phone to Oliver as I walked in the door, but that didn't stop my dad.

"Ask me the best way to get to Heathrow from Stoke Newington Church Street. Go on!"

"Che! I cannot do thees on my hown... Reechard," I continued into the phone.

I was attempting to give my trusty legal advisor a flavour of what had just happened, in the ill-concealed hope that he would proffer another dollop of essential advice, without my actually having to beg for it. I didn't mention the Somerset House business. I must have sensed, even at such an early stage, that he might not entirely have approved.

"You on the phone, Rick?" asked my dad. I grunted – no point in being rude. "Dinner'll be ready soon as little Ushma's done with her lesson," he persisted. "You seeing our little Sophie tonight?"

He made me sound like some sort of child-molester. Everyone younger than my dad is automatically 'little', even though they are usually taller than him. I had to get away from the man and his blether and the relentless accordion music and into the sanctuary of an upstairs room.

My bedroom made my office look spacious. It had a desk my dad made when I was thirteen, a bed my mum made every day of my life, posters I should have taken down a long time ago and enough cocaine in a drawer to make the Law Society strike me off forever. I kept this for special occasions and nothing had struck me as special for quite a while.

There was one other item in my bedroom worthy of note that evening. A smiling, ginger-haired child called Emily, who had apparently managed to heft our massive Threadbear all the way up the stairs and into the one place that should have been totally out of bounds. I tried to ignore her, as I carried on talking to my solicitor.

"I'm not 'up to' anything, Ollie," I protested. "It was *her* bloody idea! Hey, it's not exactly my dream Friday afternoon." I heard myself and realised that I had already made my decision. I supposed it wasn't such a big deal. After all I would be a few more hours in her company – and it would get me out the office. "… Of course I'm still with Sophie – *Oliver, for fuck's sake, the woman's a client!*"

I could feel Emily listening intently. Actually I could feel Threadbear listening intently, which made me think that neither of them should be anywhere near me.

"Can you go somewhere else please, sweetheart? And take nice big bear with you. That's a good girl… Oh, by the way, you were right Ol, it *was* a one-way ticket."

I wasn't great with kids. Some people aren't. Which doesn't suddenly make you the Childcatcher or Jimmy Savile or something. But it was actually relevant to the subject under discussion with Oliver, until he changed course and invited me and Sophie to his parents' house for dinner that same upcoming Friday night. I accepted immediately – Jewish people take their food seriously and Friday nights for them are like Christmas for us, only it happens fifty-two times a year, excluding their own Christmases, which are even more brilliant.

It was going to be a busy day.

THIRTEEN

"And you didn't want his money!"

We were in a parked black cab, staring across a smart, tree-lined, South London avenue. Each house was different and the sprawling, detached mock-tudor in question was one of several serious properties in a suburb I had never had occasion to visit, but in which I decided at that moment I would one day live. Or somewhere quite like it, you can't be too prescriptive about these things.

There were some equally grown-up cars in the circular, gravelled driveway. But Isabel wasn't looking, she was just tormenting that mangy giraffe in her handbag. Even the cabbie, staring at us in his mirror, could see how ill-at-ease she was. I met his eyes and shrugged.

"It's gone five o'clock, Isabel... *Isabel?*"

She kept throttling the giraffe. "What if he does not know me, Rick?"

I didn't know what to say to this. She seemed in such a panic that I knew I needed to lighten the mood.

"How many Argentinians is he expecting?"

Isabel managed a small smile – let's face it, I hadn't just cracked off a zinger. But it did the trick. She pushed open the door of the cab and stepped out onto the pavement.

"We'll try not to be too long." I told the driver, adding softly "My dad's a cabbie."

"Then have this ride on me." Sarcastic bastard.

I was right behind Isabel as we reached the front door. She seemed a bit unsteady on her feet, which I thought odd for a dancer. I took her arm and gave it a reassuring squeeze.

We were about to ring the bell when the door opened and a tall, slim man, probably in his late fifties, emerged. Laurence was older than I expected and the luxuriant silver hair surprised me.

"Mr Menzies – I'm Richard Davenport…"

Before the man could reply, he was joined by a younger, more portly guy with a sandy, medium-stubble beard, designer T-shirt and khaki cut-offs, who was holding a large, crystal tumbler half-full of Scotch and smiling broadly. He had an easy warmth to him that was both appealing and subtly chilling, like someone with whom you really want to be friends, even though you reckon you probably shouldn't. Or someone you'd rather like to be but are pretty sure you never will.

"Ah, traffic jam," he said, then patted the older man on the back. "Bye Hugo, have a good weekend."

"And you, Laurence."

The silver fox smiled at us as he walked to one of the smart cars. An Aston Martin, I think. I remember he gave Isabel the once over, but very swiftly, so you'd hardly notice. I don't suppose she caught it, she was staring so rootedly at her ex, but I picked it up. You couldn't blame the old bloke – even when she was hard in the face, she was easy on the eye.

With all the contempt that seemed to be lasering his way, you'd think Laurence Menzies might be a bit disturbed. But he had this look of mild amusement and that was the look I would always associate with him. Along with the Scottish accent that was so posh you'd have to strain to find Scottishness in there at all.

"Work – the curse of the drinking classes," he smiled, raising his glass.

I know now it's a quote, because I looked it up, but at the time I just thought it was really witty. So I smiled, which I would have done even if it was mega-corny, as there's no mileage in being impolite to the other side. They're not the enemy. But when Isabel caught me smiling at her ex, you'd think she'd found us in bed together.

"Mr Menzies, I'm—"

"I heard," he said, but not in a rude way, then turned to my client. "Hello, Isabel."

"Where is my son?"

That's Isabel – cut to the chase.

She launched herself straight past him into the huge lobby. There was a staircase smack in the centre, going up to what I assume was a whole cluster of bedrooms, each and every one probably ensuite. Sophie would have loved it. But Isabel paused at the foot of the stairs, looking uncertain, because of course she had never been in this house before and had no idea where Sebastian might be.

Laurence grinned at me, so I grinned back. We might have stood like that for ages, exchanging grins in a manly fashion, but a splash and yelp from outside sent Isabel scurrying onwards. You could almost see her ears prick up and you could definitely see her steps falter. For one swift second she turned back to me, eyes wide and mouth quivering. I tried to convert the matey smile I was giving her ex-husband into one brimming with compassion, just for her. Laurence gently waved her on, in the right direction.

"Done this before, Mr Davenport?" He seemed genuinely interested, even though he was talking over his shoulder, as he followed his ex-wife outside.

"Too many times, Mr Menzies." Which I thought sounded pretty good as I strolled behind him into the sunshine.

If there was a magazine called *Wife and Garden* this guy would make the centre-spread. The moment you stepped through the patio doors onto the gleaming, hardwood deck you were hit with a ravishing fusillade of colour. I recall huge beds of lustrous, expertly-arranged flowers, greenery, trees, shrubs and dangling things, none of which I recognised (or were probably even permitted to grow in Hackney), plus an impossibly blue, diamond-shaped pool, large enough to have a proper swim in. It was just beckoning for a good old splash.

Standing at the edge of the pool, wearing a bikini not much bigger than her smile, was a tall and healthily-slender woman, with short – and I reckoned expensively cut – auburn hair, who could only be Mrs Menzies Mark-Two. Barely thirty, she appeared to glisten in the sunshine, as if it was in her marriage-contract to be personally lit from on-high. This was an extraordinary week for women, in my opinion.

The new wife greeted Isabel very politely, but my client wasn't for turning. Every cell in her body was tuned to the frequency of son, who was splashing about right in front of her, yet paying her no attention at all. Perhaps he hadn't realised she was there.

All I could see was a goodly helping of jet black hair, attached to a small, brown, wiry body which was wiggling around like an eel under a huge, two-seater inflatable duck.

"He insisted on a swim," said the young woman, with a surprisingly warm smile. "We get so few fine days, don't we? I'm Rebecca."

"Hi, Rebecca," I responded, trying desperately to stay on her face. I wondered if in time lawyers switch off this bit of themselves. Maybe they just learn to hide it better.

Isabel wasn't having any of the social stuff. It was probably hard enough for her not to jump fully-clothed into the pool. Her and me both.

The kid certainly didn't look like he was in any hurry to jump out, so she squatted by the side, her flowery skirt soaking up water from the tiled surround, and quietly spoke to him in their language.

Of course I can't be totally certain what she said, but what I do know is that her voice had a tear in it – that's tear as in crying, yet it could just as easily have been tear as in ripping. She sounded as if she was in enormous pain. It was like one of those TV shows that always set my mum off, where they reunite long-lost relatives after years of fruitless searching.

"*Oh! Mi querido hijito, veni con mami, amoroso.*"

The boy remained in the water, floating in the sunshine. Yet his body seemed rigid, like he was doing a really bad imitation of carefree. Or a really good imitation of driftwood. Rebecca bent towards him and spoke in a gentle, soothing voice. "Sweetie, say hello to your mummy. She's come all this way to see you."

Sebastian swam as far away as possible to the other edge of the pool. I watched Laurence as he came to stand next to Rebecca, resting a hand lovingly on his fetching young wife's bare shoulder. Curiously, it was to me that he turned.

"This is all so traumatic for him," he said.

"Like snatching him isn't." I have no idea where that came from, yet it seemed to find its mark. Laurence threw me a look that felt like a game-changer, as if time had just run out for two city-guys bonding.

"I'd choose my words carefully, Mr Davenport. And my facts. Okay?"

"Yeah, okay. Sorry." I realised I had better cool it with the snappy responses, but Laurence hadn't finished. He beckoned me over to a spot at the edge of the garden, right by some rose bushes. As he talked the thorns kept pricking at my good suit, which was maybe what he wanted. He probably just threw his own thorn-pricked suits on his weekly bonfire or gave them to the Portuguese gardener.

"You think you know this woman," he said, "because you've had what, two – three meetings with her?" He was spot-on. "And fine, it's your job – to take her side. Hear her 'story'. But you don't look to me like someone who takes on custody cases by choice.

Hey, who would?" He smiled understandingly, so I joined him. "I'm guessing a stepping stone – to what, Corporate? Big Business? Mergers and Acquisitions?" Jesus, the guy was good. It was like he had read my application forms. "I know people, Mr Davenport. I know my ex-wife and I know my son. Remember, I was married to her. We loved each other – for God's sake, we made a child!"

The man could certainly talk, which was a whole lot more than his ex and the child they made were doing right now. "I do realise it's not your place as a lawyer to give my feelings any credence. So I'm asking you, as a human being. Keep your mind a little bit open – and your mouth a little bit shut."

He would have probably banged on even more, he was clearly well used to people listening, but we were interrupted by a piercing, high-pitched scream.

"YOU SPEAK IN ENGLISH!"

I turned. Isabel was frozen into her squat, looking totally stunned.

Finally, after a mortifying few seconds, the kid climbed out of the water. But he made sure he wasn't going anywhere near his mum. I could take a good look at him now, as he clambered lithely out – a skinny, olive-skinned, little guy wearing his ribcage almost on the outside and a pair of tiny speedos below. Unfortunately, he didn't have his mother's looks.

I know he was a bloke but a bit of that bone structure and a pair of those full-on lips wouldn't have done him any harm in later life. The deep-brown eyes with the tiny flecks and long lashes might work for him, along with his skin-tone, but there was a sullenness that wouldn't make him the most popular kid in the class. And a brooding anger that might get him into all kinds of trouble, but probably not the fun kind.

'Oh. Si. Yes, of course, *cielo*. Darling!"

She was making a real dogs-dinner of it but she probably hadn't spoken to the kid in English for years. I didn't see why he should be demanding it of her now, he couldn't have forgotten his Spanish since Christmas.

Laurence smoothed his way in front of Isabel and wrapped a huge towel around the boy, who was beginning to shiver despite the weather. "Hey pal, why don't you go and get your togs?" Still smiling, he held his son gently by the shoulders and looked straight down at him. "Remember our little chat about the weekend?"

Sebastian didn't respond straightaway. Laurence tightened his grip a tiny bit. "Sebastian, I'm talking to you."

The boy nodded. "Be polite. Keep my clothes clean." Which immediately set him apart from any kid his age I had ever met.

I watched Isabel, whose unblinking gaze never left her son, as Rebecca put a slim arm around him and led him gently back inside. I thought Isabel might look at me but it was as if she had forgotten I was even there.

"So, doing something nice this weekend?" asked Laurence.

"Oh, just looking at some more flats," I said, then realised that the question was of course for Isabel, who wasn't nearly so chatty.

"He see his mami! Is 'nice' enough for you?"

She shot him another killer-look, then stomped off back to the house. I could see as she passed that she was making a massive effort not to cry. Her whole face seemed like it was about to explode, which made me feel seriously uncomfortable. I was intruding on something very private, that I had no business being anywhere near. I wished I hadn't come.

Laurence just gave a huge sigh and a shrug. I suppose the whole thing was quite embarrassing for him too. "Not married are you, Richard?" he asked, wryly.

I shook my head, a bit harder than necessary. But at least it made him smile.

In other circumstances I would have been happy just to chill with Laurence Menzies on a lounger by the pool, Jack Daniels in hand, and ask him how he had achieved all this and whether he could do the same for a gifted young man from Hackney. But we had a taxi on the meter and I was probably going to end up paying.

FOURTEEN

If Sebastian had parked himself any farther away from his mum, he would have been dangling out of the cab window. I was opposite them, on the pop-up seat, which gave me a great view of Isabel but a less enjoyable one of the drama being played out within touching distance.

Perhaps I was just pissed-off because he was turning his lack of charm on me too, pinching up his face and scowling, like I was the one responsible for his being taken away from home. We had one angry little boy here, a boy who most certainly didn't want to be anywhere near his mum, glaring daggers at an unfamiliar male who most certainly did.

I tried to change the subject and ease the mood. For Isabel's sake obviously, but also for my own. "So what line is your husband in, exactly?"

"He is not my husband." Yeah. Okay. "I do not recognise such a big boy," she continued, which I knew was going to get her nowhere. "And he looks so handsome, doesn't he, Mr Davenport?" Er – no. "This is Mr Davenport, he is my—"

She didn't have time to explain what manner of beast I was, because suddenly the cabbie was chirping in. *"You're Ronnie Davenport's little boy!"*

Jesus!

I didn't want to answer – or to reveal my dad's calling – which I suppose was quite snobby, but back then it didn't seem information likely to further my ambitions. Not that I had the faintest idea of what my ambitions were. Or even whether I wanted them furthered.

"Er, yeah," I said quietly. I wanted to close the glass partition but I decided to let it ride.

"See you tell him Terry Magnus sends his best." That'll happen. "Here, did you know your dad was the one who discovered the Balls Pond Road Corridor?"

I took that as rhetorical. Christ, it was hardly the North-West Passage.

"Hi, Sebby," I said, attempting to get back on track. I caught Isabel glaring. Okay, so not 'Sebby'. "Hi, Seb-astian. I'm Rick. Your mum's solicitor. Ciao."

"That's it – *Rick!*" chipped in my old pal Terry. "Your dad's always banging on about you."

"That's great," I said. "Excuse me, Terry, I'm sort of – working?"

"Say no more, Rick. You and me both."

Isabel was rummaging again. I knew she was looking for either Mister Sad the giraffe or those little denims. The giraffe won – and lost. Sebastian gave it one disdainful glance then buried his head in anywhere else.

"So, what do we do tomorrow?" she ploughed on, gamely. No reply. "I know! Si! Why do we not get up early and go to Madame Tussaud's!" If possible the silence was deeper. "Oh – oh yes – I know this. *The London Zoo!* Sebastian, he love the zoo, Mr Davenport."

She was looking at me now, totally helpless. I felt like one of those Saturday dads, trying to think of some way to bond with my kids, so that their love would last me through the week.

"I've got the DVD of *Evita*," I volunteered. But even I knew this was shit. And I didn't have it actually, I'd given it to Help the Aged.

"*What about Wonderworld?*" Terry to the rescue. Who asked him? "They got that 'Leviathan' there."

"What is it?" asked Isabel. 'This Wonderworld."

"I have seen this!" yelped Sebastian. "Levi – this one."

We both turned to him – well, all three of us, if you count Terry in his newly-adjusted mirror. The little boy's face had changed, some of the sullen creases had flattened out and he looked almost excited. As did Isabel, as she watched this unfold. It didn't turn the kid into Macauley Culkin but at least you didn't want to push him out of the cab.

Terry again – and I knew what was coming. "I'll do it for seventy. Both ways." I'm not a cabbie's son for nothing.

"Oh," said Isabel, suddenly disappointed. "It is far away."

Sebastian seemed crestfallen, but it was Isabel's face that concerned me most. On it was the saddest, most desolate look I think I had ever seen and she was sending it right my way. I had absolutely no idea what to do with it.

Terry caught my eye in his mirror. I could see he was trying to puzzle out what the hell was going on. Join the club, Tel.

"Sixty," he said. "As you're Ronnie's little boy."

FIFTEEN

"L'hadlich nair shel shabbat."

Oliver used to tease me when I said his home was really Jewish – 'What do you think we do – cut six inches off the chimney pot!" Apparently it's a very old joke that still makes Jewish people laugh – they find anything about circumcision hilarious, which is sort of weird.

As soon as the family have said the prayer over the candles and passed around a beautiful silver cup with this sickly-sweet wine in it (which you're silently praying is not what you're going to drink with your meal) and a tiny bit of some great, knotted bread on a silver dish, that you hope to God you will be seeing more of, then they go around the table and kiss each other, even men on men. Which is actually a lot more pleasant than it sounds. You're supposed to say *'Shabbat shalom'* while you're doing it, which means have a peaceful Sabbath.

Only nothing is ever that peaceful in Ollie's house and it certainly wasn't on the night I came back from collecting Sebastian. Sophie and I were honoured guests and naturally I had no intention of informing her where I had just been. I was sure that sooner or later I would get round to keeping her up to speed – okay, telling her the truth – but there never seemed to be a danger-free zone. And, unsurprisingly, the longer I left it, the less palatable it was going to be.

"So Rick, how's matrimony looking?" asked Cyril Rosen, dumping me straight in it.

Cyril, whose first name I still found hard to use back then, was an old-school family lawyer. Compact, balding, with glasses even thicker than Oliver's and eyes that totally disappeared when he smiled at you; Mr Rosen was trustworthy, astute and simply a really decent man, who could be a tricky sod when he felt like it.

One of the many things he shared with Oliver was an infinite capacity to spill food down his shirt and Mrs Margo Rosen to fuss around him, cleaning him up.

Right now this equally short and cosily pretty lady, with the sort of blonde hair you know isn't real like Sophie's but equally doesn't look like one of Linda's Hackney-rinses, was giving her husband an admonishing stare. Because she assumed he was referring to Sophie's and my future relationship. Knowing him, he quite possibly was.

"It was a professional question," he smiled.

But Sophie – who looked exceptionally good and delightfully overdressed that evening – wasn't smiling. She was staring at me quizzically, while I sneaked Oliver a glare for telling his dad the truth.

"I… just help the team out. Y'know, when they're busy." I hoped this would satisfy Sophie. There was something specific I had to tell her anyway but now wasn't quite the time.

"Maybe you could help Oliver out," said Mrs Rosen, with a smile. We all knew that she was desperate to see her only son married and a father, to a point that she would even entertain reversing the order of those ceremonies. Defiantly she would face the elders of her congregation with wedding photos in one hand and silver foreskin-case in the other, although I'm only guessing on that last one.

Oliver made his usual, mortified protest "*Mum!*" but it was as much a ritual as the lighting of the candles. He moved on to one of his favourite subjects – property.

"Rick and Sophie are looking to rent a flat. Do we know anyone?"

Before Mr Rosen could respond, Sophie added happily, "We've set aside all of tomorrow to find something."

I know it could have waited until later but for some self-destructive reason I ploughed on. "Er Soph, I've got a client to see tomorrow. I'm really sorry. It just came up."

Oliver threw me his creepiest leer, enjoying a double-entendre I had never intended. But I could feel Sophie stiffen beside me.

"Show me a City lawyer who works nine-to-five, Sophie dear," explained Mr Rosen, kindly. "A demanding client, Rick?"

"You wish," said Oliver, who deserved a good kicking.

I swiftly grabbed some food – any food – that was on the table and shoved it into my mouth, although no one had told me I could start.

"These are terrific, Mrs Rosen," I mumbled. "Truly excellent. What are they called?"

But Sophie wasn't giving up. "Where are you going tomorrow?" Here it comes. "I can meet you afterwards. Is it just the office or are you going to court?"

They waited while my mouth unblocked.

"Wonderworld," I mumbled.

I didn't look at her but I could feel Sophie's incredulous gaze searing into my face.

"Pickled cucumbers," responded Mrs Rosen. It didn't help.

SIXTEEN

We didn't accept Terry-the-cabbie's kind offer to double the price of a day out at Wonderworld.

Mind you, by the time we had reached the motorway, with Isabel squeezed into the tiny rear of the MiG without prospect of breath and the adorable Sebastian next to me (because he gets sick in the back), happily picking away at my front trim, I was half-wishing I had left them both to it and was inspecting another dozen perfect flats in darkest Hoxton. But at least the kid's little fingernails were bitten down to the quick, so he couldn't do the poor car too much damage.

I've been recalling the great weather that summer. Saturday had to be the exception. They say God saves the crap for weekends – well, he was certainly playing a blinder today. It hadn't rained yet, but it was threatening, and with the MiG's canvas roof unfurled, the dampening wind was almost strong enough to blow Sebastian away.

If only.

With mist and gloom on the road, the only seasonal view was of Isabel's long legs in her short, summery dress, as she struggled to make herself decently comfortable and, preferably, not pass out. Yet again she caught me looking – women must have an antenna for this stuff – so I reverted to flicking little Che Guevara's hands away.

"Don't do that, please," I told him, with admirable restraint. Then added, just to make him feel I wasn't a total bastardo, "So what team do you support, Sebby–astian?"

"*Independiente, no es cierto, mi amoroso?*" came the squished voice from behind. I could have told her she was going to get zero mileage out of that one.

"*NO!*" There you go. "Tottenham the Hotspurs!" Then he added – presumably for my benefit but just as possibly working the room – "My father has a big BMW."

What could I say to that? I just flicked his hand a lot harder and we travelled in silence for another thirty miles. I suppose we could have made conversation, had I not opened all the windows and gunned the engine, but I doubt that it would have improved matters greatly.

Suddenly I sensed excitement frothing up on my left, as a huge poster for the 'Leviathan' sea-monster ride swam into view. She looked like the seventh circle – or seventh lots-of-circles-fused-together – of hell. Sebastian didn't say anything but he stopped demolishing my car, his hands freezing mid-pick, so I knew it was having an effect.

"I've heard 'Leviathan' is really scary," I said, because I felt like it.

"Rick!" from behind me. *What*?

"I am never scared," said Sebastian, in a voice that made me pretty sure he was. He had an Argentinian accent (I assume – I'm no expert) but I have to say his English was excellent. "You will come with me," he ordered. Yeah, that's going to happen.

"Oh no, sorry Sebastian. That's Mummy's job," I told him. "Right, Mummy?"

"*Si, mi amor,*" she said. "*Me encantaria ir con vos!*" This woman didn't learn.

"*In ENGLISH! Woman!!*"

Told you.

***

Leviathan looked seriously terrifying.

It was as if they had conceived a fusion of every bone-shattering, stomach-churning fairground ride that man, in his infinite sadism, had ever invented, then turned it on its head and hoicked the speed up to brain-damage.

We stood there, our curious little threesome, staring neck-achingly up at the monster, as screams of all ages and sexes filled the candy-flossed air. Leviathan was all twisted, blood-red girders and demented, circular ramps. Pods of horror whizzed over and past us. We were totally mesmerised, much as Isabel's ancestors must have been when they first set eyes on the Spanish fleet arriving in their unimaginable ships. If, of course, they docked in Argentina.

"You are going to be so sick," said my little passenger.

"I told you, pal, I'm not going with you," I repeated. "Sorry, but it's your mum's job."

The current Leviathan crew broke the shriek barrier just feet away from us.

"It is not!" he stamped. "You come. And then you will do poo in your pants."

What is it with kids and poo? I looked to Isabel for help. Wisely recognising that she was persona non-screamer in this scenario, she stepped aside like it was nothing to do with her. Thanks, señora.

Five minutes later I understood why God wasn't paying attention to the weather and quietly sent him an apology. He was devoting all his energies to saving me from total humiliation. When it was our turn at the ticket booth, the gentleman in charge just stared down at my overexcited nine year old, then pointed to a big notice that read, in quasi-handpainted lettering, *'No one under 4'10 inches allowed on ride'*.

Thank you, Lord!

"Oh dear, what a bummer, Sebastian," I said, turning to him to make sure the little chap had absorbed his full share of the day's disappointment. He had, judging by his instantly teary face, but I reinforced it just because it felt so good. "It looks like you're too squitty. Never mind, pal. We'll have a lovely ice-cream instead – and then find us a nice little ride for short people."

Crying never actually works with me, not sure why. I suppose watery eyes and wobbly lips aren't very attractive. But Isabel was there in a nano-second, tissues to hand, trying to comfort her sniffling little offspring. Even in extremis, the kid wasn't having any.

"No! You are a not-English toilet!"

Which wasn't the snappiest insult I had ever heard, yet it did what it said on the tin. Isabel recoiled like her child had just wired his T-shirt up to the mains, then glared at me as if it was all my fault and I should have seen to it that she got a taller kid. But I was totally unprepared for Sebastian's next move.

"You must go on it." Staring straight at me. "And then you will throw up."

Oh no. Señor Davenport wasn't going to have a liquid-laugh for anyone, especially not all over his painstakingly-chosen yet effortlessly-casual, client outfit. But Isabel threw me that look again, the same one she'd used at Somerset House when I told her about the Friday night pick-up. It was like I said to Oliver – I was all the poor woman had in the world. She was lost without me.

I plodded off towards Leviathan, stifling my grumpiness and trying to make it look like I was doing something way beyond noble. Sydney Carton in *Tale of Two Cities*. Then it started to rain. Terrific.

"Maybe it'll make him grow," I said. But I don't think they heard.

SEVENTEEN

There's another problem with driving rain. It makes it even harder to rid the smell of Leviathan vomit from your car, because you can't open the windows or the roof without drowning your passengers.

Mind you…

So while Sebastian was picking away gloomily at my dashboard, I was scratching away equally gloomily at the gobs of rushed breakfast solidifying on my best – and unfortunately full-price – GAP slim-fit shirt.

I glanced at Isabel, who was still squirming in the back. I wasn't interested in her legs this time – well, not just her legs. I was trying, without making it too obvious, to gauge her mood. Desolate would probably best describe it. If Sebastian had been cross with her before, he hated her now, this woman he hadn't seen for months and who had most probably abandoned him. This Spanish-yapping monster in bright clothing, who had suddenly turned up out of nowhere and dragged him away from his lovely big house to a fairground ride she should have known he was too short for, in the company of a disgruntled stranger who patently didn't like him.

Even my violently uninhibited chucking-up, both on and off the ride, hadn't given him quite the charge he was hoping.

Which might have had something to do with my saying 'Happy now, you sad little bastard?' under my breath, as I staggered queasily out of my stinking pod and back into the deluge.

The silence in that rank, overcrowded car was crucifying and I realised that I was swiftly losing whatever goodwill I had achieved with Señora Isabel Maria de Alences Velazco. In my line of work, goodwill is hugely important. If you fancy your client something rotten, I imagine it is imperative.

"O-kay," I began, turning to Mister Grumpy in desperation. "So what *do* your mates call you, then? Seb? Sebbo? The Sebster?" No luck there. "Who's your best pal at school?" Nothing. It was like he was deaf as well as foreign. "Come on, sausage – you must have a best pal. Everybody's got a—"

"*Rick…?*" from the back again.

I could tell that she was concerned by this line of questioning. It wasn't like I was water-boarding him but in my experience mums can be pretty sensitive.

That was when I had the idea. I suppose it was looking at him and seeing his miserable little face. I knew that I had to cheer the grumpy fellow up – okay, more importantly, I had to get his dispirited mum back on side before it all went totally pear-shaped

"Ever been to Hackney?" I said, veering off the motorway.

***

As the MiG and her gloomy cargo splashed to a halt outside a dingy, graffiti-ridden block of flats, I realised that Isabel was taking Hackney-in-the-Pouring-Rain to be the crowd-pleasing new London attraction I'd had in mind for her child and was distinctly underwhelmed.

I left mother and son in the car to puzzle it out in silence, as I ran through the downpour. "Just stay there," I yelled at the boy. "Hands in pockets! *Capisce?*"

Linda was already waiting – I had primed her on the way. I knew Gerald would be around with the same confidence that I knew she would have slept with me to take him off her hands for an hour.

"Love your hair," I said, without looking.

"I did it myself," she said.

Gerald emerged from the lobby, where he had probably been opening other people's mail. He was holding a scruffy football in one hand and his testicles in the other.

"Will you get your bloody hand out of there, Gerald," said Linda, without much hope. "You've got company." I had known a lot of children over the years and all the boys had this ongoing infatuation with their apparatus, but with Gerald it was the real thing.

"Where is the little fucker?" he said.

"Language!" said Linda. Good luck with that.

I dragged Gerald towards the car and shoved him in the back next to Isabel, who didn't look thrilled. In fact she stared at him like I had just scraped up some roadkill and given it to her for Christmas. I thought I had better make the introductions. "Gerald, Sebastian. Sebastian, Gerald. Got you a pal. Okay?"

We drove off with Linda waving us a grateful goodbye. I wondered if she ever thought wistfully of her son going off in a stranger's car, but it was probably just the Velazco case lingering in my mind (as opposed to my desk, where cases usually did their lingering).

"What team do you support?" asked Gerald, as a kick-off, which was friendly enough, although he probably didn't need to grab Sebastian by the collar and pull him closer to his ketchup-stained face. Sebastian failed to respond and I did seriously worry that he might have gone into shock or asphyxiation. But he finally managed a few recognisable sounds.

"Tottenham the Hotspurs."

That was the first time Gerald hit him. Not hard – more to

get his attention and correct his erroneous affiliation. "*SPURS?* They're fucking wankers!"

I caught Isabel's look in the mirror, aiming straight at me. It was the look someone gives a person when it starts to dawn on them that the person might well be insane.

The rain suddenly seemed totally appropriate.

***

London Fields is usually full of people. But today they had either looked out of the window and seen the weather or looked down the road and seen Gerald. I wasn't unduly concerned, as I reckoned an audience would only offer more opportunities for Sebastian's new playmate to build up loyalty-points on his ASBO.

The moment I managed to extricate him from the now fetid MG, Gerald was off and running with the ball, unfazed by the pelting rain, splashing mud in every direction but mostly on himself. Eventually it dawned on him that he was a man alone, so he turned and watched as poor Isabel tried bravely to burst free from the tiny, green cocoon that had been her home for so long.

Meanwhile Sebastian had wrenched himself away from his trim-picking duties and taken up position as far away from mother as was possible without sinking into the mud. He was biting his nails like a masochistic cannibal. It was all going really well.

My despairing client, by turns, glared at me and smiled bravely at her son. The little boy was already starting to shiver, as the weather gained purchase on his flimsy summer clothing.

It occurred to me, not the first time, that what had started off this morning as a reasonable idea was, by this afternoon, approaching threat-level imminent. Mother and child could not have looked further apart if there had been an ocean between them, which pretty soon there would be. No one seemed to be taking into account that it hadn't been my best Saturday either.

"Are you bloody playing?" cried Gerald, who was growing hungry and needed fresh meat.

I tried to encourage Sebastian to move onto the sodden grass but he wasn't having any. And then of course déjà vu struck again.

"You come!" he demanded, staring up at me.

Oh no sunshine, not this time. "I'll just stay here, Sebastian, and keep Mummy company. You lads go and play. Don't you worry about me."

Sebastian just crossed his arms and threw me a pout. I hate it when kids do that. Do they actually think it works?

"What are you fucking waiting for, Tottenham arsehole?" yelled Gerald, his hand happily back inside his trousers.

"The mouth on him," muttered Isabel.

I turned to look at her and our eyes met. It was extraordinary – even with her hair dripping and plastered to the sides of her head and our miserable English rain mingling with the almost perpetual moisture in her eyes, she was still the most beautiful creature I had ever seen. It was as if some exotic animal had escaped from a private zoo and sought refuge in the mean streets of East London.

"I'll just get them started," I told her, with a reassuring smile and strolled, in my cool, blue-leather, soon-to-be-ruined-like-everything-else Office shoes onto the soggy pitch.

Even with yours-truly squelching right there beside him, I could see that Sebastian was still pretty tentative. Okay, terrified. He was no budding Maradona. Or, as he might have preferred, a member of the England squad.

Gerald, either out of sportsmanship or sarcasm, kicked the ball very gently towards him. To his credit Sebastian kicked it gently back, at which point Gerald charged in with a powerhouse right-footer and slammed the ball into the smaller boy's tiny chest. Sebastian flew backwards, like a felled tree, into the mud. Shit.

Before a distraught Nurse Isabel could steam in and make things at least ten times worse, I stretched down to pick up her son. But I didn't need to. To my surprise as much as his mum's, the boy drew himself up from primordial London East 8 and kicked the ball with more force than anyone would have given him credit for. It didn't actually reach Gerald but it was more than respectable.

Gerald was clearly impressed. "Shit a brick!" he complimented and booted the ball back into Sebastian's proudly-soiled chest, sending him arsewards once again.

This time the plucky kid bounced back even more determinedly – almost balletically – and shot the ball in my direction.

It was bound to happen. With Isabel's eyes on me and the boys primed excitedly to evaluate my soccer prowess, I gave the muddy ball an almighty slice, slipped in my own footprint and landed on my side, my useless legs horribly twisted beneath me. Smart/casual client-outfit looking not quite so smart but a lot more casual.

I heard loud cheering. Both boys wore beams like their birthdays had all come at once. I gazed across at Isabel to see that she too was smiling, but fortunately not in a way I found totally demeaning. Which was why I decided to fall over again on my way up. And again. By this time Gerald was wetting himself – and that's not me being descriptive, it's Gerald having less control than a normal person might, perhaps because he plays with it so much.

That was how the game proceeded. Two contented little boys and one much bigger boy, playing kick-about in the pouring rain to a soundtrack of relentless obscenity, combined with some admittedly expert farting. (Interestingly, bum-trumpets transcend international boundaries – Sebastian was clearly a fan.) All of this while our glamorous soccer-mother looked on in bemusement, occasionally trying to cheer for her muddy son, which he totally – and, I think, quite deliberately – ignored. No change there.

Inevitably, in time, everything bar Gerald's mouth and anus reached saturation point and we decided to call it a draw. Or at least I did.

"We fucking sorted you. ARSE-nal. Did you hear that? Arse…"

But this time the North London team's new signing from Buenos wasn't taking it lying down.

"Tottenham the Hotspurs are o-kay!" Still a way to go.

Gerald gave his new opponent a huge but respectful grin from a filthy face, which the smaller boy returned in kind. Then the Arsenal player punched him on the shoulder, hard yet not without affection. In the circumstances I reckoned Sebastian's yelping reaction wasn't altogether bad news.

Isabel seized the moment to step in and try to clean Sebastian up. For one brief moment he just stood there and let her. I observed the scene, and what followed, almost as if I could see inside his brain. A message suddenly came through that this was not how things were supposed to go and he shrugged her off pretty forcefully. So, my turn again. Mr Fix-it.

"Right – who wants McDonalds?" I cried. I was sure I could put it through expenses.

"Shitting ace," beamed Gerald, as Sebastian put his hand up. "Oh, not the one near us, Rick. They went and banned me, the cu—" I covered his mouth just in time and we hungry lads strolled towards the MiG.

I glanced back at a suitably grateful Isabel, nodded wisely and gave her the reassurance only a top-notch lawyer can give.

"You just went to the top of my pile."

I hoped she didn't notice my smacking her son's grubby little hands off my car.

EIGHTEEN

The week that followed the classic Arsenal-Spurs game was probably the busiest of my working life. Which, considering I was working on just one case, probably doesn't speak much for my industry to date.

Sophie was the first to challenge me, because she had grumpily re-arranged all our property inspections for the following day and I think she could sense I wasn't in the zone.

The heavily-pregnant woman showing us around the third flat must have picked up something too, as she kept leaving us alone in the tiny rooms. Either that or the baby was pressing on her bladder.

"Still in Wonderworld?" asked my prospective co-habitee, when she caught me staring fixedly at a wall, which probably wasn't the most notable feature of that particular living-space.

"It was a one-off, okay!"

I found myself taking serious umbrage at the insinuations she was making, which I suppose she had every right to make, considering that we were about to spend the rest of our lives together. And, of course, that they were true.

"So, what's she like?"

"Who? What's who like?" I replied, trying not to sound like I was stalling. But Sophie just looked at me, so obviously that hadn't paid off. "Oh, her. I dunno. Late-forties, big, sort of y'know, *peasanty*. Cries all the time. Really hard work." I was getting back into my rhythm. "A solicitor shouldn't have to be 'supervising' pre-trial parental contact, Sophie. It's a new system, Law Society approved obviously, but I'm not alone in thinking it's hardly fair." *What?*

"Poor you." She was genuinely sympathetic, which only made things worse. "Poor her too, I suppose. Not allowed to be alone with her own child!" I shook my head. So unjust. "Are you coming over tonight?"

I know I should have said yes but I had experienced this vague niggling all day that I should put in some actual, billable hours on the Velazco case. It had dawned on me that the way to keep the attention going – attention which, for some reason, I desperately wanted – might be to focus even briefly on why my client was here in the first place. (Although, like a dog chasing a car, I had no idea what to do with this attention once I'd got it.)

"Big merger," I muttered. "Mega. Gotta work."

Sophie and I descended into a silence that was as pregnant as the lady who owned the apartment. She could sense it the moment she waddled back in.

"It's been a happy flat," she said.

***

If you're picturing me at all that long-ago summer, it may well be as a young, rangy, not too horrible-looking guy (in a sort of unformed, English, could've-been-in-a-boy-band way), smartly but not stuffily dressed, crammed nine-to-five behind a wonky, overburdened desk. Perhaps dribbling the odd, cheesy string from his melting ciabatta, while he pores over the case that's now firmly at the top of his ever-mounting pile. And letting the cobwebs settle over Mrs Armitage, the angry Irishman and all the others who unfortunately failed the Davenport legs, face and sexy-accent test.

But this would be to ignore the London Eye, Hampton Court, St James Park and the pond on Hampstead Heath. All of which I visited those heady weeks with Isabel, who apparently was no fan of conference rooms either (and no way was she coming anywhere near my office).

Gradually, as we walked and talked, she unpeeled layer after layer. Not of herself unfortunately, although the hot weather didn't exactly hurt, but of her life in Buenos Aires, which unsurprisingly is a world away from Hackney and the Edgware Road.

"Si, of course there are the bad places," she explained. "The *villa miseria*. The slums, yes? Like here, like in everywhere." I think, personally, she was doing her slums down. "But I live with Sebastian in a good part. Far away from the danger. San Telmo, she is the oldest *barrio*. Many dancers, much art. You would like this place. You like the art?"

"Of course. Who doesn't? It nourishes the soul. And it's an excellent investment."

I tried to imagine her life in Buenos Aires with Sebastian but I'm not great at picturing things way outside my own experience. I even bought the *Evita* DVD again (Cancer Research, Stratford, 25p), but of course it told of an earlier era. It also said in the end titles that they filmed it in Budapest, so that was a waste of an evening. Curiously, however, I could imagine Isabel in her dance studio in a leotard without much difficulty. In fact it was becoming harder and harder not to.

I remembered to take proper notes these times, and not just stare into those bewitching eyes, because even I could see that I would have to do some proper lawyering pretty soon. (More pleading calls to Oliver, to ascertain what I needed to know procedurally and to update him on the sort of things he didn't need to know at all.)

If I were to take time out to elaborate on the arcane

mechanics of the English legal system, I guarantee that within two paragraphs you would lose the will to live, as I did on a regular basis. And even now I can't pretend that I've got everything totally right in my head about how things went down back then. Legally or chronologically. It's funny how the mind can jumble things that you were convinced at the time were indelible. Just ask two accident-victims, or even onlookers, how they recall a car-crash.

But briefly, to build up a picture for the all-powerful judge of what life had been like, and would be like, for little Sebastian Jorge Menzies in Buenos Aires, I would need to secure concrete information. Cartloads of it. Hard facts, full details. You can't just waltz into court and say, 'This kid would be living like a prince, Your Honour, with a golden X-box and all the fajitas he could munch.' I needed names, dates, school reports, apartment spec, witness statements, bank statements, medical and dental records. Facts, facts, facts. And tons of signed affidavits.

Even though, as Oliver kept assuring me, it wouldn't make a scrap of difference.

But that wasn't my problem. You have to just do your job as best you can and not get too involved in the consequences. How do we think doctors stay sane and sleep nights? (Or hostage negotiators.)

Naturally Isabel was more than happy to give me all the background I might need. I realise now how accustomed I had grown to English reserve, the reticence that had to be overcome, the wheedling, the obfuscation, the going round-the-houses to reach the required destination. But Isabel was like an emotional satnav, she got there straight away without the diversions and dead-ends. It came as a shock to my pallid system to encounter barely-prompted outpourings of the most intimate facts and emotions.

The truth, the whole truth and nothing but the truth. Or so I assumed.

Each day, when I returned to the office, I added more facts to the file, made further costly international phone calls (a first for me and quite exciting) and requests for detail, did everything that Oliver told me to do and that behoves a good family-lawyer, albeit a family-lawyer surviving on non-existent fees from one solitary, impoverished client.

I chose to ignore the 'hello stranger's that Leila hurled my way, and the 'where the fuck have you been?'s that Dimpy whispered over-loudly, as I whipped past reception and its bemused clients. And, of course, Barney was far too busy doing real law and lunches to give me the time of day.

As to the regular phone calls from the forty-five other people on my desk-top Matterhorn, I evolved a response that Oliver didn't actually provide, but of which I think he would have been proud (even as he was appalled).

"Hello, Mr Davenport, how's my divorce coming along?" was the type of question.

"Absolutely fine Mr/Mrs X. We're just waiting on a major decision from the House of Lords that could affect the outcome. Won't be long."

"Ooh. House of Lords, eh?"

And they would contentedly put down their phones, flattered beyond measure that the dissolution of their marriage should be so important that the greatest legal brains in the land were up nights concerning themselves about it. Never underestimate the gullibility of the British public, when confronted by a randy young lawyer with a hot foreign client.

***

I was working late on the Velazco case one balmy summer evening, when my dad knocked on my bedroom door. It struck me once again that should Isabel discover I still lived at home with my parents, it was game-over on the impressing front. (I

92

had told her that I was renting an old Cambridge pal's flat in Knightsbridge, while he was working undercover at an Embassy overseas.)

"Big takeover?"

Dad had brought me a cup of tea and a KitKat, which he set down next to the papers on my desk. I still have that desk. It was made of sturdier stuff than the one in my office, because Ronnie Davenport had built it for me out of love and reclaimed pine when I was thirteen (and Oliver was getting truckloads of gifts for his bar mitzvah.)

"Yeah. Something like that."

I assumed he would catch on that I was pretty busy and just back away, but for some reason he hung around, blocking my light and smiling loopily at me. I realise now, of course, that he was almost paralysed with paternal pride but right at that moment I wished there was some sort of parent-repellent I could spray into the air that would encourage him to leave.

Eventually he sensed that a nice, summer evening guy-chat wasn't on the cards, so he turned for the door. But I knew this wasn't the end, because my dad has the cabbie's trick of conducting a conversation over his shoulder, at whoever happens to be behind him.

"Yeah. Well don't overdo it, son." And here it comes. "Hell of a pile-up on the Old Kent Road this lunchtime. Fact." Just don't say anything and perhaps he'll— "Had to go all round the houses." Maybe just a nod.

"'night, Rick."

Result.

I went back to the Velazco case. Contemplating my new acquisition, in anticipation of a possible, albeit unlikely, merger.

And then my mum came in with some crumble.

NINETEEN

"Your dad doesn't need a corporate lawyer, does he?"

It was always better to catch Oliver first thing in the morning. Not because, like some solicitors we both knew, he would be at his most sober, but because his day was usually pretty blocked-out with clients or court.

"I'm in a black hole here with Barney," I continued, to genuinely sympathetic 'tsk's or 'oy's. "He never talks to me, Ollie. Especially not about my prospects. I might as well not exist. And there are fuck-all jobs being advertised."

I had the legal-employment pages stacked up in front of me but there was no one out there exactly screaming for a guy with my impressive dearth of qualifications. I turned away from the phone.

"Sorry, Mrs Chen."

Mrs Chen was my first client of the day but I was sure she didn't mind my making a phone-call. She seemed to be too busy sobbing into my first Kleenex of the day. And I had to catch my more-learned friend Oliver, so that I could plead with him to look through the wealth of Velazco material I had somehow cobbled together. I needed reassurance, before it went into the system. It was very important.

If poor Mrs Chen knew how little work I had been doing on

her case, she would have had even more to sob about. So I put the phone down and gave the diminutive, middle-aged Chinese lady the full Davenport attention.

"I'm afraid there's not a lot we can do regarding your divorce, Mrs Chen. At least not until—" Until what? The Year of the Goat? Think, Rick! "Until that new Act of Parliament comes in next month. The Chinese… Divorce Act."

The phone rang. I braced myself for more human misery – you don't get many jolly phone calls in Family. But it was Dimpy, with the worst news ever.

"*HERE?*" I screamed, making my tiny client jump. "*She doesn't have an appointment!*" I slammed closed the barely-opened Chen file and just as swiftly encouraged its subject out of my pathetic office and back towards reception.

"Top of the pile, Mrs Chen," I told her, helping her out of the chair. I hadn't made allowances for her lightness. She came up with alarming speed.

I virtually carried her out into the corridor, past a bemused Leila, who I knew was going to say something about a Chinese takeaway when we were alone. (You don't want to know what lawyers say about you after you've left.) I could see the angry Irishman standing at the far end, staring ruddily at me, but he wasn't the person I was concerned about.

It was of course the angry Argentinian, who was parked beside Dimpy's desk with full glare on. Dimpy had warned me on the phone that Isabel was demanding to see me straightaway and our impish receptionist had added, a bit unnecessarily in my opinion, that it didn't look like she'd settle for a trip to the zoo.

I felt like one of those unbelievable heroes in an action movie, who has to assess and respond to lethal threats coming at him from all directions. Go for the closest first – "You know your way out, Mrs Chen," easing her streetwards with a gentle shove to the small of the back.

Now I was ready to tackle the Irish challenger. "Mr Ryan, something I need to talk to you about. A letter's being faxed through as we speak. So give me just a few minutes, okay?" (I'd need far more time than that. Should've said pigeon.)

Finally, I turned to my most dangerous and unpredictable adversary, who could destroy with three little words.

"*Your office. Now!*"

I managed a swift look at Dimpy, who shrugged. She knew the score. Defeated, I led Ms Velazco down the corridor like dead lawyer walking, the scary silence broken only by Evan opening his door and sighing enviously in Welsh as we passed by.

It didn't take long for Isabel to absorb the Family Department of Darcy, Cracknell, Solicitors-at-Law in its shameful entirety. "They're decorating my new one," I explained lamely. "This is just a stop-gap…"

"You lied to me!"

"*Lied*?" I roared, in outrage. Then blew it slightly. "About what, specifically?"

I dusted the seat from Mrs Chen, not that she had left anything but it's a courtesy, and offered it to Isabel. She clearly felt, however, that her venom would be best delivered standing.

"I talk with Laurence last night."

Bugger!

"You talked to him! What the hell for?"

"He is my husband. Once. We have a child." I supposed this made sense. "And he tell me he *agreed* to the weekend visits. He say he is okay perfectly with this."

What could I say?

"It was his lawyers, Isabel! Bastardos. I told you, they play ten kinds of hardball."

She suddenly softened, yet curiously the softening seemed somehow worse. "Mr Davenport," she said, quietly, "Rick. You are all that I have. Please do not screw with me around."

Understood. Sort of. But unfortunately, as she was dialling her anger down to quiet desperation, I had instinctively ratcheted my own boiler up a click or six and was now entering a white-hot mood of barely justifiable self-justification.

I grabbed a handful of papers from under the stale bagel that served as a paperweight until munched, and waved them in her face.

"Look – see? All yours! Your flat in Buenos, your bank accounts, Sebastian's school reports. Medical reports. Dental records. Your mother's death certificate. Testimonials! Affidavits! *SEE!*" I had finally been doing my homework and this time, even as I berated my favourite client, I was impressing myself just a bit. "If Barney gets wind of how many hours I'm spending just on Menzies v. Velazco, I won't be able to handle a – a bagel, let alone a major merger."

She looked at the ream of stuff I was brandishing and nodded contritely. With a huge sigh she pulled the chair out a bit further and sat down.

"Perhaps, if you win this," she said, "your boss, he will give you what you really want."

She was offering me a half-smile and I glancingly took on board that maybe she knew me better than I had assumed. I didn't mind. She must have realised after my outburst that I was genuinely on her case (albeit for not entirely selfless reasons), so my own long-term ambitions shouldn't concern her. It wasn't as if she figured in them.

"Isabel," I began, as if the recent misunderstanding had never happened. "Is there anything else you should tell me? Anything we might have missed?"

"How would I know this?" she sighed. "What things?"

"Well, for example, that one-way ticket. You still haven't—"

She leaned across the desk, not raising her voice but somehow conveying her displeasure by making it even raspier.

"I keep telling this!" she insisted. "I pay it from Buenos Aires.

Laurence, he promise to me he will pay return home later. He tell me it is cheaper." She sighed as a different and deeply troubling thought slithered in. "But I do not know what he speak to my little boy – about what is in his 'awful' mami's mind, when I am sending him away."

Even I, with my non-existent experience of custody cases, knew that poisoning a child against the other parent was a common accusation and quite probably an equally common reality. Who knew what reasons Laurence had given the kid for not packing him back home after his Christmas break?

I recall the sense of relief washing through me as we talked through the documents together at my desk and slowly re-entered the shallows of calm. I should have realised, knowing Isabel as I was beginning to, how deceptive this could be.

Her question had seemed so innocent. "What else do you need to know?"

Of course I wasn't exactly sure, so I thought I would make it safely all-embracing. "Just enough to prove you're a good mother."

Oh shit.

Instantly she was up again, with a dancer's spring, fury rising in her eyes of flame like a newly-stoked furnace.

"Isabel, I didn't mean…"

"I AM THE VIRGIN MARIA OF GOOD FUCKING MOTHERS!"

She didn't give me a lot of time to endorse or question this clamorous self-assessment, as she combined it almost simultaneously with a mightily well-aimed kick to the big pile of files beside my desk. Followed by another kick, another pile.

It was almost as if she had choreographed the whole routine, right foot, left foot, this client, that client, the full eleven o'clock number. *West Side Story* meets the Edgware Road. And, with every movement and displaced file, a word emerged from her livid lips, lyrics timed exactly to the staccato beat linking her head to those ten toes of fury.

"Ask all of these, your customers, no – your 'clients' – if their children they are happy with them!" Kick, kick. "Ask them if they laugh with them, play with them," kick-kick-kick – "*dance* with them."

Papers were flying everywhere. Staples popping. The world was about to have Hurricane Katrina that year. I had Hurricane Isabel. But she hadn't finished.

"Listen, 'Mister' Davenport. I have given up everything – *everything* – to do what I am doing here. Because everything, it mean nothing! Nada. *Comprende*? I have no life here in this goddam awful place, this not-friendly city. No money, no job. So what? Is not forever."

The door opened and Dimpy popped her head round. I imagined it was to tell me that Angry Irishman had added 'Impatient' to his name, or maybe she had just heard the commotion. She never managed to pass it on, because she was out of there in a traumatised instant. Isabel, of course, was only into Act One.

"I live for this day only," she said, clearly expecting me to ask which day. 'You know which day is this?" It probably wasn't August Bank Holiday, which was the one I was suddenly yearning for. "The day when my little boy, he will call me his mami and he will say to me, 'Mami, I want to come back with you home'. *IN SPANISH!*"

In other circumstances I would have thought 'Don't hold your breath'. But with affidavits swirling like snow and long legs kicking, I don't think I thought at all. I do remember hearing the phone ring and recall that it was suddenly whizzing out of my hand towards the window, sent on its way by a deftly-placed, high-heeled shoe. Darkish blue, if memory serves.

"Is this what a 'good mother' does? You tell me, *por favour*."

The descending pitch on those last words gave me hope that she had finished. I took a chance and answered the phone that had fortuitously bounced off the glass and was now dangling over the side of my ravaged desk. "Yeah? Out in a second, Dimpy." I pointed to a file, whose contents were scattered beside my chair. "That one," I informed my unscheduled client. "Mr Ryan. He's waiting."

I had no idea if it was this exact file, such was my lack of familiarity with its contents, but it seemed to work. Still panting from the dance of the sugar-plum maniac, Isabel squatted down with astonishing elegance and helped me shove all the papers back into their folders. Or any folders. She would never bag a job as a filing-clerk.

Our knees were rubbing on my cheap-as-chips carpet and our faces were so close that I could actually feel her hair brush my cheek. Even after all the drama – or perhaps because of it – this was electric. Her warm breath dusted my ear and instantly my own breath stopped. Our eyes met and lingered perhaps a fraction too long. I'm not ashamed to say – well, I suppose I am a bit – that her colossal anger had really turned me on.

I was totally unsure where this would lead, nor even where I was hoping it might. Life had suddenly become too heady for my lukewarm Hackney blood. Yet I knew before the words came out of my mouth that I was going to go for it.

"But I'm free tonight. Isabel."

TWENTY

It was well after seven-thirty by the time I hit accordion city. Not late by City-lawyer standards but midnight-oil for me.

My mum was on the case the moment I pelted up the stairs. "Ricky – is that you, love? Come in and say hello. Linda's here."

"Can't stop, Mum. Hi, Linda!"

Cue my dad coming out of the living-room, where he had doubtless been listening to that secret, 24/7 news channel to which Oliver and I believe only London cabbies are subscribed. The one that knows stuff to which ordinary news-gathering organisations either aren't privy or have unforgivably overlooked.

"They're closing the northbound M25 because of terrorism."

"No, they're not."

I was at the top of the stairs and I could hear him behind me. "You in a hurry?"

"Yeah, sort of. Sorry, Dad."

"We don't seem to have supper together any more. Y'know, just the three of us. Me, you and your mum." (In case I thought he meant the Pope and Elton John.) "Are you taking her somewhere nice?"

"Who?"

"*Who!* Who d'you think? My little Sophie."

"Oh… yeah. You know."

"Yeah. Sounds lovely. How's the flat-hunting?"

"Dad, I'd love to chat but I've still got to change."

"I know. Sorry, son. Still it's nice you're dressing-up for your girl, isn't it?" He beamed. "Mind you, someone's pretty dressed-up already, what with that new whistle 'n flute."

Even though he was a genuine Eastender, I still winced whenever my dad lapsed into his somehow not totally convincing rhyming-slang. Although my dearest wish right then was that he would slope off back down the apples and pears.

"Yeah, well, you have to make an effort," I smiled.

I was almost inside my mini-wardrobe, also built by my dad, wondering what you wore for an invitation bestowed by the most attractive kneeling-client on record, asking you to meet her at some address you had never heard of, but which could be a highly discreet club, an intimate hotel or even a friend's apartment. For purposes unknown but imagined all the way home. Along with the leotard.

Didn't somebody famous say power was an aphrodisiac? Somebody quite unattractive, as I recall. So, at the very least, I should probably shower and shave and splash something on. Or would a woman like that prefer the earthy, unshaven Rick Davenport? It was hard to know with foreigners.

It was also hard to know when to tell her about the phone call I had received shortly after she had left my office. I was sure it would all fall into place.

"You having a shower?"

I know my dad was only making conversation but was it any of his business? He'd soon be asking if I was considering a poo before I shot off. We really had to find that flat.

"Dad, I'm sorry, but—"

"I know. Just think before you drink before you drive, okay?"

"And Mr Kipling makes exceedingly good cakes."

***

My dad would have known exactly where to find the street that Isabel had chosen for our first 'out-of-hours' assignation. But I certainly wasn't going to ask him and learn the six best ways to get there from space. Thankfully GPS had been specifically designed to avoid these conversations.

As I cruised along the sedate suburban avenues in the less sedate MiG, I could see rows of large Edwardian houses, all a lot smarter than the house I had just left. Number 23, however, wasn't a house. Or a block of flats. And it certainly wasn't a discreet hotel.

I heard the music first. South American I assumed, although I couldn't have told you what category other than loud. It was blaring out through the open windows of a small, one-story, redbrick building that looked like some sort of Sixties village hall.

It turned out to be the local scout hut, which discovery didn't exactly make my head swirl. At first I thought Isabel had simply made a mistake but soon realised that it was I who had misread the signs.

If I was now expecting Isabel to be entertaining a group of overexcited little boys in shorts and woggles, correction was at hand. The moment I entered the place I could see that I was the youngest guy by far. And Isabel the most youthful woman by decades.

The unfamiliar but unashamedly sexy music that I had picked up from the car, and which was now syncopating through the small, scout-scented hall, was coming from a Tango album that Isabel had presumably loaded into her ghetto-blaster. This exotically upbeat yet enticingly lazy sound was insinuating itself out of the speakers and into the bodies, hearts and hearing-devices of at least a dozen elderly couples, all dressed to kill and chest to chest, entwining with enviable vigour under the tutelage of their devoted teacher. The accordion had never sounded so good.

"This is it, people," encouraged the expert, "match the movement to how you feel. Si? Surrender to the passion that is burning inside every one of you. Especially you, Mrs Waterstone."

Mrs Waterstone, an ample, white-haired lady in her late sixties, ramped up the passion to the delight of her partner, a tall but stooped black gentleman, who suddenly found his right leg in a far from matronly, Home Counties vice.

Isabel didn't even notice me. If the others did, they certainly weren't paying me much attention. The leotard of Davenport fantasies (flame red with real, painted flames) was not on display. Instead she had on a simple, tightly-fitting black dress, slit on either side, revealing appealing lengths of sheer, black stocking. The effect was still sensational. I looked on the tiny beads of perspiration that glistened across her upper chest and forehead as elegant grace-notes I berated myself for having so far omitted from my dreams.

There was no way my client could keep her lithe and lovely body still. She was Tango-ing alone – or perhaps with an imaginary partner – but more to inspire the others than simply instruct.

Then she saw me. Yet instead of acknowledging me with any of the several limbs or joints at her disposal, she suddenly grabbed hold of a stout and swarthy partner, about my dad's age, with as much wiry, grey hair sprouting through and over his shirt as he sported on his head. He seemed both surprised and utterly thrilled at this embrace.

"Come on, Mr Demetrios. Let us show them how we do this when I am living here."

Of course Isabel was as consummate as I would have expected, flowing like mercury all over the wooden floor and down the less-wooden Cypriot. Long legs striding and sliding and going places you can only go with permission. But tubby Mr Demetrios was no slouch either and I began to realise, as the locked pair danced almost as one, that in Tango you can make up your moves as you go along. I suppose they have to conform to some sort of regime; you can't just interpolate a slice of Gay Gordons or Riverdance, but you still have a lot of leeway.

"Feel the music, amigos! The Tango has only the one rule – yes?"

I thought this was rhetorical but suddenly everyone in the room was yelling out "FREEDOM!" and stamping as vigorously as their pacemakers would allow. (Cheap shot – they were a lot better and fitter than I was.)

Perhaps it was simply the way this particular dance goes, but at the very moment the happy couple passed my stationary and totally fascinated body, Isabel threw her head and torso back with such ferocity that it seemed she was going to disappear between her own legs and roll around the hall. Her tightly ensconced yet unapologetically wonderful breasts were just centimetres from my face and those blazing eyes caught mine, which were of course following her every move.

I could have watched until rigor mortis set in – certain parts of my body were already practising – but I suddenly felt a tap on my shoulder that was more like a thump. I turned to see a tall, Indian lady, even older than my mum, beckoning me with smiling determination.

"You," she commanded. "Tango!"

Before I had time to decline, which I would have done most readily, the old leg was up and intertwined with my thigh and a strong, sweaty hand had its clasp on mine. The lady's greying head suddenly hurled itself back as if commanding me to thrust my own forward and make one writhing body out of two. It was like wrestling to music.

In seconds we were swirling around the scout hut, cutting a Latin-American swathe through the old-time Tangoers, my partner's head held high and proud, suffused with the arrogance that only comes from being really good at something that someone close-by really isn't. I could hear laughter and it pissed me off, until I recognised it as Isabel's, then immediately all sensations moved from angry embarrassment to pure mortification.

But the next moment I was handed on like a baton to a highly nimble lady of restricted growth and thence to Mrs Waterstone, who seemed to be surrendering to the passion with admirable lack of restraint. As she moved confidently backwards her generous, varicosed leg curled round my ankle, causing me to topple into her grandmotherly breasts. She was graciously allowing me to lead and I felt like a bull pushing an enormous wheel of cheese.

Finally, after working the room, I ended up at my inevitable destination. Isabel was laughing and sweating and glowing and having no trouble summoning up some of the happier sensations that must have been interred for a while beneath all the anger and pain of the past few months. I caught a revealing glimpse of how she must have been, at a time before I knew her and in a place I knew I never would.

As she Tangoed me round that suburban hut, transformed for those few glorious minutes into a *milonga* in Buenos Aires, the feel of her firm hand in mine and her warm breath in my face, the smell of a magical scent from somewhere foreign intermingling with an earthier one from much closer to home, all conspired to intoxicate me to the point that my dad's warning of breathalysation might well have been more prescient than I had thought.

"Move the centre first then the feet will follow," she whispered.

I wish.

"Bonjourno," I said, which of course was Italian, but the sentiment seemed to get through.

"Buenas noches," she corrected.

"Olé," I responded, thereby exhausting my list of expressions that can piss off a Hispanic, before we took off at even greater speed.

The sound of applause filled my ears, which was either aimed sarcastically at me or sympathetically towards Isabel, but apparently marked the end of Pensioners' Tango 101 for the evening.

By way of an encore my teacher fell into my arms and sunk down to the floor, clutching my legs as she collapsed into a sultry black heap, causing Mr Demetrios to whoop and Mrs Waterstone to raise a pencilled eyebrow. Clients don't normally do this (and personally I hoped that Mrs Armitage never would), but somehow it felt perfectly acceptable in the circumstances. I just wished I knew what the circumstances were.

She was still down there as her little troupe left the building.

**

"I am lucky my students they still remember me."

We were sitting on a bench, mopping ourselves. Or rather Isabel was mopping – rather sensuously as I recall – and I was awaiting the towel.

"You're lucky they remember anything," I responded.

She smiled, waving an admonishing finger. "Now you take me home." A command I was only too willing to obey.

I recall that my heart was pounding, which it would have done anyway after all that unaccustomed exercise, but this was different. I felt giddily lightheaded, especially when I noticed that she was looking straight at me, as she carelessly wiped the last stubborn beads of sweat from her torso. She was still smiling with those perfect teeth as I walked her to my car.

"For a moment I am in Buenos Aires!" she yelled into an avenue that probably wasn't used to elation. "Is good to dance, no?"

"No... Yes. It was fun. Thank you."

I say thank you a lot, it's something my mum taught me. I wondered what else I might soon be thanking Isabel for, as I opened the car door for her and she slid in. Why is a woman getting into or out of a car so bloody sexy? I suppose she has to look okay in the first place but a tight, black, tasselly Tango-dress doesn't hurt.

As I started the engine and once again heard those sounds that told me poor MiG was ailing, Isabel suddenly smacked the dashboard. It must be something genetic.

"Now things are going well, yes?" she crowed. "What judge would say I am not fit? I am bloody fit, eh mister Davenport?"

"You are," I agreed. "Fit. Where am I going, exactly?" She waved me forward impatiently, like I should know the area. "This street here?" Another nod.

She moved in even closer, which is pretty close in an MG.

"And I am still the top of your list," she said, softly. "Richard?"

Oh God, how she said that name. But I wished she hadn't brought up the case, just when things were going so well.

"So!" she said, as we moved slowly down the street. I wondered if the loud American was home. Hopefully she was in a four-hour Shakespeare somewhere. "What is next?"

This was so not the right time.

"Well, it's all fine, Isabel," I reassured her, my eyes firmly on the road. But I could sense her nodding, all serious again. "Everything under control, yeah." I paused but I could tell that she was waiting for more, almost as if she knew what was coming. "The Child Welfare Officer – we call them CAFCASS– it stands for Children And… er not sure, but she – or he – just wants to see you. You know, with Sebastian. It's standard practice."

Silence.

I turned to her. The tan had appeared to fade on the spot. She looked completely terrified. Which wasn't what I had hoped but can't say I hadn't expected.

"Stop the car. Now!" she demanded.

"There's really no need"

"Si. Here is where I live." I stopped. "Why do you not tell me this? The CAF—"

"I only heard this afternoon."

"No. Is too early!"

"They need to observe you with him," I explained gently. "That's all. And just to talk to him. You know, on his own. It's no big deal. Can I come in?"

"NO!"

Oh.

"Is too bloody soon. For this – child person. After these months, when I am not being with my son. And after the lies his father tell about me."

I had no idea how to reassure her. Oliver had briefed me about CAFCASS, so I wasn't totally out of the loop, but knowing about it and having experience of it were quite different things.

"It's not like it'll happen tomorrow, Isabel. And things can – change overnight. Maybe I can come in and we could talk about it?" Worth a shot.

"I am very tired, Rick."

She hadn't been tired five minutes ago but she certainly looked wrecked now. I wished I could cheer her up but it wasn't in my gift and I couldn't very well change the subject. There only was one subject.

"*Richard…?*"

Her voice had changed, like the music earlier, when it had lost its arrogance and become for a moment mournfully plangent. The anger had gone and there was a softness here, a nakedness which plucked at my heart as on a string of one of those Tango guitars, even when I didn't want it to. I had to remain professional, especially when I was intimating that the evening shouldn't end in my car.

"Yes, Isabel?"

"Sebastian, he wish to see you again."

Whoa! This came out of the blue. Why on earth would

the kid – *any* kid – wish this? I know I had introduced him to Britain's future most-wanted but that had nearly gone so wrong. And Wonderworld had been a total disaster. I was her (trainee) solicitor for God's sake, not her childminder.

"This Saturday, yes? Is okay?"

You're having a laugh!

"Of course it is, Isabel."

To my own surprise I knew exactly where we would go.

TWENTY-ONE

"I think I've found a flat."

It wasn't the best time to tell me.

"*Sophie!*"

"What?" she protested. "You're either in meetings or in me!"

She had a point. I hadn't devoted much time to her that week (and I certainly hadn't told her I had taken up Tango), so there had been precious little opportunity for the conversation we were clearly about to have, the only likely interruptus being Kim/Cypress deciding to thump on the wall.

"We can see it on Saturday afternoon," she persisted.

"Oh."

"What – oh?" She had turned on the bedside light, which is never a good sign. Her face was red, but I would be flattering myself if I thought it was all the heat of the night. "Booked a conference call with Spongebob Squarepants?"

"Oh, come on, Soph!" I hated sarcasm. "I got tickets – for the Spurs game."

I had managed to buy them, for around half my life's earnings, through Cyril Rosen. He had a season ticket and knew people. (I wished that I knew 'people'. Back then I only knew people.)

"I'm *sorry?*"

I could see that Sophie wasn't sorry at all. She was outraged. She shifted herself well away from my yearning (arousal) but aching (Tango) body and just stared at me. "Rick, you hate football."

Ah.

I didn't say anything – what could I say? But my guilty silence gave her the chance to work things out for herself. "*It's that Mexican – with the kid!*"

"Argentinian," I corrected, for no useful reason. "She's Arg—"

"Like I fucking care."

I was quite shocked, Sophie doesn't usually swear. But what she said next shocked me far more.

"Well, seeing as I'm not doing anything…"

TWENTY-TWO

I had seen four football matches in my life and quite enjoyed them. I had a feeling that this tradition was about to be broken.

Attending White Hart Lane that sweltering Saturday was like walking into a windowless bakery in the Mohave Desert. Even the grass was sweating.

Where we sat was an unbroken bed of white and navy, as thousands of overheated Spurs fans sang, yelled and spat their support for their unparalleled London team. But even with all the verbal virtuosity, few could touch the rival chant coming from a scruffy, ten-year-old fifth columnist right there in their midst.

"You're shite, Tottenham. Shite in white! Ha! And blue. Wankers!"

It was amazing that young Gerald wasn't stabbed by some dementedly loyal home-team fan. Or indeed a player. Or me. But that particular afternoon was full of surprises.

Sophie's was the biggest of them all. Unsurprisingly, it occurred at the exact moment she caught her first glimpse of Isabel.

I had given my client the match-tickets for her and Sebastian, who had apparently been thrilled, so we didn't meet them until they were in the West Stand, awaiting kick-off. I decided to bring

Gerald along, for Sebastian's sake (and for his mum's, obviously), but also to provide me with some sort of ill-conceived protection against the inevitable.

Everything happened at once.

While Gerald was greeting his delighted new friend ('Arsehole!') and Isabel was sending me a strained but still dazzlingly grateful smile, all I could really hear was Sophie muttering '*Big peasant?*' a bit too loudly and too often in my ear. I reckon Isabel heard this too but I couldn't very well tell her that it was a criticism aimed solely at me and not some sort of gratuitous insult emanating from the delicate mouth of a fragrant English rose.

The match hadn't started, so we were all still on our feet, arranging who would sit next to whom. What I did notice, however, as soon as I arrived, was that Sebastian had no intention of sitting anywhere near his mum, however humbly she asked him. So I parked him between Gerald and myself, which rather unfortunately set me down next to Isabel with Sophie on her other flank.

I didn't need a tactician to tell me this was an utterly disastrous formation. I tried immediately to rearrange things, so that I was between Isabel and Sophie, but then Sebastian moved next to me, squidging Sophie out. And Gerald leapt right up and moved himself next to his new mate on the Sophie side.

Don't bother working all this out. Trust me, it didn't work. I was beginning to wish I'd had a note from my mum, like schoolboy Oliver would present on a regular basis when Mrs Rosen didn't want him involved in a potentially bruising sport.

I could see Sophie sniffing the air around Gerald and shuddering. I think she would have changed places with a St John's Ambulance stretcher-bearer just to avoid spending a second more with Hackney's own wild child.

After this pre-match entertainment for the merry Spurs fans around us, the game itself began. Not that I was in any mood for watching. Even when I wasn't checking her out, I could sense Sophie's eyes coldly sizing up our exotic interloper. Isabel was doing the same but without the exotic bit. I found myself wishing my client didn't look quite so stunning in just her worn, skintight denims and some sort of tight-fitting, creamy T-shirt, but I knew it wasn't her fault and the feeling lasted about a nanosecond.

I tried hard to concentrate on the game and enjoy the unrelenting, yet generally good-natured, banter from the crowd around me. I managed all of five minutes before I sensed Isabel's hand reaching towards my lap.

I froze, horrified, knowing Sophie would be picking all this up. With my luck it would be on *Match of the Day*. But the hand wasn't for me – it was crossing over to touch the smaller hand of her own son, something he reacted to as if she had dug a steak-knife into it. With a huge sigh she withdrew the offending object and deflated back into her seat.

I looked across at Sebastian, because right then he was probably the least contentious person to look at. He was doing his angry pout again, which did him no favours, but he seemed genuinely cross and upset. More than that – he seemed totally confused. I couldn't imagine what his time alone with Isabel was like. (Actually I could, because Isabel had told me. It was dire.)

"I used to get cheesed off with *my* mum, matey," I confided. "Still do. I think women are just hardwired to annoy us."

He responded but so quietly, amidst all the clamour, that I had to strain to hear him. "Did you ever wet your bed?"

Did I *what*? "No, of course not!" He was staring at me intently – and I noticed for the first time that his eyes were not unlike his mother's. Sadder, a shade darker, but with the same great lashes. "Well yeah, okay," I admitted. "Sometimes I did. Rarely but... yeah. Do you?"

He hesitated. "... Of course not!"

Well, that settled that.

I looked back to Sophie, to check if she had picked up any of this or had simply closed down to avoid catching a nasty dose of Gerald. But she was staring straight at me and mouthing something I had absolutely no problem catching. "*Are you shagging her?*"

Outraged, I shook my head violently and honestly, if you can shake a head honestly, because of course I wasn't shagging her. Nowhere near. And – it occurred to me, with what I have to confess now was a guilty regret – most probably never would.

Then Isabel joined in, from the other side. "Will you come tomorrow to see us?"

Great timing, Isabel. Sebastian, for some reason, seemed to be hanging on my response.

"I can't, Isabel," I said, as quietly as I could. "Flat-hunting."

"No. This is good. I understand."

She was very sweet about it, until she rested her hand on my knee. No mistaking it this time. Nor her face, as she looked up at me with a resigned smile. "You have your own life – Richard."

Without respecting the situation one jot, Spurs' newest continental signing chose this moment to score the first goal of the match. The crowd rose with a roar, or at least the home crowd did. Gerald shouted, "Stupid foreign twat". Isabel jolted a tad. And Sophie walked.

It took a second for me to notice and then a few more to struggle past Gerald, who had his hand down his trousers again, so wasn't quite as flexible as I would have wished. Sophie was moving at incredible speed, marching out as the Spurs went marching in, not caring what ecstatic Tottenham toes she trod on with her tiny, spiky heels.

I looked back to take in my little guest-list. Isabel had seized on my absence to move closer to her son, but he was grabbing a similar opportunity to shrink even further away. Gerald was wiping his nose on the scarf of the kid in front of him. I couldn't help musing on why everything I touched seemed to turn to shit.

My panic continued to rise as the crowd noises receded. Sophie was clacking down the steps with dangerous urgency, clearly anxious to be as far away from me and Tottenham as possible.

"Sophie," I yelled, "there is nothing going on!"

She turned, her angry face a portrait of disbelief. "Her hand was on your sodding knee!"

"She's foreign!" I countered, as if this explained it. "I swear to God I haven't done anything."

"But you wouldn't half like to!"

It's amazing how a nanosecond of delay can change an entire lifetime. "Great," she continued. "Oh, that's great. Why did you lie to me, Rick?"

"About the Corporate department?"

It just came out, as if I'd been flicking too swiftly through my mental Rolodex of deceits and haplessly plucked the wrong one.

"About that woman! Hang on… what *about* the Corporate—?" She didn't even finish the question. She didn't need to. But she arrived at the answer pretty fast. "You're not in Corporate, are you?"

"Not quite," I admitted. "But if I can maybe win this…"

Now she was crying. I think I told you earlier that tears don't usually work with me. Well, these did. "And you couldn't tell me? Oh my God, Ricko! Is that what you think of me? Oh my God!"

I didn't know. Was it what I thought of her or was this far more about how I thought of myself? And why was I still wondering what was going on with Isabel and her son just up the staircase behind me, even as Sophie and I were downstairs breaking up?

I knew that I didn't want Sophie to go. I'm still sure of this. There was no way I had suddenly found her less lovely or appealing. My heart hadn't hardened, in fact quite the reverse. It felt almost as if it had expanded. How bizarre was that? Even as

117

I watched my poor girlfriend's tears and felt on the cusp of my own, I was uncomfortably aware that I yearned for the heat of Isabel's hand through my chinos, as it settled back on my knee. What do therapists call this – conflicted?

"Sophie…"

"Who *are* you, Rick?"

It's like that joke, isn't it? The hard ones first.

"Sophie – I'm me!" Oh brilliant. "Nothing's changed," I ploughed on. "I'll get Corporate. If not at Barney's, then somewhere. I *want* Corporate. Fuck it – Sophie, I love you!"

I realised even then that combining long-held City ambitions with protestations of love wasn't an obviously winning one-two play, but I could see from her glistening eyes that I might just – miraculously – have made a vital inroad through her defences. And if I hadn't chosen that moment to take my eye off the ball and look back at the stadium, she could well not have stomped off with the middle finger of her right hand up in air.

And the result might have been totally different.

TWENTY-THREE

If someone asked me to describe that capricious summer, the closest I could come is that it was like a bumper box-set. We all experience drama in our lives, I'm far from unique. But doesn't it tend to the episodic, with some sort of normal service resuming in-between? Surely it has to be pretty unusual when the routine, boring bits get so mercilessly squeezed out that all the action comes in one huge, unbroken, overwhelming splurge.

Welcome to my August, episodes one to ninety-six.

The week began with Leila, and even she seemed to be telling me off.

"So, how's the Family man?"

That wasn't it. She was building up.

Leila had squeezed into my office, filling it almost to capacity, and was giving me her grade-A sardonic, single-eyebrow-raised smile. Most mornings we would stop for a chat here or by the coffee-machine in the firm's tiny kitchen, trying to avoid Evan. Trying also to hoover up the good client-biscuits, before Miss Collins could snatch them away for the good clients.

Leila seemed to have taken a shine to me, almost as if I needed protecting. More often than not we'd have a very swift drink after work, before she scooted back to her husband, a stay-at-home dad minding their two year old. She called it her 'shot before the tot'. Leila was forever showing me photos of the little girl, who I suppose was pretty cute, but I would always find myself having to stop her feeling guilty for not being back at home with her.

It made me think of the parents who left their kids with my mum, some of whom seemed ecstatic to pass on the responsibility to someone else. For life, if possible.

This day, however, I didn't have time for a chat. Actually, I wasn't in the mood. So I just shook my head and kept on reading.

The Velazco file, as usual, was the one lying splayed open on my desk, as I struggled to make sense of the unfamiliar world within. Today was a particularly bad one in Buenos Aires and I felt curiously troubled.

Leila knew about the case and had spotted Isabel on several of her visits, so she picked the file up and pretended to sag under its weight. It was then that she said the something that really hacked me off.

"There's always one that's more interesting than the rest." Here it comes. "But they're all people, Rick."

What did I think they were – Smurfs? It seemed like she was angry with me, something I didn't need just two days after the great White Hart Lane disaster. Especially not with the document that had just landed on my in-tray this morning like a primed IED. The sort of document that made having any sort of cordial, time-wasting chat with a colleague, the stuff of normal, workaday life, so totally out of the question.

"Fancy a drink later?" she persevered.

I knew I had been a bit remiss on the helping-Leila-to-believe-she's-still-a-great-mum front, but these were unusual times. Even so, I could have done with talking to someone about my own recent break-up with Sophie and, unsurprisingly, Oliver Rosen wasn't my first port of call. He may well have been Sophie's – I really didn't know. He wasn't even answering my texts.

120

"Er no, I can't today. I'm sorry, Leila." I tapped the document that was eating into my drinking time. And my soul. "And before you say it, yes – she could well be coming in today."

"I know," she said. "Barney just grabbed her."

***

I don't remember dropping the papers back onto my desk or even steaming past Miss Collins, who must have been at her usual station, percolating the morning bile. But I do recall flinging back the door to see Barney at his desk, chatting to a seated Isabel and Evan.

Evan?

What the hell was he doing there – aside from gurning unashamedly at my client?

"And here is Mr Davenport now."

Barney Cracknell was smiling at me. I can't say it was one of his nice smiles but then I had never seen one of his nice smiles. I found myself, amidst all the fear and puzzlement, just praying he wouldn't call her señorita.

"I was just explaining to the señorita here…" I looked across at Isabel, who was glowering at me, like I was the one who had snatched her child away. "… that when a client comes to Darcy, Cracknell, he – or she – has access to the *entire* firm."

"EVAN?" I splurted. "He's done even less Family than—"

Best not to go there, even with Evan putting on what he obviously considered his caring, family-man face. All he needed now was a mac and a bag of sweets, in my opinion.

I turned back to Barney but no words seemed to come.

"So, we're all agreed then," said Barney, rising from his chair. I suddenly felt my entire life disintegrating like a bomb-struck building. And there was absolutely nothing I could do about it.

"No, we are not 'all agreed then'. *Señor!*" Guess who?

Isabel was up from her chair, dominating Barney's posh

carpet like Xena, the Warrior Princess. She turned away from my stupefied boss and pointed straight at me.

"You. Conference room. Now!"

Talk about assertive. She might as well have picked me up and folded me under her arm. We were out of that room in seconds, with the others just watching in awestruck silence. Even Miss Collins, who – from the way she shot back into her chair – had probably been listening at the door.

I just managed to ask Dimpy if the room was free – not that I think it would have bothered Isabel if the International Court of Justice had been in there discussing Mrs Armitage. Dimpy nodded, clearly gagging to know what was going on, but I was in no position to tell her. Or to breathe.

The door slammed shut when I was only just inside. Isabel took up her position behind the table, right in front of the framed Cambridge prints.

"How many more lies do you tell?"

I tried hard not to stare at the prints.

"What? *None!* What did Barney…?"

'That you are just – how do you call it – a trainer?"

A trainer? "Ah. *Trainee.* Well, I'm not sure I actually said I wasn't." *Move on!* "Isabel…"

"And he say to me I need someone who will work faster."

I felt ridiculous for having been so cocky. Barney had clearly been watching and noting exactly how much time I was devoting to the case he had specifically instructed me on day-one not to spend any time on.

"*Cheaper*, he means cheaper," I told her, my voice growing stronger in tandem with my outrage. "Less hours. Oh and yes, what's that other thing – less commitment? He's onto me, Isabel. Didn't you see his face?"

As I was berating her, I slowly began to realise just how precarious my situation had become. "I'm on my final bloody warning – that's what you just saw in there – and if I lose my job here, I can fucking whistle for another one. I'm damaged goods. Oh and I've already lost my girlfriend!"

"Your job is not my problem" she hurled back. "Your little girlfriend is not my problem. My son is my problem."

O-kay. Clear enough. Thanks for that, Isabel.

"*He is your problem too now,*" she threw at me.

I turned my back on her and walked to the door. I could feel her sudden panic like a tremor in the ground. Her voice came at me shakily, as she moved swiftly round the table.

"Where do you go?"

"I do have other clients, Isabel." I moved into reception. "They're all people, you know."

I walked back towards Dimpy, who smiled expectantly at me, but I wasn't in a smiling mood. The morning had seen to that. And this time I wasn't just playing at being serious, which I can do so well that sometimes even I can hardly distinguish it from the real thing.

I sensed movement behind me but I carried on walking, straight through our busy reception and out onto the narrow landing. I heard those heels of fire catching up, so I closed the firm's outer door and turned to her. This time I met her eyes and read the sudden terror, which only spurred me on.

"Oh, want to join me, Ms Velazco?" I spoke very softly. She stared at me in puzzlement. "You can tell me about the abortion on the way."

TWENTY-FOUR

The trouble with making a dramatic exit is that not everyone around you is in on the drama. The cabs going down the Edgware Road certainly weren't – not a yellow light in sight.

So Isabel had plenty of time to catch me at the kerb. By then I was on my mobile, trying to talk to Sophie, who hadn't exactly been rushing to take my calls since the big match.

"Hi Sophie… can you pick up please?" *Come on, Sophie!* "How many times can a guy say he's sorry!"

About 127 so far.

I truly was sorry. Sorry to have hurt her so badly and more than sorry to have lost her so messily. Perhaps not forever, although it certainly felt like it. But I was floundering back then. I'm not making excuses, I doubt if even I could think of many. I'm just trying to be as true as I can to how I felt at that time.

Weirdly, I was also feeling like a man betrayed. Betrayed by my client and by what she hadn't told me. Betrayed by what she had done before I even knew her. Go figure, as her theatrical American friend might say. Or shout.

'Rick…?"

There she was behind me, her of the noisy shoes, and I knew what was coming next. *"Richard."* There you go. "Please, do not be angry with me. This I cannot bear—"

I could hear her voice breaking up, the huskiness at barely half-strength, interrupted only by a taxi finally swerving towards us. I had to think of a suitable destination.

"Law Courts. Strand." A personal favourite.

I wrenched open the cab door and leapt in. Isabel followed, as I knew she would. Which probably looked to anyone watching like I was simply a badly brought-up young man in a hurry. (Hardly fair to my mum, who had been quite firm about this sort of thing.) The cabbie certainly didn't look impressed – he was staring rather than moving.

"Here, aren't you Ronnie's…?"

I closed the partition. Had my picture suddenly been posted on CabbieNews 24?

"I meet someone, in Buenos Aires."

I wasn't looking at her and I don't think she was looking at me. It was like we were both talking to the Edgware Road and the back of our cabbie's head. I just hoped he couldn't lip-read in mirrors.

"We break up," she continued, 'before I find out that I am…'' I didn't say anything. I felt her swivel towards me and almost shout into my appropriately stony face. *What else does Laurence know?*

Jesus!

"*What else IS there, Isabel?*"

I don't know why I asked the next question, especially as the last one had demanded such an urgent response. Even with this unfamiliar, unwelcome rage ripping through me, I knew it was absolutely none of my business. "Did you love him?"

"Who – the father?"

"Well I don't mean the sodding baby!"

She stared at me, her mouth open but no words available. I could tell that she was appalled and utterly thrown. My first thought – is *this* how she's going to be in court? – was replaced before we hit Marble Arch by the shaky realisation that I had been hugely inappropriate. Even for me.

I suddenly felt an overwhelming, unfamiliar need to justify my behaviour. Sure, I wanted her to feel bad, for jeopardising so much, for such a massive failure to disclose. But I didn't want Isabel Velazco to hate me. Not now. Not ever. Which meant, even though I was genuinely incensed, that I should probably work just that bit harder at not being hateful.

"Everything matters, Isabel," I explained more gently. "Can't you see? The parties… the men. They can twist things. If they even need twisting. I mean, how many others?"

Before she could answer – or count – another thought hit me. One which, considering my form to date, almost verged on the responsible. "Did little Sebastian know?"

"Boludo – you think I tell my son?"

It was another of those file-kicking, paper-flying moments, but fortunately everything in the cab was screwed-down. So she took it out on the mangy giraffe instead, the one which, despite its provenance, she clearly hadn't been able to restore to its original owner.

"I say to you always the truth, Rick. I am not a *puta*… but I am not a nun."

I didn't actually think she was a *puta*, if that meant what I thought, and I bloody knew she wasn't the other. But yet again her barometer suddenly plummeted and I observed the white-hot anger instantly dissolve into a cold, bottomless panic. I could see that her hands were shaking. I almost felt for the giraffe.

"Rick, please. I am good mami – mother. You see me only with Sebastian here, now – and he does not trust me. You *see* this! And why in the hell should he, after his father has—" Her voice became even softer, more wistful. "Is not always like this. It is… we were…"

She didn't finish but I was already into my own thoughts. I suddenly found myself wondering if I could believe a single word she said. If indeed life back home with Sebastian had been anything like the sunlit idyll she had described. I realised then that I had seen absolutely no sign of it.

She looked out of the window, as if she was drifting off into memories in which I played no part. She spoke so quietly that I could hardly hear her.

"Do not close the door on me, Rick. I am begging this. He is all that I have." And then she turned back to me to say the one thing that suddenly changed everything. For better or for worse, I had no way of telling. "You are all that *we* have."

Before I could reply, if I even knew how to reply, she took my hand and gently stroked it with those long, cool fingers. They moved so exquisitely slowly, as if my skin was something wondrous, like a rare manuscript uncovered for the first time in centuries. I sensed her shifting so close to me that I could feel the sudden heat of her summer-warm body against my thigh.

I looked down at our two hands, our melding hips, as if from a great height, trying to work out exactly what the hell was going on down there. Was she coming on to me or was this just another crazy dance? How would I ever know?

She opened the cabbie's window. "47A Bedford Road, SE23" she said.

Now I knew.

I wondered briefly who was going to pay for the cab.

TWENTY-FIVE

I'm not going to journey back through every thrilling stroke and response of that morning's wholly unanticipated, yet much imagined, encounter. Despite the fact that each tiny detail seems to be engraved forever in my mind, like a rose etched into a diamond. But what happened that day in Isabel's tiny, darkened bedroom, in her friend Joanne's Victorian terraced house – the one in which I couldn't even set foot just a few days earlier – set the seal on all that was to follow.

Let's just say that Isabel took me into her unmade bed and her extraordinary body, which was naturally everything I had pictured, yet still somehow totally different. My pedestrian mind could hardly match that singular vision of whoever dreamed-up Isabel Velazco. She moved beneath me and around me like the dancer I expected her to be, ablaze in her virtuosity, every twist and turn a marvel, every muscle toned and tuned to the task in hand.

But of course she took me nowhere near her heart. Not that I cared so much or even wished for it. I was too busy exploring Argentina, lost in its exotic contours, its peaks and valleys, its miraculous scents and sounds.

We needed each other, if not in the same way, but I could sense an urgency rippling within her, a demand for some sort of instant, mindless release that I'm sure wasn't just my fragile ego running amok. Yet I don't think I could take in what was happening for a single second.

You can see why people have selfies taken with celebrities. It isn't just so that others will believe them – it's because they can't quite believe it themselves.

I don't know how to explain how different it was. I had slept with girls in the past, attractive girls, young but not unadept, yet just now I had made love to a woman. Alright I had made love to a woman who was also a client, and a client who was at a pretty low ebb, but if anyone thinks those caveats were crying havoc in my mind right then, they haven't been paying attention.

And it wasn't as if I had pounced on her, was it? Quite the reverse.

Finally I flopped back onto the pillow, spent. If something was missing, if Isabel's response hadn't exactly shattered the suburban silence, I wasn't going to let it impinge on the sense of triumph I felt. My legal high. Like the new Spurs signing, I had justified the confidence of my team. But, as yet, the only cheering I could hear was my own.

"Okay?" I said, turning. She had pulled the sheet tightly around her, the ogling sun just catching her face and naked shoulders through a gap in the curtains. She stared at the ceiling, unblinking. "I mean, was it okay? For you. I've never done it with…"

"A grown-up?" she said, without shifting, which wasn't what I meant, although God knows what I did mean. A client – a foreigner – a mum?

I made it worse by checking my watch. "I don't think this is what Barney would call billable time."

If linking sex with payment was somehow meant to lighten the mood, a mood which right now felt considerably more sombre than my expectations, it failed spectacularly.

I rose from the bed and began to dress. I wasn't completely

unclothed, it had all been too swift for that. The following her up the narrow stairs, the pawing on the landing, the falling onto the midday bed, our mouths locked.

My assumed trajectory now was out of the door and into a cab, hopefully driven by a total stranger. It wasn't the time to hang around for a chat or a case conference. But I was momentarily halted by a narrow shelf over what would once have been the fireplace. Aside from the usual knick-knacks and a small vase of flowers, there was an assortment of photographs, ranged in a line, each in a small, lightweight frame.

They were all of Isabel and Sebastian, but an Isabel and Sebastian I had never encountered, like one of those films where bodies are snatched and replicated by unfamiliar beings. The two of them on an impossibly white beach, smiling into the sun. At the zoo, waddling stupidly beside penguins. Dancing a rudimentary Tango in a pretty, candlelit room. And surrounded by leaping kids at an outdoor party. A mother and her son, so together. So – conjoined. Why did she never show me these? Perhaps she just assumed that I would know.

At the very end, almost toppling off the shelf, was a tiny photograph of the pair of them with an old and rather elegant lady in black, who I had to assume was the recently deceased grandmother. *(His grandma had died while he was away! It had simply never occurred to me.)*

Even though I knew I should be leaving, I couldn't wrench my eyes from the whole display. I picked up one of the frames – the sunny beach photo of the pair, with little, bronzed Sebastian holding a beach-ball almost as big as himself – and just stared at it as if they might suddenly invite me in to join them.

Would they ask me if I was content with what I had just done?

The dim room seemed to be closing in on me, making me dizzy and oddly claustrophobic. Traffic-noises from the street, unnoticed until now, began to lodge in my head like a tune I couldn't set free.

I suddenly felt scared and way out of my depth, with a cavernous emptiness inside that seemed totally new to me. Or perhaps it had always been there but I was simply now, for the first time, aware of it. I had to leave, but I couldn't move or even drag my eyes away from those bloody pictures.

"Anybody home?"

That unmistakeable voice, the one an audience could hear even from the theatre next door. I looked at Isabel but she had turned away. I remember regretting even then that she hadn't chosen to light up a cigarette. Was this really how I saw the world – in trailer moments?

I passed Joanne as she was coming up the stairs.

"Oh Jesus!" she said.

I didn't say anything. What could I say? It wasn't until I was in the happily anonymous taxi and crossing the Thames that I realised I still had that last framed photo in my hand.

TWENTY-SIX

I hadn't spoken to Oliver since my break-up with Sophie.

For reasons I still can't fully explain, I dearly needed to speak to him that evening. Perhaps I was looking for some sort of absolution, except that this probably credits me with more substance than I deserved. Let's face it, I wanted to crow – what's the point of doing something momentous, if there's no one around to share the moment? But even then, as I recall, my actual elation at the event was more muted and less comfortable than I might have wished.

Because I had shamelessly taken advantage of a vulnerable client? Or because she hadn't called me all afternoon and I suspected we weren't on for a rematch?

All the other solicitors had gone home, to partners and families, except of course Evan, who was probably kerb-crawling somewhere. I was at my desk, trying to work but mostly staring at my mobile or the framed photo that now smiled accusingly at me from beside my appropriately cold Americano.

The phone rang and I grabbed it without looking. There was something I needed to tell her, a piece of information that had nothing to do with what had happened earlier that day. Yet, despite this imperative, I knew even then that it had to be Isabel who made the first move.

"How's the 'big peasant'?"

"Oh… Hi, Ollie." It took me a second or two to cotton on. "You spoke to Sophie." No response. "She okay?"

"Not great," he said, coldly. "She's forgotten your name. Keeps calling you Dick."

I wasn't used to his angry side, barely aware that my sweet friend had one, but I was still locked-on to my own ignoble trajectory.

"Ollie, I've got to tell you something."

My door opened and Barney filled the room.

"You *shtupped* her, didn't you!"

I switched off the phone in a panic.

"If that was the Brazilian ball-breaker, you're history," said my boss pleasantly. I could smell whiskey on his breath, which curiously made it more palatable than usual.

"No – it was… Mrs Armitage. Poor woman."

"Never give 'em your mobile number. Not if you want a life. Unless, of course, they're important, which yours aren't." He wandered around, which was hardly a stretch. "And to what do we owe this rare personal appearance, Mr Davenport?"

I wasn't entering into that discussion. "I thought you'd gone ages ago."

"New client. The thirty-year-old malt kind." He saw the pile of cases on my desk. I just hoped he wouldn't notice that beneath their shiny covers they were still in total disarray. But he simply thumped them with his podgy fist. "I want bills for all this lot by Friday. Not a sodding charity." He leaned over towards me. It really was a very good whiskey. Peaty. "You'd better start earning your keep, matey."

It wasn't the time to use the old 'you pay peanuts…' retort, not if I wanted to hold onto a job that seemed to be dangling from an ever-thinning thread. He had lurched off anyway, his point made.

"*Argentinian* ball-breaker," I corrected him, in a voice just loud enough for him not to hear.

I checked the mobile again (do mature Argentinian women text?), then strolled over to the window. The rush-hour traffic was long gone but Edgware Road still hummed. It could probably lay claim to being the kebab centre of Northern Europe and the warm, spicy smells spiralled tauntingly upwards through the toxic London air and through my tiny open window. Making me realise I hadn't actually eaten all day.

I was about to correct this when I noticed a figure down below. The sharp-suited man with his coat under his arm was leaving our building at a businesslike pace. I watched him instantly commandeer a passing cab with an aplomb I somehow knew I would never master. I could only glimpse the top of his head, with its rich, silvery-gray hair, but I had a vague feeling that I had seen him somewhere before.

My phone rang again and this time I knew it was Oliver. I just let it ring. It wouldn't be a fun conversation and there was somewhere I had to be.

TWENTY-SEVEN

"Sophie… hi, it's me… Rick. If you get this, ring me? *Please?*"

I was in the MiG, outside Joanne and Isabel's house, watching the street. I knew it was Tango night – Jesus, had it only been a week? – and that hopefully Isabel would emerge through the Forest Hill darkness very soon. I recall wondering if it was safe for her to be on her own at this time of night and being surprised that I should feel so protective about someone I hardly knew. Someone who could patently take care of herself, even if she wasn't quite so assured about the one small person she had sworn to God to protect.

I failed to notice the large BMW approaching from the other direction, until it began to slow down opposite me. Turning off my phone, I slipped down in my seat and watched the driver leave the car. He walked up to the house.

Laurence moved with a confidence that seemed so natural I felt he must have been born with it. Although I suppose most of us arrive with a god-given assurance and have it drained out of us by parents and life. Even when Joanne answered the door and greeted him with a hostility you could have weaponised and fired from drones, he simply nodded politely and strolled back to his car.

Like me he was content just to wait, yet contentment is

hardly the best description of how I felt that evening. I would have had no words to express the turmoil back then and I'm not finding it much easier now, all these years later.

I don't suppose you ever really know a person fully and one act of love doesn't automatically make you joined at the soul. But curiously Isabel and the workings of her head and heart were even more a mystery to me now than they had been this morning. How can a shared coffee or pizza or a kids' manic soccer game in the mud and rain – even a barely provoked attack on an office filing-system – be so much more intimate than two nearly-naked bodies urgently joining?

How could I have expended such effort only to jettison so much?

I didn't have unlimited time to ponder this as Isabel was turning the corner, still wearing her lacy, black Tango-dress and holding the barely-portable boombox.

She seemed smaller somehow, as if diminished by her thoughts. Tired, deflated and terribly alone. I thought of the vital, muscular person with whom I had tangled just a few hours earlier and found it almost impossible to reconcile with the sombre figure walking towards us.

Laurence was out of the car and on her case in seconds. I couldn't hear a thing they were saying but I could tell that her preference was for not saying anything. She tried to pull away but he took hold of her arm. I wouldn't swear on oath that he was aggressive, yet he was clearly unwelcome and I realised I could hardly just watch like a dummy. Although I had no guarantee, despite – or maybe because of – events just hours earlier, that I would receive favoured-nation treatment.

"Ms. Velazco!"

They turned to me as I crossed the quiet, suburban road. Laurence had that faintly amused look, the one that was just starting to get right up my nose. Especially when matched with a faintly amused comment.

"Graveyard shift, Mr Davenport?"

I looked towards Isabel, as if to an ally, and saw in that wintry stare what I realised I had been fearing all day. Everything had changed. Even if I wasn't totally sure what 'everything' was, I knew now what it hadn't been. It hadn't been hostility, fear and a chill that sucked away what remained of the day's excessive heat.

"Mr Davenport has come – to talk about your lies!"

Nice one, Isabel. Not true of course. This wasn't my reason for turning up so late at her door and she had no idea what the real reason was – but well played.

The man with the BMW looked even more amused.

"Why don't we three discuss this over a nice bottle of wine?"

***

I don't imagine the local pub was exactly his hostelry of choice, nor the wine his preferred vintage, but Laurence sunk to the occasion and played the gracious host. Isabel wasn't drinking. (And attracting no more attention than any stunning foreigner in a tight-fitting, black Tango-frock might expect to attract in a suburban, South London pub on a weeknight.)

"We drivers can't finish this on our own, can we, Rick?" I was now Rick apparently, getting them in with my drinking buddy. "Chilean Cabernet Sauvignon, best wine for the heart, so they tell us." He turned to me as he poured another glass. "It used to be Izzie's tipple of choice."

Isabel was glaring at him, saying nothing. But she occasionally managed to wrench her eyes away in order to glare at me and say nothing. Lest I forget.

"Mi amor," continued the ex, in a softer, more wheedling tone. "What do you and I both want? The legal phrase, Mr Davenport. Remind me?"

Hard ones first again. I thought for a scary moment that he was asking me for some Latin but thankfully I remembered. "Er

– 'best interests' – of the child. Obviously." He nodded. "But it's up to the judge to—"

"On the basis of the evidence," interrupted smart-arse. "And we've all read the evidence, haven't we?"

This was clearly for Isabel's benefit. I could see her face reddening, without benefit of Cabernet. "You have twisted everything!" she growled.

That trademark smile again. "Have I – really – Isabel?" he said, then stared into her eyes. "You are looking good, you know."

I had seen her looking better, but the fact he even said it was astonishing, at least to me. He was *flirting* with her, his ex-wife, the one he was taking to court! The one he was battling to secure his only son. What was that all about? Worst of all, I could tell that he was enjoying my confusion.

"You're a family lawyer, Rick. Do you know how many couples still have sex after they're divorced? Some say it's even better."

This was so creepy, but at least he didn't ask if I knew how many divorcees have sex with their lawyers. I supposed nothing was going to surprise me after that bombshell, but then he took his ex-wife's hand in his own and gently stroked it. I felt certain she would rip her arm away, maybe rip his own off in the process, but she didn't. She just turned her face to look at me, as if to check whether I was watching.

I remember thinking, *I am so out of my depth.*

"You aren't going to win this you know, my dear." They were ignoring me entirely now. "I think you do know. Mr Davenport certainly does." Oh hello, back in again.

Isabel turned to me and my face must have unwittingly confirmed what Laurence had said. I immediately tried shaking my head, as if to imply total and utter disagreement, but I could sense it still read as a ringing endorsement for the opposite side. The trouble was, unfortunately, that I did believe him. Especially after today's news. Mr Menzies was on the money.

"Look at that wee boy's life over there," he continued gently. "In that poky flat. Not a tree for miles, Rick. And poor Isabel, on your own, hoofing away all hours of the day and night." Isabel said nothing, but I could tell she was listening intently. "See how Sebastian is here with us. He has his private school, his lovely big home, adoring step-mum. Puppy."

"What puppy?" asked Isabel. "He has no puppy."

Laurence just smiled. Again. I think I expressed my shock with an involuntary but still quite British intake of breath while Isabel – being Argentinian – cried something involving a 'puta' and his 'madre', then picked up the half-full wine bottle and swung it at Laurence's head. Flirting season was clearly over and I just managed to grab the weapon in time.

"So shitty," I said.

"Puppies usually are."

I'll say one thing for him, he was quick. I usually think of stuff like that when everybody else is tucked up in bed. But the smile had disappeared along with the contents of his glass. Turning to me, he became all serious and businesslike.

"You'll be receiving an offer tomorrow. Reasonable contact. Generous settlement. I'll pay airfares – *both* ways – and more besides. I would advise your client to take it, Richard – if I were you." He paused and turned back to Isabel. "Or you could lose everything."

If people truly can self-combust – and I remember Oliver gleefully showing me pictures at school of just such phenomena – then Isabel would have been on anyone's watch-list. Having failed at the bottle-swinging, she finally managed to throw the contents of her untouched wine-glass at her ex, which can't have done his heart a power of good, let alone his suit, but credit where it's due, he never lost the smile.

In that moment I realised that I – and the rest of the Queen' Head – had been given an exclusive, un*Hello*-like glimpse of the first Mr and Mrs Menzies at home.

Isabel was half-way to the pub door by the time I realised that the wine-hurling had been her parting shot. I had just leapt up to join her when I felt my arm being grabbed by Laurence, who was clearly an arm-grabbing sort of guy.

"Be careful, Mr Davenport." What happened to 'Richard'? "You have no idea what you're playing with. And I ain't as lovely as your client when I'm angry."

It's not something I'd boast about but I was seriously intimidated by Laurence Menzies, even if somewhere deep down I still wanted to be him. Yet perhaps just a tad less than before. I eased my arm away and backed off towards the door and – hopefully – Isabel. I could hear her dark mutterings before I saw her stomping through the busy car park. Unsurprisingly, she could move pretty fast.

"You got what you wanted today, *Mister* Davenport," she said a bit loudly, because I hadn't actually caught up with her. I tried to ignore this bulletin, even though customers pausing by their open cars clearly hadn't, and concentrated on the relevant.

"He's just trying to rattle us, Isabel," I said quietly. "You don't still, y'know, fancy him – do you?" So much for the relevant.

"I am very tired," she sighed. "Why did you come here? No, let me guess."

This was hardly the warmest of responses, considering the day's activities, but I took a moment to answer her. Because I knew that what I had to say wouldn't exactly lighten her mood.

"The CAFCASS officer. You know, child welfare. It's this Saturday, Isabel. I couldn't put it off any longer."

Isabel just stared at me, the fire extinguished.

"But you will be there – with me and with Sebastian – yes?"

I shook my head. The look she dashed back at me, eyes narrowed, perfect nose flaring, told me, as clearly as if she had spelled it out in a neon news-flash all around Piccadilly Circus, exactly what she thought of me. Then she told me exactly what she thought of me.

"*Al pedo como teta de monja.*" And when I simply looked baffled rather than rebuked, she kindly translated it for me. "Useless like the tits on a nun."

I'm sure this made great listening for anyone in the vicinity, but this time, as she walked away, I didn't follow. Glancing back at the pub, I saw Laurence in the doorway, just watching. Thankfully he wouldn't have heard anything, nor hopefully understood the context, but he could surely see that his points had been well made.

I think it was at that moment, on a balmy night in the dimly-lit car-park of a South London pub, with cheap Chilean wine in my belly and the thrum of Tango still in my head, that I had my first seismic revelation.

I wanted to win Menzies v. Velazco.

The second, far more dangerous one, was yet to come.

TWENTY-EIGHT

'*LAWYER WOULD PREFER TO WIN CASE!*'

Not exactly the stuff of front-page headlines. Or the killer slogan on a movie poster.

But it was heady stuff to me. Up until this point it was '*lawyer would like to get into client's knickers*' and we'd already been there. It might have been that I knew I had zero chance of going there again, so I had better find a new way to occupy myself.

Or, and I like to think this could be nearer the mark, perhaps it finally took what came to pass in Isabel's tiny room that lunchtime, and then again at the pub with Laurence, to make me see this truly desperate, yet highly accomplished (and yes, okay, stunning) woman – the type of person whose path would never normally cross mine, except in my most ambitious dreams – for the first time.

I'm not overly impressing myself as I write this. I suppose I'm not really writing this to impress. But driving home that night, still shaky from what had gone before, I began to tell myself that it was probably time for me to stop trying to use my position, the so-called 'fiduciary relationship', to my own advantage.

Or at least not *solely* to my own advantage. I hadn't suddenly turned into Mother Teresa. Also – and perhaps I'm not on such unassailable high-ground here – I seriously wanted to shaft Laurence Menzies. For being so bloody condescending. And so fucking successful.

Don't get me wrong, I still wasn't crazy about Sebastian – we're not talking early Daniel Radcliffe – but at least I could just about understand why this was. And why the boy wasn't exactly at his most appealing back then. More importantly, I was beginning to latch on to why his mother probably *was* crazy about him and so viscerally wanted her son back home again with her. I imagined it could have been like this with me and my parents. Although, hand on heart, I was a really cute kid.

So I even felt a mild affection for my dad – or at least diminished irritation – on seeing his familiar cab in the street as I quietly turned the key, after that incredibly long, weird day. And then, just as I was trying my best not to wake anyone on my way up, he scared the shit out of me by walking down the unlit staircase with Threadbear held out in front of him, overstuffed arms akimbo, totally obscuring his own compact frame.

"Hello, son," he said concernedly. "You been working all this time?"

"The New York Stock Exchange doesn't close till eleven."

"Oh yeah," my dad nodded sagely, "I forgot. You look tired, Rick… Your mum worries."

We just stared at each other after that, neither of us with the least idea what to say, until we both said 'goodnight' at the same time and he continued down the stairs with his furry friend.

I went straight to my bedroom that night and took the framed photo from my case. The one with the beach-ball. For some reason I had brought it with me from the office. I set it on my bedside table, next to my executive travel alarm-clock. (Which had actually travelled as little as I had.) I just wished the CAFCASS person could have been there, on that distant South American shore. As I imagine he or she would too.

143

As I was dozing off, I suddenly thought of Mrs Armitage. Someone I had never thought would feature in my dreams.

***

"I didn't ever want this, Mr Davenport. I still love the bastard."

This wasn't my dream, it was all too real. The poor woman seemed totally washed out, yet the kindly way she was looking at me, head cocked to one side, gave me the clearest indication that she thought the same about her lawyer. She kept nodding sideways at my sandwich, which was still under wraps and well away from where she was sitting, as if to suggest that I should eat it before I passed out.

I found myself speaking softly to her, which might have been pure exhaustion, but I like to think was something more. "He's going to get this divorce, Mrs Armitage." She nodded, resignedly. "But we'll make sure he won't get away without really supporting you all. That's a promise."

How many times had I made these people promises? I remember from some childhood story my mum told me years ago, that every time you tell a lie a fairy dies. This must have been a particularly good year for fairy undertakers. I wondered if today's could be the promise I might just keep.

She noticed the framed photo on my desk.

"You don't look old enough," she said. I could have just shrugged and moved on, but for some reason I smiled, almost flattered, and said "Child bride", which had to be the least smart thing I had said for some while.

"I'm so sorry for just dropping in like this, Mr Davenport," she concluded, getting up and packing her things away. I noticed her own, home-made sandwich in her bag.

"Hey, who you gonna call – Ghostbusters?"

This time she smiled, but I noticed that for once her eyes were joining in, steering it well away from her usual, over-apologetic offering. Suddenly she didn't seem quite so old or grey. I handed her my smartly embossed card. "Any time, Mrs A. I mean it. Any time."

She looked at the card in surprise, feeling my bumpy name with her fingers, as I escorted her back to reception.

Oliver was sitting there, chatting to Dimpy, on an unexpected but not wholly unwelcome visit. I swiftly saw Mrs Armitage out, before he said something inappropriate.

"Bye, Mrs Armitage… Hi, Ol?"

"You shtupping her too?"

There she blows.

I dragged him away from Dimpy, who had ears like a receptionist, only to bump into Barney coming out of the conference room. He nodded curiously at Oliver, whom he knew of course because of Cyril Rosen, then stared at me the way you would if one of your own were consorting with another firm in your lobby.

I pulled Oliver out the door. "Just off for lunch." But my guy kept on talking.

"*100 easy ways to screw a client. You had to go for Screwing 101.*"

"Oliver, shut the… Who told you I was screwing her?"

"You did. Just now."

TWENTY-NINE

We went to the local, cheap 'n cheerful Thai Restaurant, one I often frequented with Leila, but I suppose taking Oliver was tempting fate. On a good day he'll share a bowl of rice with his shirt, but when he combines industrial-scale slurping with throwing me his almost biblical looks of righteous indignation, it's bonus time at the dry-cleaners.

And, of course, there had to be two pretty girls eating their sparrow portions at the next table. Oliver seemed to attract good-looking women into his vicinity with a magnetism that had its polarity reversed immediately he opened his mouth.

He began reasonably well, taking some important-looking documents from his bag and handing me a typed list.

"Barristers," he announced, tapping the paper. When I said nothing, he added. "They're the ones with the white, curly wigs."

I had forgotten that I had asked him to recommend someone. When I was a kid I'd had dreams of being a barrister, because they get to dress up and make dramatic speeches like you see on TV, but you don't get many kids from council estates going to the bar. At least Barney paid me the Law Society recommended minimum wage for the work I wasn't doing.

"And the CAFCASS Family Court Adviser is the one who sees the kids with each of his parents. So, on balance, it's probably better if mum's not giving you a blow-job when they turn up."

That certainly got the girls' attention.

"It was just one time, Oliver," I said quietly, hoping he wouldn't broadcast this back to the eager crowds. "There won't be—" I really didn't have to go into this with him. "So what do they look for, y'know, the CAFCASS lot? Lovey-dovey stuff?" He just nodded. I shook my head sadly. "Ain't going to happen, pal," I mumbled. "War zone."

Then I looked up from my steaming plate and stared straight at him. "I have *got* to win this, Ollie."

He appeared as stunned to hear this as I was to be saying it out loud. The words had been pinballing around in my head but now they shot out with an urgency that made my jaw clench. My buttocks weren't far behind.

"I bet she gives great thank you," he responded, uncharitably.

"She's barely talking to me. Blames me now for sodding CAFCASS! She'll blame me even more if that all goes tits-up, which it will. I blew it, Ollie." I didn't wait for him to come back with a mucky response, although I could see it on his lips along with the diced chicken. "And I think Barney knows I'm rubbish. You saw for yourself how he looks at me."

I recalled a recent conversation, one that I suspected I would never forget. "Sophie told me, the day we split up, that I don't know who I am any more. She's right, you know. She's well out of it."

"Do you still love her?" he asked, softening. "Did you ever?"

I didn't answer straightaway. Sometimes you don't have to. But of course you can't take too long about it, especially in a fast-food place. "How do you know if you love someone, Ollie? I mean, really know."

He didn't answer straightaway either. "Look at my mum and dad," he said, finally. "They know. And yours, probably." He smiled at me with more sympathy than I had ever seen him show to anyone, and he's a kind person.

"From one lawyer to another?" he said, scraping the food off his tie. I nodded. "You are in such deep shit."

THIRTY

Who'd be a CAFCASS officer?

It can't be the easiest job in the world and it's certainly not the best paid. Attempting to assess the state of a parent-child relationship, making recommendations that could change lives forever? That has to be a tough gig. I hope at least that it's rewarding, because it's not like people such as Isabel are flinging wide their doors, singing *Deck the Halls*, it's CAFCASS.

Worst of all, parents can't rally the troops in support. My client was all on her own that critical Saturday. So it wasn't until later that I heard exactly what had happened.

Shortly before the visitor turned up, Isabel and Sebastian were playing Snakes and Ladders on Joanne's living-room floor (her sensible landlady and kids having taken refuge in a nearby lido). Sebastian had apparently thrown a triumphant six, but when he discovered that this would send him scuttling down a long and slithery snake, he shunted himself to the relative safety of the square next door.

"Hey," laughed Isabel, "you move a seven."

"No, I did not," insisted Sebastian. I hate it when kids lie, which probably sounds rich coming from me. But at least I'm better at it.

"You did, cheeky," said Isabel, still laughing. Perhaps she

was simply lightening the mood or maybe she genuinely didn't foresee the dangers. "You go straight over this wiggly snake."

"No, I move a six. YOU ARE A LIAR! I hate you! I hate you everywhere!"

Isabel was stunned. I wouldn't have been but this clearly wasn't the Sebastian she remembered and it rocked her. It must have scared her rigid too, that particular afternoon.

"Sebastian, is a game. Is only a—"

"*Rebecca lets me!*" Of course she does. "You are shit!"

"No. You must not say this… Is very… The person will be here soon."

"I do not care," he muttered, his face reddening. "Where is Rick?"

I'm not adding that, he really did ask for me. I really wish he hadn't.

"I am your mami – your mummy." She was holding on tight to the tears, but doing less well than her nine year old.

That was when he kicked over the board and sent the pieces flying. Family tradition. Isabel was frantic – there was no way on the planet her child was going to calm down before the visit. So far as she was concerned, it was all over bar the screaming.

"I want my puppy!" he yelped.

I don't dislike animals as much as I do children, probably because our house didn't double as a kennels, but had I heard that demand I would willingly have wrung the mutt's neck. (I say mutt –Mungo Menzies was more likely the most inbred dog on the planet.)

Of course that had to be when the doorbell rang.

Isabel dragged herself slowly up from the floor and gave Sebastian one final, imploring look. The kid wasn't having any, and he wasn't rushing to clear up the debris either, so she walked like death-on-a-stick out of the room and into the hallway. By this time she had half-decided to tell the unwelcome guest to go away and take the rest of the day off.

Standing at the door was a tall, taciturn young man, holding a card. "Ms… Velazco?" he said, reading from it. He didn't look particularly friendly or professional, but how was she to know about these things?

"Yes. Hello. Come in. Please."

The man didn't move from the step. "Where is… Sebastian?" he asked, checking his card again.

"He is…" She turned to call him. "Sebastian! SEBASTIAN!!"

They waited. Nothing. She shrugged apologetically, as if to say 'kids'. The man didn't respond, which she found less than comforting. Finally, the little boy sloped out of the room in almost teenage-sullen mode. This was never going to be the most fun for him, but he acted like he had just been given permanent school detention without hope of parole or lunch. Isabel could only sigh and wait for the inevitable.

The visitor now did something totally unexpected. Instead of moving into the house, he stepped aside, beyond Isabel's range of vision. She wondered momentarily if he had brought some sort of equipment but was at a loss to think what this might be.

What it was unlikely to be was what the man eventually produced. It was a huge, oddly-shaped object, all curves and protrusions, awkwardly packaged in reams of the most gaudily tasteless wrapping-paper she had ever seen. The man shuffled with it towards Sebastian.

"I was told to give you this," he said, in a jaded monotone.

The young boy looked at it with a confusion quite as massive as the object being presented to him. After a few seconds he began to remove the paper, tentatively at first and then with increasing fervour as he gradually realised what lay beneath.

"*Sodding bloody ace-shit!*" he yelled.

As you would, of course, were you to be presented with an enormous and extremely mangy old teddy bear, sporting the brand new strip of a player from celebrated Tottenham the Hotspurs.

"Fucking Spurs arsyhole!" he further explained to the world-weary delivery man.

So perhaps, in a way, I was there after all.

THIRTY-ONE

I had chosen the Lido Café in Hyde Park that scorching morning, because it can make you feel on holiday, even when you're not. Only it didn't. The young women in their flimsy summer-dresses might as well have been nuns. I was in such a nervous state that four office walls, in embarrassingly close proximity, simply couldn't have contained me.

Isabel had called me immediately after the lady from CAFCASS had left, so I knew the score and that Spurs' new signing from Teddy Land had played a blinder. But I had no real sense of the state of play between us.

Here was a woman to whom I was seriously, stupidly attracted yet barely knew, with whom I had enjoyed a sadly unedifying one-morning-stand and about whom I now cared a good deal more, yet connected with a fair bit less.

I buried myself in my work, so I didn't have to think about it. But a shadow falling over the screen made me pause.

"If you lose your job as lawyer, I think you can become tourist guide."

I smiled in some relief, as I began to close down my laptop. "Not even as a joke!"

I still hadn't looked up but I could sense that she was smiling back down at me. Then another shadow consumed the entire table. I raised my head very slowly.

"Not going to chew your balls off," said the larger figure. "Not just yet. You did good for once, kiddo."

They sat down but, curiously, Joanne didn't seem to diminish in the process. The shadow was just as overwhelming.

"What is even better," laughed Isabel, clearly still full of Saturday, "it is when Sebastian he tell the visitor lady that Arsenal are the 'fucking wankers'. "

"And know what," continued Joanne, like they were a double act, "he sure didn't get those choice words from his Argentinian mami, did he?"

I smiled at the image. "Win, win," I said cheerily.

Of course it's just an expression but the way it immediately lit up Isabel's face made me feel wretched. I needed so badly to reach out to her and this time it wasn't randiness, I didn't want to cop some sort of quasi-legitimate feel or a not-quite-accidental brushing of limbs. Not even a quick and sweaty Tango. I suppose I just wanted to comfort a friend. Of sorts.

"No, no – sorry Isabel. I didn't mean— Yes, it's good news. It's great and I'm glad it went well. But it's like – well, it's like your dance class. You know, tiny steps. Sometimes forwards, sometimes back." What was I talking about – it was nothing like dancing. "Please, all I'm saying is just don't get your hopes up, not yet. We haven't even had the woman's report. She could…" I might as well have been talking to the pedal-boats.

"No," she steamed on. "I know this will be fine. Sebastian will be fine." I caught just the slightest flicker amidst the elation – I must have been getting better at picking-up emotional subtleties. "Even if I know this is not because of me," she sighed.

I shrugged. What could I say? Bit late for lying.

It was what Isabel said next, however, that threw me right off my stride, even though it was the most obvious thing in the world.

"But when I go back with my little boy to Buenos Aires, this will be good again."

I just stared at her. She stared back curiously, as if reflecting the set of my own puzzled face.

"*Buenos Aires?*" I muttered.

"Where then, Epping Forest?" Thank you, Joanne. But even she was looking at me oddly.

"Right. Yes. Okay," I steamed on. "Can we talk barristers, Isabel? They're the ones with the white, curly wigs."

I had no idea how I kept talking or even what was going on in my head. But watching the two women as they listened with genuine interest to the stuff coming out of my mouth, I had the suspicious feeling that I was setting off on a voyage to join the grown-ups and an equally powerful sense that I hadn't even begun to pack.

My phone buzzed. A text from Dimpy: '*Barney wants you. NOW! Can I have your stapler when you leave?*'

***

Dimpy's face didn't reveal a thing as I rushed back into the office. It wasn't that she was being professional, simply that – to her deep regret – she knew no more than she had told me. Miss Collins was equally uncommunicative. I thought I would try out the new-found warmth that was pervading my body like some sort of benign, yet still somehow disturbing, virus.

"How's your mother, Joan?" I asked kindly.

"My mother died several years ago," she said. "Why are you asking now?"

What can you say – you seemed like someone who went home every evening to tend to an ailing parent? Perhaps it was her father, but I couldn't go through every member of her family.

"I wish you long life," is what I actually said, which is what Oliver and the Rosens say when someone dies, but maybe that's only if everyone's Jewish.

155

I hoped I would have more joy with Barney. I wasn't banking on it

"How's your girlfriend?" he asked, before I had even closed the door.

Shit.

I had to say something quickly, but nothing sprung to mind that wouldn't take me deeper into the ordure.

"Eva Peron?" he continued. "You know. The hot tamale." The *what*? "You winning?"

I had no idea why he was taking an interest. "Barney, she's… just one my clients. My many, equally-deserving clients." Who talks like that?

He smiled and shook his head, but not in his usual, arsey way. 'Okay, okay Mr D. Don't get your knickers in a twist."

He reached into the drawer beneath his desk and pulled out a bulging file. *Not another fucking divorce*, I thought, in the way that family lawyers do. Barney slid it across the huge desk and it eventually landed on my side. I reasoned that the least I could do would be to open it, which I did and was immediately baffled.

"This isn't Family," I said.

"You didn't go to Watford Tech for nothing," he smiled.

"*It's a University now!*" That just sounded pathetic, yet I felt Watford needed all the help she could get. "Barney, are you taking me off my cases?"

He shook his head. "No, Señor Davenport. I am adding hugely to your workload."

I stared at the meaningless file before me, like someone who has just been handed a stupendous treasure map and realises he has lost all sense of direction. Perhaps it was simply the fact that I had given up all hope of this ever happening.

"At least pretend to be grateful," said my boss.

"Oh, sorry. Sorry, Barney. I am – grateful. Very," I stuttered. "I'm overwhelmed."

"You bloody will be. Read it, then we'll talk. Now push off."

I just nodded and picked up the file. It weighed a ton. I couldn't believe it, after all these months. *Corporate.* I don't know how I managed to get up and reach the door. Not from the weight of the file, obviously, but from the infinitely more onerous weight of trust and responsibility. I had assumed the conversation was over, but just as I was on the threshold…

"Oh, what *is* happening on Velazco?"

I turned back. He was already flicking through another file. "We're still awaiting the CAFCASS report," I reported, "which is looking quite hopeful. I also did some very extensive research and instructed a barrister. Quentin Shaw."

Barney nodded. "Good man." I wasn't sure whether he meant me or my choice of counsel. Although I had a pretty good idea. "Keep me in the loop."

I nodded, thinking, *Like you give a toss*, but my mind was already on the bulging file in my hand.

Which was probably another big mistake.

THIRTY-TWO

Isabel must have forgotten how mercurial our English weather can be. The coat she wore that day we went to meet Quentin Shaw in his chambers was well-tailored but dangerously flimsy. I could see that the threatened summer rain was already mocking her, as she moved towards me across the famous square.

Lincoln's Inn Fields is enormous and rather attractive, I suppose, if you like that sort of thing. I'm not into buildings, but even I could see that the ones we were approaching, in another square confusingly called Old Buildings, were what the guidebooks would call 'of architectural merit'. When you've spent all your life in a council house, distinguishable from its neighbours only by the quality of the flowers around its door or the graffiti on its walls, I think your sense of beauty has to be carefully nurtured and mine probably wasn't.

Isabel just nodded as we met. We had clearly talked ourselves out on the phone and she was saving herself for the hour or so ahead.

I wanted to cheer her up after the news we had received that morning, or at least die trying, but I didn't have the material to work with. So I was left hoping that our esteemed counsel could niftily dredge something up from his years of serious legal experience, a seam I couldn't as yet mine for myself and most probably never would.

You can't just stroll in and knock on a barrister's door. After a short walk up a very narrow but beautifully-wrought staircase, we were welcomed into the unexpectedly modern lobby by the clerk of the chambers, a dapper, balding, middle-aged man in a smart pinstripe, who looked quite distinguished in his own right. Naturally he began his conversation with the weather.

"He'll mention the weather," I had said to Isabel, hoping for a delayed smile when the inevitable actually occurred.

"Miserable day," said the clerk, on cue. "Looks like rain."

Isabel just nodded, which was bad form. If you come to our country, you should at least respect our customs.

"We need it though, don't we?" I responded. "And it'll save watering the garden."

"Oh absolutely, Mr Davenport. Absolutely."

Not even the hint of a smile from my client. That particular raincloud had just grown bigger. The clerk led us through and knocked on another door, which he proceeded to open.

"Mr Shaw...?" he said.

I looked at Isabel and squeezed her arm. It was like hugging a robot. If fear had a texture, this would be it.

Even though it wasn't so many years ago, I cannot recall a single thing about the room we entered. I know exactly why this is.

Quentin Shaw.

I met someone recently who had once seen Bill Clinton across a crowded room and said he had felt charisma coming off the ex-President in waves. I think this could have been my experience on first meeting our barrister. Unfortunately I could sense that this was exactly how Isabel was feeling, which may well have been what turned me against the man from the outset. That and his name.

Quentin Shaw was in his mid-forties and about six-foot-four, which of course gives you a head-start straight off. (Unless you're Kim/Cypress, when you might as well get yourself felled.) He had a nose you could use for opening letters and straight, straw-coloured hair in need of a good cut, which he kept sweeping back from his forehead with exceptionally long fingers, like it was such a nuisance but what can you do. He spoke in the poshest voice of anyone in this story, and that includes the judge.

There was a confidence here that matched Laurence Menzies' in degree but was totally different in kind. He didn't need to rub it up against others to give it a sheen. More all-embracing than intimidating, it clung to him like an outer skin, as if it was one of those auras natural healers can see but ordinary mortals can't.

He had risen from his seat as we came in and was across the room with his hand in Isabel's in what seemed like a single stride.

"Ms Velazco? Do come in. Please, take a seat… Mr Davenport." He managed to make my name an afterthought and my presence a sideline. He really was very good.

"Disappointing weather," he began. Oh not you too.

But Isabel was there in an instant. "Perhaps the rain will clear the air," she said, as she sat down. He gave a 'we can only hope' nod.

"Good for the gardens though," I contributed.

This of course went for nothing. He just picked up his chair and moved it closer to Isabel. He wasn't hard of hearing nor was she softly spoken, so this all seemed a bit unnecessary. As did my moving my own chair closer to my client's, but I did it anyway. We looked more like a conspiracy than a consultation.

"So. How is Buenos Aires?" he asked with a smile. "Avenida Nueve de Julio?"

Seriously?

"You know this?" she said, clearly impressed.

"Not well," he continued, with a modest shrug. "A school-friend's father was one of 'Our Men in BA.'" Of course he was, whatever it meant. "I took a trip in '91 – just after we stopped being *persona non grata*."

I must have looked a bit confused by this, so he kindly explained. "The Falklands War?"

As I was nodding to intimate that of course I knew, how could he possibly think otherwise, he was off again with his Spanish and Isabel was responding in kind. I thought of saying something witty like, 'I'll go fuck myself, shall I?', but he was already back into self-deprecation mode.

"Schoolboy Spanish. Perdon." His face became serious. "Not a nice story, is it?"

I reasoned that after my less-than-stunning Falklands opener, I should at least show that I was up on the law.

"The report does clearly recognise the bond Isab— Ms Velazco – has with Sebastian. Which is a result." Thanks to the kid-in-question running around with a Spurs kit and a potty-mouth, both courtesy of yours truly.

To her credit Isabel ran a small smile my way. A sad one but not ungrateful. Quentin, however, was looking even more serious, as if there was a facial scale for barristers and he was gradually running down it.

"Indeed," he said, gravely. "Yet it still suggests, Mr Davenport, that the boy's interests might be best served by his staying here." Deep sigh. "With his father. And stepmother. In the country of his birth…"

This was the news we had heard just a few hours earlier and the reason Isabel was looking so glum. It had come as a bit of a surprise to me too, although I suppose it wouldn't have done, had I known how the system actually works. Oliver, of course, hadn't been in the least surprised when I told him, but to his credit there was very little I-told-you-so in his voice. Just enough to make me want to deck him.

"… where he spent his formative years," continued the barrister, like we hadn't read the report.

Isabel looked more desolate than I had ever seen her. Her nodding took on the characteristics of people I had seen on TV with mental illness or deep religious conviction. Quentin tried to ratchet Mister Gloomy-face up a notch.

"It isn't conclusive, Ms Velazco. Or may I call you *señora*?"

She nodded graciously. Of course. Call me anytime.

Naturally, I was right in there. "That's what I told her, Mr Shaw. Not…"

"It is, however, persuasive," he continued, ignoring me totally. "And, I am afraid, predictable. Regardless of blame or fault or indeed unscrupulous behaviour."

I could sense another file-kicking moment coming on. Isabel slowly rose from her chair. Quentin didn't know what he was in for.

"Why do you not say it?" she said, in a voice growing ever more strident. "We can have every expert in the world… *'His mami, she make him nice breakfasts…' 'His mami she always give him the clean clothes…' 'His mami she take him to the bloody zoo…'* But I will be flying back to my 'poky' little apartment on the awful side of 'Avenida Nuevo de Julia' on my own!"

Quentin sat back in his chair, as if the blast of her words had propelled him there. He looked at me but I surely wasn't going to give him any help. Been there, pal. Yet far beyond the way Quentin Shaw was making me feel, which I supposed I could live with, something was hurting.

It was a curious sensation to experience someone else's pain. Not in the way they did, obviously, but perhaps not so far from it as you might think. I didn't like it. Yet even worse than this was the agony of knowing that there was absolutely nothing on earth I could do about the situation. I had felt helpless in the past – it was practically my default mode – but it had never felt like this.

For some reason I suddenly had an image of Sebastian in the MiG, that day of the Leviathan, his busy hands picking at the trim. Tiny hands, nails bitten down to the quick. I sneaked a

162

look into my open briefcase. The photo was there on top, Isabel and Sebastian on the beach, the little boy holding a brightly-coloured ball. The nails on his slim, olive fingers perfect and unchewed.

"Did you go to boarding school?"

I was back in the room. *What?* Why did she suddenly ask him that? Had I missed something?

"From the age of eight," answered Quentin, to which she just nodded, like this explained everything. I felt like a kid who had sneaked downstairs when his parents had guests and caught a snippet of baffling adult chat.

"Ms. Velazco, I do think we have an opportunity. To regain custody of Sebastian."

I was still processing the boarding-school bit. This sounded like we had suddenly moved on. I had no idea how we could possibly have the slightest opportunity to regain anything, but that was probably why he was an eminent family lawyer and I wasn't. (Although, as we know, I was now also Our Man in Corporate.)

"Hang on," I said, "you just…"

He smiled as he talked over me once again.

"Much of your husband's case is based on the sort of life Sebastian would have in Buenos Aires." Isabel just nodded but she was leaning so far forward she was practically in his lap. Which he clearly wouldn't have minded at all. "And, of course, on how unsettled the boy would be – a child who was born here and grew up here, who speaks our language – having to move back there yet again. After…"

"After I send him away forever!"

She practically spat that out, into a silence that on my part was simply that, empty and blank, but for Mr Shaw was clearly contemplative. Finally he looked towards the window, steepling his bony fingers, as if thinking out loud into the damp City air.

"How would you feel, Ms Velazco, about staying here?

Permanently, I mean. In London?" He smiled very slightly at this point, as if this might cushion his words.

"What?" she said quietly.

But she heard him. We both did. Only neither of us could take it in.

"It's the best advice I can give you," he said, almost apologetically. "Yet it's still very far from a guaranteed solution. And, I don't doubt, equally far from ideal."

I felt I had to contribute something of a positive nature, because I could see that, yet again, the colour had drained from Isabel's face. Even more scary when that person until a few seconds ago had a gloriously healthy, unBritish tan.

"I'd help you find somewhere," I said, breaking the polar silence. Which clearly wasn't the right thing to say at all.

She began to shake her head vigorously, something I found even more disturbing than the earlier nodding. Without saying another word, she rose and walked towards the door. I immediately stood to accompany her but she waved me angrily back towards my seat.

In what seemed like seconds she was back in the square again. By this time the much discussed and universally predicted rain was bouncing off the pavements and doing the grass the world of good. Both Quentin Shaw and I watched with equal helplessness as our mutual client walked slowly in her open shoes, her useless coat unbuttoned, into the deluge and out of sight.

Quentin was still watching when I left the room. I hoped that the extra time wouldn't show up on our bill.

THIRTY-THREE

With all the turmoil that was going on outside, I should have been grateful that at least my home life was proceeding very much as normal. But I wasn't heavily into gratitude that summer. And, to be honest, normal was still pretty irritating. Of course my parents probably didn't have quite so much opportunity in those final few weeks to get up my nose, as my nose and I were simply less around.

Looking back, I realise that I had made an art-form of avoiding them, which is what you do when you're an adult who's still living at home. By gliding quietly in and out of barely-opened doors, shoelessly tiptoeing up and down staircases, slipping round corners you barely knew existed, you somehow pretend to yourself that you're happily ensconced in the bachelor-pad of your choice, blissfully unencumbered. And simply ignore the odd grunts and smells and locked bathroom-doors that might give away that you're not.

Because the moment you bump into the older residents and listen to what comes out of their mouths, no matter how neutral the subject or how genuinely respectful of your opinions they try to be, you feel as if you're about ten again. Back then, with all that was going down, I really needed to feel that I was at least twenty-seven. (Even though I rather appreciated the in-house washing and ironing service.)

The corporate project that Barney had generously entrusted to me was unfortunately far less stimulating than it was time-consuming and of course I only had this one chance to make a halfway respectable fist of it. Especially with the man himself poking his flabby neck round my door every five minutes to ensure that I was giving it my full attention. At least it pissed off Evan, so every cloud…

Right now, however, my priorities were Isabel and Sebastian and I had the cruellest feeling that I was letting the pair of them down.

Isabel wasn't even returning my calls. (With most lawyers, as you may well know, it's the other way round.)

When I tried to contact Joanne, she told me curtly that her friend wasn't there but she was sure Isabel would be in touch 'as and when'. It was like someone had pressed an enormous pause-button, yet there was no cup of tea in sight.

So when Oliver asked me to join him the following Saturday at a new club that had just opened in Shoreditch, I agreed to go. Not that I had any desire to be a single clubber again, after all those years with Sophie, but I needed to be with a friend and there was only one friend who knew exactly what was going on in my life. Or at least knew enough to make him believe he knew it all, which is often all you need in a friend. And I knew what was going on in his life, which was exactly nothing and was why we were going to that club.

∗∗

The place was called Vortext, which sounded vaguely Germanic and totally baffling until you walked in and the secret was revealed.

The lighting, of course, was dim – or moody as they would probably prefer me to describe it, if they still exist, which I doubt. Jets of colour flashed across the floor, the tables and the patrons with an insistence just inside the epileptic guidelines. The music was loud, but not as ultra-loud as usual, as this might undermine the conceit of the whole establishment.

On each table – and there were plenty of tables – was a terminal and above it a number, which would flash intermittently. The idea was that if you saw someone at another table with whom you wished to communicate – and I'm not talking the correspondence of a lifetime – you would use the keyboard to text them (Vortext – see?). It makes me feel old just to recall it and it wasn't that many years ago.

I was content to nurse my beer while Oliver pecked furiously. Actually I was nursing a goodly number of beers, while Oliver was doing what seemed like an unhealthy amount of pecking. He looked beaten down, poor guy. It's not easy being rejected in print and the responses being barely literate didn't make it any more bearable.

"*How wld u 2 ldies at Tble 7 like to ease yrself dwn to 2 solctrs on Tble 4?*"

He would speak it aloud as he texted and you can only imagine how much fun that was.

"Can't you make yourself a bit more interesting?" I moaned.

"*I specialse in Conveyncng n my frend ds Famly.*" He nudged me conspiratorially as he added "*nd now Corprt.*' Send!"

I looked at him and felt a huge rush of affection, entwined with an almost overpowering sense of wanting to be somewhere – anywhere – else.

"What are we doing here, Ol?" I moaned. "I should be working on Barney's sodding project."

"I'm trying to get meaningless sex," muttered my friend.

"You're not into meaningless…"

"If I had it, it would mean something!" he snapped but then he felt his line pull and his rod stiffen. "Ooh, oh oh, incoming!" He began to read, like I couldn't see the giant screen with

200-point lettering directly in front of me. *"We wrk all dy wth solctrs! Srry."*

"I don't even know where she is," I continued, on my own tack, which was I'm afraid the only one I was bothered about back then. "It's like she's just given up, Ol. After what that smarmy barrister went and suggested."

"Which was probably the only thing he could suggest, in the circumstances," said Oliver.

"Yeah, okay. Mebbe." I shook my head. "I thought we were friends again."

"We are, Ricky," he said, still typing. "Okay, I was a bit disgusted that you went and shagged…"

"Not me and you. Me and—"

"Sophie? Dream on."

Oliver!

He was off again. "Look. Look. In the corner! Table 9. O-kay. *'Prfessnl gys – G.S.O.H – keen on trvl. Cn we join u?'"*

He beamed at me with pride. It was very sweet and yet incredibly sad. All that childlike enthusiasm simply made the inevitable disappointment so much worse.

I had to get up. The floor with its swirling patterns suddenly rushed up into my eyebrows. "I'm driving over there right now!"

Through the haze I could see that the girls from table 9 were on the move, although I seriously doubted that we were the destination.

"Eh? Driving where?" said Oliver. His eyes were fixed on that table. His sweat glands were revving up. "No! *The hottie?* I thought you didn't know where she'd gone!"

I just shook my head, which didn't have space for such trivialities.

"Rick!" he yelled frantically. *"They're coming over!"*

He turned to me and his face seemed to change, like a cartoon child registering open-mouthed shock. Even with all the colours of the spectrum gliding over him, I could see that some of his own colour had departed.

"Oh my God," he said, a bit too loudly. *"You're in love with her!"*

Perhaps it took Oliver to say it. Or perhaps, because it was Oliver, I took it. But standing there in that weird club, wobbly from drink and weak from work, I knew without question that he was right. I think. Even if this felt like the sort of conversation two girls would be having, not grown men of almost twenty-four with LLBs.

It feels like the only way to convey any sense of how it was for me is to say how it wasn't. It wasn't like anything I had felt in my life up until that point. Okay, I'd never felt heartburn or haemorrhoids, but I have now and it's different.

I had also drunk a table-full of beers before and I knew the difference between that and the lightheadedness that was propelling me to the door. Or at least I knew that alcohol couldn't explain the surge of adrenaline that was roller-coasting through me and leaving me chilled yet burning hot. It was probably like that ecstatic fear people experience when they're doing something stupidly dangerous by choice, like cycling a sheer mountain pass in Bolivia or leaping out of a tiny plane. Scary as shit but not wholly unwelcome.

"Go for it, Ol," I told him, as the two girls approached, whilst I struggled up from our hot-desk and angled towards the exit. But bless him, my best pal couldn't let me go, even with table 9 almost at his terminal. So he made the ultimate lawyer compromise – he handed the prettier of the two arrivals his business-card.

"So sorry. Really," he apologised. "I'm in the office most weekdays. Best before 5.30 – but I have been known to stay late."

He gave the young woman a shrug and she returned it in kind, more than a little bemused. With that he followed me out of the club.

We found ourselves beside the small canal that ran alongside the rear of the building. Weirdly, at the same time as I was trying so hard to regain my bearings, physical, mental and emotional, I could also feel myself watching the whole thing as if from a chopper hovering overhead. Like it was tracking me on the way to where I vaguely recalled having parked the MiG. I was going pretty fast, considering the twin conditions affecting my balance, but Oliver easily caught up and became the dominant male.

"Give me the keys. Come on, gimme Rick," he said. "*Now!*"

I stared at him. This man who had accused me of losing my heart and my motor-skills. He took out his mobile and made an elaborate dumbshow of what you do when you're calling someone.

"I'll buzz the fuzz and say you're legless. They'll believe me. Add that to your other… derelictions." It took him a while to get that one out, so I realised he wasn't exactly temperance league himself. "*Hello, Law Society!*"

He was extending his hand. Through the haze (and the whir of the non-existent helicopter), I could still sense that there was some wisdom here. So I surrendered my key-ring. But even I could perceive that the wisdom-level was diminished somewhat by his throwing the whole bunch into the canal.

"I thought you were just going to drive me home," I said, as I watched them disappear, with hardly a ripple.

To his credit Oliver looked like he could kick himself. To my shame this is exactly what I did.

THIRTY-FOUR

My dad notices things.

Such as my coming home at one in the morning, without keys or a car, and having to ring several times on our doorbell that plays the theme from *Taxi Driver* (a birthday gift that went way over his head). Or the fact that the colossal teddy bear, who had been one of the family for so long, had mysteriously taken himself off on a gap-year.

But I wasn't ready for a chat or a confrontation when I surfaced that Sunday morning, especially not after a sleepless night and my head in the shape it was, so I just ate my breakfast and pretended that nothing was going on.

"What's going on, Rick?"

"Nothing."

I don't imagine that snippet of conversation has added much, but actually the tenor of it was pretty different to our normal weekend chatter. My dad didn't usually challenge me so brusquely, even though, as I've indicated, my responses to however he talked were generally fairly noncommittal.

What *was* going on?

Dad, I've fallen in love with this much older South American woman, who's asked me to help her win back her angry, weird kid and she's been told the only way this could possibly happen is if –

and it's a massive bloody if – she jacks in her whole life and shunts a million miles away over here. To a place she hates. Only now I don't even have a clue where 'here' is, 'cos she's not answering my calls and her landlady won't tell me. Oh, and yes, I shagged her last week, because she was so helpless and lost and frantic and you know me, I'm a bit of a rogue.

"We're worried about you, pet," said my mum, dangling an unfamiliar child on her lap. Where were the parents on a Sunday?

I was also worried about me. I know twenty-three isn't that young and during the war there were younger guys commanding fighter-squadrons, but shooting down Germans felt much more straightforward, although technically probably not that easy.

"Sorry, Mum," I said.

Yet, as I heard myself, I realised that this wasn't my usual apology, the one I generally threw out if I was skipping supper or after locking one of her charges in the shed. I really was sorry, although I wasn't exactly sure for what. For everything I suppose, in the past and in the future. It was as if I knew there was going to be a lot more to be apologising for, which was sort of scary.

I rose from the table. "Gotta get the car – then do some work."

"Old Barney piling it on, is he?" asked my dad.

It was strangely exhilarating to be (sort of) honest for once. "Yeah. New client. A big one. Corporate – obviously. Kind of a test, I think."

"Well, you're good at tests," said my mum, referencing some mental-arithmetic challenges from a long-ago primary school, most of whose alumni are now probably counting days until their release. Only not as deftly as I would.

I could fail to chat all day, but I needed to find Isabel. Actually, I needed to find my car and then find Isabel.

Locating the car was a whole lot simpler, and discovering it with the wheels still on was a bonus. It seemed to know its way to Joanne's house, which was great, because I was still losing the plot after the night before and especially after Oliver's girly yet shocking pronouncement. I wondered if I looked like a man in love as I drove down the ever-busy Sunday streets. London never sleeps and I felt much the same way, so my eyes were finding it hard to stay fully open.

They opened a bit wider when Joanne came to her door and told me I looked like crap. It was the end of summer, her kids were still home and apparently this was taking its toll.

"Know the two most feared words in the English language? 'Long' and 'vacation.'"

"Joanne," I said, "I have to speak to Isabel. Please."

She just looked at me and I understood that Isabel's whereabouts were clearly still off-limits.

"I'm her lawyer, for fuck's sake!" I protested, then apologised to her kids who were staring at me from the hallway. "Sorry about the 'fuck', guys." (I was very tired.)

I could tell that Joanne was weighing things up, mostly because she was an actress and her face was doing what she thought weighing things up would look like. Finally she told me and it made even less sense than when she hadn't.

My car didn't know the way this time but fortunately the satnav did, although I could tell from her voice as we approached that she didn't want to be there. (I recall Oliver and his dad inventing a Jewish satnav that made comments about why you were going and whether you shouldn't be doing something that would take you somewhere so much nicer. I was quite envious of how two guys could just riff like that – we didn't do so much of that at home.)

The small block of flats at which I finally pulled up that morning was seventies, shabby and soulless. And coming from a housing estate in Hackney, this is saying something. At least we had what you might call a community there – here it looked like everyone was sealed-in and screwed-down.

There was no one on the streets and no reason why they should be, although I wouldn't say it felt dangerous because this would at least give it some character. Here there was more an absence, as if the place had just been discovered and colonised and was waiting for history to etch in the local colour.

I walked into the nondescript lobby and up the stairs to the third floor. Standing outside flat 3C, a good part of me hoped that Joanne was telling the truth and an equally large part hoped she wasn't.

Isabel opened the door.

I'm afraid that I just stood there and stared at her for a second too long. She looked like she went with the place, frayed and worn and dusty. I can't say she didn't look beautiful, because to me she never seemed anything less, but I recall my first thought being that she looked her age. Which I suppose is the last thing a woman ever wants. And beyond the last thing you would ever wish to tell her.

She just nodded resignedly, like a wanted criminal discovered after too long on the run, and turned back to the hallway.

I noticed she was wearing yellow rubber-gloves and that even they looked good on her. When she used the back of her hand to brush away a stray wisp of hair that was falling over her eyes, my attention was total. I tried not to think that this was the woman with whom I had slept just a short while ago and tried even harder to accept that this would probably never happen again. To be honest I wasn't even sure I wanted it to – at least not in the way that it had.

The tiny, two-bedroom flat was depressingly spare and rundown, but at least was well on its way to being clean. The walls had clearly once been white and were now what I suppose you'd call off-white, stained by neglect and life. I didn't know much about furniture, never having bought any, but I imagined this stuff was as cheap as it looked.

On a small table in the kitchen was a glass vase in which Isabel had arranged some very pretty flowers. Don't ask me what they were, yet they managed somehow both to brighten the place up and make it look even sadder.

I didn't know what to say.

"It's nice," is what I said.

She just looked at me. She knew that it was as far from nice as it was from Buenos Aires, but it was in the rough vicinity of the Menzies home. Sharing a slice of postcode, if not the same air, it was clearly all she could afford.

The new tenant returned to her chores. I thought I had better keep talking, because she was clearly not in a chatty mood and I hadn't driven all this way for the silent treatment.

"When we win, we'll get bastardo to pay for something much better," I told her, with a confidence that even I found surprising. "You're not getting your child back unsupported. Not with me on the case."

Isabel threw the cloth she was using right across the kitchen and into the sink, then turned to me like she was going to give me a hard time. Perhaps I had overdone the confidence bit.

"You know where he is this week? My son?" I shook my head. "*Fucking Paris-Disney!*"

I was shocked. "What kind of a shit-head takes his son to Paris-Disney?"

Which was kind of a stupid thing to say, as I wouldn't have baulked if my own dad had rolled up that minute with tickets to Disneyland Paris. But his motives of course would have been totally different. He would have found a more direct route for Space Mountain.

"Please now, you have seen me," she said, more quietly. "I would like you to go." I didn't move. "You can put this in your big file. Good client does what her barista tells her."

"Barrister. Barista is Starbucks. Okay, I'll go if you want. But let me come back this evening. To help you a little. To – I dunno

– to talk." I paused, hardly able to look at her. "We do need to talk, Isabel."

"Today I work," she said and noted the surprise on my face. "There is an Italian restaurant near this." She gave a wry smile. "Italian – Argentinian. Who is caring? Ha. Is my first night. Will they clap me, I wonder?"

She looked very brave and determined yet it wouldn't take a research-fellow in human nature to realise that the stuffing had been knocked right out of her. Not totally – the spark was still there in those inflammable eyes – yet I wondered how long before that too died out, like a barbecue in the rain.

"You must go now, Richard," she sighed.

I nodded and was just turning away, when a thought occurred. "Could you – maybe – leave the key under the mat?" She looked at me with huge suspicion. "Trust me, Isabel," I said gently, "I'm a solicitor."

Which are probably the least convincing words after 'the cheque's in the post' or that other one. And, of course, they weren't actually true. But at least this time I meant well.

THIRTY-FIVE

The restaurant was called Casa Mia.

I was sitting outside it in Auto Mia that night, listening to the radio and waiting for Isabel to emerge after her shift. She hadn't told me which casa she was actually working at, so I had spent the latter part of the evening driving around, until I'd spotted her leaning over a table and lighting a young couple's candles. I have to admit that it was good to see those legs again and clearly the young man felt the same way.

Finally, all the lights went off and seconds later Isabel emerged, waving goodbye to whoever was locking up and looking even more worn out than before. She was holding a small bunch of flowers. As she raised them up to her face, to sniff whatever scent lingered on after that pungent kitchen air, she closed her eyes and swayed as if in a gentle breeze. For a moment she seemed to be somewhere else.

She caught sight of my car. A soft, and I believe genuinely grateful, smile restored just a touch of the former glow to her face as she walked slowly towards me. I should have slid out of the car and opened the door for her, but I can forget these things in the heat of the moment. I'm afraid I forgot it with Sophie quite often.

"How was it?" I asked. "Your debut."

"They give me flowers."

This was all she said as we drove off down the empty road. Which was fine – there would be time to talk and I was excited about what was going to happen when we got back to her flat.

I would be lying if I say I had noticed a car further up the road pulling out at the same time. Perhaps it didn't do so that particular evening. But, as things turned out, I wouldn't be at all surprised if it had.

***

"Do not tell me. You have built the inside swimming-pool."

I was relieved that Isabel could joke after her long day and had been equally encouraged earlier that afternoon, after she had left for work, when I found her key under the mat. I was in a state of childlike anticipation as I drove her home, wondering what she thought I had been doing in Casa Isabel while she waitressed. Most probably something allied to DIY, but as I can't knock a nail in, that wasn't going to happen.

What I had done was infinitely more imaginative.

"Think *Pirates of the Caribbean*," I said, equally jokily, although perhaps the Disney reference wasn't all that clever. Happily, it sailed right over her head.

Once we were in her tiny hallway and she had removed her coat (but kept hold of her bag for some reason), I threw open the door to what would be Sebastian's room, at least for the few weekends remaining until we went to court.

"Da dah!" I said, which you have to say in these circumstances and which, frankly, the transformed little room deserved. "Da dah dahh!"

The place was unrecognisable.

An explosion of old toys, cuddly creatures, board-games, pieces of Lego, puzzles of every size and complexity, books with words and books with pictures, cars, planes and anything else the district's car-boot sales, flea-markets and junk shops – in fact anything cheap and open on a Sunday – could provide. All over the floor and the shelves and the flimsy furniture. In boxes, out of boxes, in pieces, in piles, infinitum. Hamleys-lite. (Or my mum's kitchen-diner on any weekday afternoon).

It had taken several trips in the MiG to furnish this impressive toy-land. Anyone watching would have thought Christmas had come early or the local child-molester was building a franchise.

I turned to look at Isabel and wondered what the Spanish was for gobsmacked. Her glistening eyes were huge, her hands moved instinctively upwards to conceal her gaping mouth and then – *result* – the tears began.

It was time for me to do modest and self-deprecating.

"Hey, hey. It's okay Isabel. I liked doing it. And it didn't cost me nearly as much as it looks. Really."

"It is so – pathetic," she murmured, through her tears. Not the word I would have used, but it wasn't her mother-tongue.

She slumped onto the near corner of the bed, which was the only piece of room Santa hadn't visited, and stared up at me.

"For who do I do this thing, eh?" she asked quietly. "*Que quilombo!*"

I wasn't completely sure what she was on about, so I said nothing. But I had this awful feeling that my much anticipated surprise wasn't quite the triumph I had been banking on.

"Is this love?" she challenged, spreading her hands around to encompass not just the room but the whole flat. And perhaps the entire undertaking. "Tell me! *Is this love?*"

I shunted aside an old box of Monopoly and sat down on the bed, keeping a good few inches away from her, so that our bodies wouldn't touch.

"Looks like love to me," I said.

And it did. I had never loved a child, in fact quite the reverse, but I hoped that if I did, this was the sort of thing I would do. I had already done the toys thing for Sebastian and I certainly didn't think I loved him. But Isabel hadn't finished.

"How would *you* know about love? Or children? How would you know about this pain – this pain that is like there is a big *jaguar* – the jaguar, si, that is eating out of the inside of your heart? *HOW WOULD YOU FUCKING KNOW?*"

Whoa!

It took me a few seconds to realise she wasn't talking about a car.

She leapt up and began to tidy the room in a frenzy, as if the Queen was coming to stay overnight and her host had only just been told.

"Isabel! Hold on," I said, stepping into the whirlwind. "*Wait*! Listen to me. Please. Okay, I may not have a little boy of my own, but I did used to be one. And not so long ago, what with being only twenty… seven. Our house is full of kids all day long. They love things messy."

"*Si – but they like to make the bloody mess themselves!*"

She was holding a *Star Wars* light-sabre (30p, beaten down from 50p) still in perfect working order – and I thought she was going to brain me with it. But just as it lit up, she seemed to lose her own charge and begin to calm down. She shook her head, yet managed to give me a small, sad smile.

"You are very kind, Rick, and my little boy he like you more than he like me. *Likes!* More than he will ever likes me, I think. Especially when he sees this place." She sank down again onto the bed, picking away at the duvet-cover with frenetic, restless hands. This time I remained standing. "I know now that we will not win. You are good lawyer… in your own way. But you are not God."

She opened her bag, which was on the bed beside her, and took out the tired giraffe. She threw 'Rafa' onto the pillow, next to the other forsaken toys I had put there. Splayed out on the clean white linen, lifeless and unloved, it seemed like a gesture of total defeat.

I had never felt more helpless in my life.

THIRTY-SIX

"What are you doing for lunch?"

Words can't flow much sweeter from a boss's mouth, save for 'I can't think what this firm would do without you' or 'Take a fortnight in Antigua on us.' And there can't be many worse ways to respond than 'Having a chicken tikka baguette', which just shows how much strain I was under.

Fortunately Barney ignored this, so I just followed him out of the office and down the corridor. I barely had time to say 'Hold all my calls' to a fascinated Dimpy and 'Suck on this' to Evan, but I managed.

I tried manfully to ignore the fact that my mind was light years away from Corporate at that moment. Perhaps a good lunch would help.

To his credit – and my surprise – Barney did ask me how the Velazco case was going. I updated him on Quentin Shaw's bombshell but he simply shrugged. Clearly he wasn't over-interested, merely mentioning that, in his experience, it really wouldn't make much difference. Then he moved on to his favourite topic. Food.

Naturally I had never been to the restaurant at the top of the National Portrait Gallery. I don't think I was even aware that the nation had a portrait gallery, let alone one where you could eat.

Portraiture seemed like a fairly narrow remit to me, but then again I only saw a handful of them as we took the escalator up to the business end.

The first thing I noticed was the view, which was spectacular. You could almost lean out and poke old Nelson in the eye, with Big Ben, the Houses of Parliament and loads of other famous landmarks laid out before you like a huge architect's model with real moving parts. In fact I was so busy taking in this unanticipated panorama that I didn't fully absorb who our host actually was.

Sitting alone at a window table – which I imagine demanded some serious clout – was a distinguished-looking man reading the menu with the same sort of informed scrutiny he had probably given his *Financial Times* on that morning's train.

It was the rich crop of silver hair that rang the first bells. When he finally looked up, I recalled where I had seen him before. It wasn't simply that evening a couple of weeks ago, when he was leaving our office so briskly – it was early the previous month at Laurence Menzies' place. The Friday afternoon we went to collect Sebastian. What the hell was his name?

"Rick Davenport, meet Hugo Sandford."

That was it. I knew the Sandford bit, it was on all the turgid documents that I had been wading through into the early hours. But I had never linked the two. I felt I had better say something, rather than just stand there staring at the luxuriant hair, like a barber admiring his work. He certainly didn't seem to recognise me.

"Oh," I said, pithily, "I think we've met, haven't we?" The man looked blank, as if he couldn't conceive of our two paths ever crossing. "Laurence Menzies? You were coming out as I was going in?"

"Ah Laurence, yes," he nodded, patently not recalling me at all. "We do some business together. Small world."

Barney was in there like a ferret down an entertainer's

trousers. (Apparently they always lick before they bite, which is how you know to whisk them out.)

"Hello, do I smell a conflict of interest?" he said, then added with a sigh. "Only one thing for it. Richard – I'm afraid you're sacked."

I stared at him like the ferret had started licking. Then both men began to laugh as if it was the funniest joke ever. Of course, I laughed with them. *Knew all the time you were joshing me, guys, I'm not that green!*

Barney got back to business, pausing only to stuff his mouth with some high-grade olives to make himself less intelligible.

"Rick's read the bumf, Hugo. Makes sense he hears exactly what you and your partners want. Words of one syllable, he's only twelve. And some decent scoff won't hurt him, considering all the donkey-work he'll be doing."

I got in my first and only joke of the lunch.

"Do they do carrots?"

Not a certified knee-slapper, but it went down well enough. After they had offered their informed suggestions as to what I should actually eat, most of which I had never tried in my life and couldn't even pronounce (*bouillabaisse?*), we moved on to 'business'. But my attention was only half on it.

The other half was on a conversation I needed to have with Oliver, which suddenly seemed a lot more important.

THIRTY-SEVEN

Of course Oliver thought I was being paranoid.

He also reckoned I was acting seriously weird that evening, pacing his office and waving my hands around in a flurry of erratic – and for the most part involuntary – movements.

The most disturbing part of my unscheduled visit, however, was that he seemed almost equally paranoid, twitchily checking his watch and his phone, opening and slamming shut his diary, shooting across to the window and staring wildly out.

It was quite disconcerting and for a moment I thought he was simply taking the piss, but I soon made the executive decision that whatever was genuinely exercising him, my problem was more important. Even though I hadn't the slightest idea what was stirring him so dramatically.

"Yeah, okay, maybe I am being paranoid," I said, as I know that repetition can keep a conversation on track. "And it was probably just one of those things. Coincidences happen, right? But Ol, I can hardly fucking breathe." I proved this by hardly fucking breathing. "It's all getting too… why are *you* acting so hyper?"

I had to acknowledge it. Oliver Rosen, solicitor-at-law, was impeding my flow and blocking my route around the room. Anyone staring in and watching our behaviour would think that we were floundering examples of care-in-the-community.

"Rick, can I tell you something?" he said excitedly.

"You should have seen her crappy flat, Ol. It was just so – sad. And now *she's* having second thoughts. Can you believe that?"

"Oh, we're back with you," said my nervy friend. "Okay."

I felt bad that we were holding our two conversations simultaneously, and that neither of us was hearing the other, but there are times when you just have to talk to someone and it's almost irrelevant whether that other person is actually listening. I bet the Samaritans get calls like that all the time.

"What if – after all this…?" I asked. "Oh Jesus, Ollie! *What if I'm wrong about her?!*"

Oliver was by the window at this point, which was pretty much where I wanted to be. Then his laptop pinged and he was back at his desk in a flash.

"No, Oliver!" He turned at this. "I am *not* wrong about her."

He dove back into his laptop. I swiftly took his coveted place by the window and caught my face reflected in the glass, as the sky momentarily darkened. More rain, probably. But then I stopped and did something I had certainly never done before and have done only once since. (Admittedly, an important once.)

I made a speech.

I'm still not totally sure why. Because I needed to hear the words come out of my mouth without pause? To make certain I believed them as much as I thought I did? Or maybe it was simply to check out that they actually made sense to somebody else. Even if that somebody was a person to whom I rarely made much sense at all.

"How often do you get the chance, Oliver," I began, "like even the smallest chance to… well yeah, okay, to change a person's life?"

I realise this doesn't sound much like me, but I'm pretty sure it was. Ollie looked up from his desk. I could see his reflection. Bless him, the old bugger was listening.

"What I mean," I thought aloud, "is, y'know, the chance – the opportunity – to make a difference. A *real* difference. To someone. People. I'm not talking cures for cancer, obviously. Or, I dunno, muscular sclerosis or something, course I'm not. But still…"

I stopped but my friend didn't say anything. Not even to correct me. He was probably letting me work myself out.

"And then what if, after all of it, after all the really crap stuff and the really good stuff too and the risks and the fighting, and maybe losing the only legal job you can ever get, because you're not that sharp, not really, only the suit, what if you can't change a thing?"

I turned to look straight at him. I could feel tears in my eyes. Real tears. Jesus! "*What if you can't change a fucking thing?*"

Oliver was really staring at me now. Okay, he was stealing glances at his watch and the door of his office, which was weird, but mostly he was staring.

"This isn't about me any more, is it Ol?" I went on. "Or even about me and her. It's about – it's about *them*. Y'know, the two of them." I felt my voice cracking – it was a bit embarrassing. "Okay, it is about me. I'm not that selfless. Because if she loses that aggravating little sod, I just don't know what I'll do."

This was getting way too cringeworthy, so I thought I had better let Oliver off the hook. "Sorry. I dunno what – fancy a drink? My shout."

"I can't, Ricko," said Oliver, which surprised and upset me, after I had just vomited my heart out. Something I had never done before in my life, because so far as I knew it was something blokes didn't do. Although maybe Jewish boys get down-and-weepy when they're alone with each other, being more in touch with their emotions because they had a terrible history and had spent fewer generations in England, so could be this was nothing special to Oliver. He'd probably seen far worse at weddings.

"Why not?" I asked.

"I've got a client coming any minute."

"Bit late for you, isn't it?"

What he told me next jolted me more than anything he had ever said before. "*It's the girl from that club!*" At first I had no idea what he was talking about. "You know! The one I gave my card to!"

"She rang you?"

"She rang me!" He joined me at the window, his face flushed with excitement. Even if it went no further, we both knew that this was a result.

"That's incredible, Ol," I said. "She was very pretty, wasn't she?" I tried really hard to keep the surprise out of my voice.

His nod, whilst enthusiastic, did appear to contain just the slightest element of umbrage. But then he said, "I think so," and I realised that he couldn't quite remember which of the two young text-goddesses was about to roll up.

"Business or pleasure?" I said.

He took this in good part, because he responded with that arm-bent-at-the-elbow, rapid pumping, deeply un-PC gesture so familiar to lads throughout our shores. I can only assume he didn't sense the door opening behind him or he probably would have left it at that.

"This from Olympic client-shagger Davenport," he continued. "Uh uh uhhhh!"

I think it must have been the look on my face that told him someone had walked in. In fact two people had – Cyril Rosen and the young lady from the Vortext Club. Who was indeed pretty, in a warm, unshowy way.

"Ah, Ms Morgan," said my old friend very professionally, spinning round to greet her like nothing of a client-shagging nature had occurred, "it's about conveying your flat, isn't it?"

I nodded to them all and quietly slipped away.

THIRTY-EIGHT

The day had to arrive when Sebastian and Casa Isabel would finally come face-to-face.

Isabel seemed as excited as if a friend had rung to say she'd just picked up some ebola and was popping round for tea. No amount of cleaning or tidying or licking of paint was going to turn her tiny, rented flat into a detached mansion with swimming-pool, games room and planning permission.

Naturally I couldn't be there on the street with Isabel when she heard Laurence's BMW purr round the corner, nor would she have wished it. Yet I could almost hear the Rosens' opinionated satnav saying, 'You *really* want to come here – seriously?' But of course Isabel filled me in on whatever went down in bleakland that grey Saturday morning. We were still just about talking, Isabel and I. Despite her despondency, I hadn't given up and I didn't believe I was ever going to.

She was at the door of the dingy block (she couldn't clean the whole building), waiting anxiously. They rolled-up en masse – Laurence, Rebecca, Mungo and Sebastian, the latter accessorised with tiny suitcase and shiny-new Mickey Mouse blouson. The Schnauzer puppy was apparently adorable.

Isabel attempted what she assumed would be a swiftly repelled hug – the Threadbare incident hadn't turned Sebastian

Menzies any more cuddly – but to her delight the little boy moved, albeit a tad stiffly, right into her outstretched arms. Her spirits lifted as she held his familiar, skinny little body for almost the first time in months and inhaled the singular, miraculous (well, to her) smell of him.

"Good man," said Laurence.

Sebastian turned to his father solemnly, acknowledging his approval, then Rebecca took him aside to say *auf weidersehn* to his dog. Isabel's mouth went dry as she realised her dutiful son was merely obeying orders.

"So," exclaimed Laurence, staring at the block of flats she couldn't totally hide with her body. "You've decided to up-sticks and move to my part of the world. Almost."

"You are not the only one who can make the surprises," she said.

"Oh, you've never failed to surprise me, Izzie." He smiled warmly. "Hey, you know, I don't want to be your enemy. You don't believe me, why should you? But I remember how you hated the winters here. You had no career. No life. You couldn't wait to get back home."

Isabel threw back a smile not quite as sunny. "So, you buy me a ticket – one way?"

She glanced at Rebecca, who seemed uneasy. Even more so when Laurence gently touched his ex-wife's arm. It can't be fun to watch your husband toy with the woman who previously held your position. And it wasn't the time to compare notes.

"My solicitor say you will help us find the better place when we win," said Isabel defiantly.

"I'm sure your solicitor does, Isabel," replied Laurence, with a dismissive shrug I have no trouble picturing. "But if you and your young advisor are imagining some division of spoils and a King Solomon-like partition of our son, I fear you could be cruelly disappointed. You know me, my love, I only play to win."

Laurence moved past Isabel towards the door, ushering

Rebecca and Sebastian forwards. "Mind if we take a wee look inside?" he asked, his tone becoming lighter.

"Yes."

Momentarily jolted, he rallied swiftly. "Well, I'm sure you've given it your usual taste and flair. Let's hope it's like the Tardis, eh Sebastian? He loves this new *Dr. Who*, except when it gets too scary." He tapped his son reassuringly on the shoulder. "Nothing to be scared of today, sweetheart. You know where we are."

Laurence turned back to the car, which was already gaining a bit of attention from some youths who had appeared in the street. Wishing they had one just like it or deciding that this might be the exact one they were about to have.

"We'll see you Sunday evening, poppet," he said. "Now, say goodbye to Mungo." The boy waved a bit forlornly at the puppy, who gave a posh sort of whimper, then he walked off towards his mother as if to his own firing-squad.

Isabel was wise enough not to take her son's hand. She just grabbed his little suitcase and led him up the stairs. She wanted nothing more than to break down and cry, yet she knew she had to put on a show. As she told me, she was good at shows. But this time she faced her most uncompromising critic.

"You must tell me all about Paris-Disney," she said, with genuine, if bitter-sweet, interest. "Was it a wonderful thing?"

For the first time Sebastian's face showed some animation. "It was very incredible."

Of course it was.

The moment Isabel opened the door to her flat, she knew that it was very unincredible. She wanted to promise her son that it was only temporary, that when he came to live with her for real they would find something he'd incredibly love. She didn't wholeheartedly believe this, in fact she hardly believed it at all, but it is what she wanted to tell him, as any mother would want to comfort a child in distress.

She wanted to tell him so many things and to kiss that sorry, confused look off his face, with the kisses only a mother can give. Yet she could find no words that might ease the pain and fear of a nine-year-old Disney-boy, deeply suspicious of a mother out of his life for months then suddenly flown back in again with talk of lawyers and courts. And she knew in her heart that there really were no workable words.

I don't come from luxury, so when I heard later about his unconcealed disappointment I might well have thought, *Spoiled-rotten kid*. And had I seen him turning his delicate nose up, maybe I would have. But maybe I wouldn't.

"Do you like to see your room?" she asked, with some trepidation.

He didn't say anything. Perhaps he was indeed hoping beyond hope that the tiny hallway was simply a deceptively bland holding-area for some miraculous wonderland, concealed until now by cheap plasterboard. He was going to be so pissed-off.

Isabel opened the door into the tight little bedroom, empty save for one sad-looking ex-giraffe. She wasn't surprised to see his lower lip quiver, the way they do as a sort of early warning for worse to come. Indeed she was half-convinced he was going to grab his mini designer-suitcase from her and walk straight back down the stairs into crapville.

And perhaps he would have done, had the flimsy wardrobe-door not suddenly burst open with a wood-splitting crack, unleashing Gerald of Hackney in his pre-soiled Arsenal strip, stocky little legs and arms waving dementedly. Followed a moment later by my good self, in sweaty T-shirt and shorts, from under the narrow bed. Wondering if I would ever stand up straight again.

"SEBASTIAN!" I yelled.

"WANKER" the feral Hackney-child yelled even louder.

There was an ugly moment when we all three still wondered whether the kid from Buenos would simply revolve on his

Nike Juniors, moaning that his poky, sodding room was now overcrowded to boot. But he only had the briefest of windows, because the thugs from E8 were on him in seconds, hurling him forcibly onto his cheap new bed and pummelling him to within an inch of his life.

To our immense relief – none more so than Isabel – the little boy didn't asphyxiate in seconds or expire of a hitherto undiagnosed medical condition. He actually beamed and even giggled. Giggles that soon turned into an abandoned, blouson-splattering, laughing fit, with obligatory cataracts of snot. Like any normal kid being beaten senseless by a lawyer-in-training and a felon-in-waiting.

Yet what made the day so very different from its predecessors was that this time Sebastian had enough reserve in his emotional power-pack to flash one of his precious, gap-toothed smiles in the direction of his wary mother. Not full-beam and certainly not one of those Duracell, long-lasting ones. But sufficient to allow me to glimpse, albeit briefly, a fully three-dimensional version of joyous, earth-mami Isabel. One that I had so far encountered only in teary reminiscences and a few framed photographs.

Like the one I always kept with me, in whatever bag I was carrying, and that it was now far too late to give back.

***

The almost-obligatory smack in the Davenport face came within ten minutes of us all sitting down for tea in Isabel's tiny kitchen. From the least expected direction.

Gerald had his head in a huge slice of chocolate cake, which made me think of Oliver and wonder how he was getting on. In fact, quite disconcertingly, I was also thinking about Mrs Armitage and the angry Irishman and some of the others, and wondering how they were getting on.

Which made me wonder about myself, as this wasn't like me

at all. But most of all I was watching Isabel as she tried to make normal conversation with her son.

It was still far from easy. Sebastian was more interested in talking cars and TV shows with Gerald, but he was a nine-year-old kid, so why wouldn't he? Yet perhaps in Argentina mums and kids chat more together than they do in Hackney, it being a Catholic country or a hot one or just different, so I was working a bit in the dark here.

I tried to help as much as I could, but I had also promised Linda that I would deliver Gerald home in time for him to visit his Nan, although I hated to think of the damage he might do to an elderly lady. Perhaps she would let him practise his mugging on her, so that he could gain invaluable work-experience off the road.

"C'mon, Gerald," I said, standing up reluctantly. "I've got a ton of stuff to do and your nan's expecting you."

"Oh, shit bollocks!" he responded, predictably.

I nodded. I didn't want to leave either.

"Do not go, Rick." That was Sebastian, which was sweet. "Please?"

It felt, however, just a bit different this time. As if he wanted me to complement the assembled company rather than just protect him from being alone with his mum. But I wasn't totally sure.

"I'll be back, Sebastian. Some time. I'm a bit pushed right now," I explained. "Can you wipe your fingers please, Gerald, before you get in my car? Which might involve you taking your hand out of there."

Isabel stood up. She didn't need to say thank you, I could see it in how her eyes glistened and the way she cocked her lovely head to one side. She was simply being a normal person, which curiously was not how I had ever really seen her.

I could sense that I was slowly beginning to make things right again between us, after they had gone so horribly wrong.

Looking at her in that tiny flat, with her precious son, I knew that I needed the trust and friendship of this desperate, bewitching woman with an intensity that went way beyond lust or adoration but left me just as weak. I had stopped sneaking frequent glances at her legs or down her blouse, or at least far less often (if no less sneakily) and was even starting to quite like her kid, which she must have noticed. It all surprised the hell out of me.

We were on our way out when she grabbed my arm. "Wait… Richard," she said, rather quietly. "A moment please." I waited expectantly. "I know you have done much for us. So much. But I ask you one more very little thing? Something you might like also, because you are working so hard."

I had no idea what this might be, this very little thing, and even when she told me, it took quite a while to sink in.

"I have the day off, from my restaurant. On this Monday. Okay, it may be not possible, I understand this, but who knows, perhaps it may be." What in God's name was she on about?

It didn't take me long to find out.

"Take me to this place you always talk about." *Excuse me?* "Your very special place."

My very special…?

Oh shit.

THIRTY-NINE

It wasn't much of a stretch to persuade Dimpy that I was too sick to come into work that Monday – or even to speak to Barney – because I was feeling almost as nauseous as my pathetic little phone-voice suggested.

Dimpy promised to save some of her mum's extra-spicy japatis for me, if I recovered, then sympathised as I pretended to retch into the phone. It's these little touches that make a story convincing.

Aside from trying to cope with the mortal fear curling and uncurling like a coked-up anaconda in my gut, I had spent several hours the day before – when I wasn't toiling on Barney's increasingly burdensome brief – diligently conducting my own research. Each time my dad came in with a cup of tea for 'Mister Corporate', which seemed like once every five minutes, I had to flick swiftly to a different page. I reckon he thought I was watching porn, which curiously I had stopped doing in recent weeks and felt all the better for it.

So poor MiG sounded much as I felt that glorious, cloudless day, as we drove into the historic city. I had kept up my side of the conversation reasonably well, trying as best as I could to steer us away from the many predictably excited questions about our destination. I had told Isabel I would prefer to make the day as much of a surprise as possible. Which was more true than I prayed she would ever realise.

"Oh Rick," she enthused, her head almost spinning to take it all in. "She is so beautiful."

Despite my total lack of interest in architecture or history, or beauty in its more spiritual forms, I had to concede that the city of Cambridge, my cherished alma mater, was indeed a truly spellbinding place. Especially for two people who had never been anywhere near it in their lives.

I could only hope that Isabel would be so utterly overwhelmed by all the mind-bogglingly stupendous stuff going on around her that she wouldn't sense my total desperation. Or smell it.

It had suddenly become beyond crucial that this inordinately special person, someone I now regarded as a genuine friend – as I hoped she did me – could look upon her legal representative as the one male grown-up in Britain she could trust beyond question. The fact I had built my credibility around a colossal and shameful (and regularly perpetuated) lie could, I felt certain, tarnish and even destroy whatever goodwill I appeared to have mustered over these past weeks. Not to mention freak her out about how the case itself was going, in the hands of a deceitful academic-midget. One who, in all probability, knew precious little about family or any other manner of law.

It could send the poor lady plummeting.

But there was no way on earth I could tell her, was there? Not after having assured her so repeatedly that those other shameless lies were simply a relic of my embarrassingly adolescent past.

And especially not now she was doing that thing I thought you only saw in movies, where the beautifully uninhibited woman stands up in the open-topped sports car and lets her long, flowing hair swing untrammelled in the breeze. Sophie had never done this – mind you, she had a sort of cute page-boy cut, so we would have had to be driving through a tornado. What you don't see in the movies is the poor, distracted driver nearly demolishing passers-by, as his head spins wildly around, because his view is blocked and he has no idea where the hell he is going.

"You see it every day for three years and it still gets to you," was how I actually responded, hoping that a sudden attack of nostalgia might explain the quiver in my voice and my steering.

We finally found a car-park, which cost a bloody fortune. "You'd think they'd let us alumnuses park for free," I protested, as we walked back through the narrow, tourist-heavy, streets into the city centre.

The first college we paused at, after a pleasantly bewildering stroll, was King's. You could hardly miss it, as it was the seriously old one that all the other foreign visitors were happily invading with their guide-books and cameras. In fact King's is the place you see in the brochures and videos, the institution with the huge church, or chapel as they like to call it, and a little river meandering round the back. Job done.

I think some of the guides were students making a few bob over the holidays – they looked so young and intelligent. I worried that I only had fifty per cent of those bases covered.

"*Deo,*" she murmured, staring at the famous chapel, "and it is probably not even Catholic."

"Well," I said confidently but I hoped not too robotically, "not so sure about that. See it was founded in er – 1441, I think, by – yes, by King Henry VI. Probably why they call it Kings." I wanted to keep it sounding effortlessly spontaneous, even though I had frantically downloaded it all into my flaky memory-bank just hours before. "But, of course, it was old Henry VIII – you know, the fat one with all the wives – who fitted it out."

"I have heard of this king!" she announced happily.

We strolled towards King's College Chapel, with me still gabbling. It really was vast, more like a cathedral to my mind. I explained to my guest that each college – all twenty-five of them – had its own special prayer-hall. I did a lot of praying myself, when it came to my finals, but had I actually been here I would have had somewhere to do it properly. Mind you, if I had been here, I might not have needed to pray quite so hard. Or at least my prayers would have been taken more seriously.

"Wait until you see the inside, Isabel," I enthused. I had seen pictures and it looked the business. No wonder they broadcast a carol concert from here every Christmas. "There's a painting in there by Rubens himself." An artist I had never actually heard of before the previous afternoon, but who apparently was very heavy-duty. Probably not in the Rembrandt or Van Gogh league, but close. "It's called 'The Adoration of Maggie', but I'm sure he didn't mean Maggie Thatcher!"

If you can embellish your falsehoods with a good joke, you're cooking with gas.

Isabel was clearly enthralled. She almost danced down the nave on her loudly-clicking heels, Audrey Hepburn neck stretching one way then the other, taking everything in. Twirling and gliding with an enchanted grace.

I decided to respect the solemnity of the chapel, and not offer up any more interesting facts until we had allowed the majesty of the place to seep right into our souls. That probably sounds like something else that Richard *Asked Jeeves*, but I have to say that even with the chaos churning up my breakfast, I was genuinely moved. Which didn't happen to me all the time. In fact up until the past few weeks pretty much never.

I supposed I could count myself lucky.

I might reason that this was all because of the quiet magnificence of the building or the thought of all those dogged construction workers from centuries ago, toiling and probably expiring over rudimentary pulleys and carts, but it was more likely that I was experiencing – perhaps for the first time in a long while – some sort of curious peace.

Cambridge was going to be okay.

Isabel was clearly onside and suspicion-free. I was simply

taking a sickie in the sunshine with a person I liked very much – okay, foolishly-besottedly-hopelessly adored – and whom I was finally, after some early dodginess, doing my level-best to support in the most exacting of circumstances.

Perhaps I could have done even more, had Barney not kindly decided to dump a shitload of City-stuff my way. But I wasn't totally ashamed of how – with Oliver Rosen's help – I had amassed some very respectable material for Isabel's fight. Not that it would do us much good in light of how much more material Laurence had garnered. Solid, plausible, judge-friendly stuff – not necessarily true, but persuasive and from considerably nearer home.

And this was something that scared me even more than what was going on today. What would happen to this lovely woman – and to a friendship I now truly cherished – if and when we finally lost?

"And *anyone* can come here?" exclaimed Isabel, in a state of awe.

I realised she meant the university, not the chapel. "Not quite anyone, Isabel," I replied with a haughty laugh, as I walked back in a Cantab double-first sort of way into the grassy quadrangle and the precious East Anglian sun.

That was when the first near-disaster happened.

We were strolling out of the college grounds, about to continue our utter-mystery tour in whatever direction my rapidly diminishing recollection of the city map (the one at the back of my dad's battered AA book) might lead, when an elderly Japanese couple shuffled in front of us.

"Excuse sir," said the gentleman, looking quite concerned, "can you tell us please, where is College of Christ?" His wife was nodding politely but rather fast. "We must meet our coach at this place."

Without a moment's hesitation I told him.

"Oh yeah, it's quite simple." I pointed in a random direction.

"You go out of here onto this Main Street, okay?" They both nodded now, listening intently to every word. "Take a left then sharp right and you'll see an arch. Big arch. Really big. Go through the massive arch and keep on going for about half a mile. You'll come to an old building, very ancient, mock-tudor. With a big… crucifix. That's Christ. College."

They were so grateful, poor things. They couldn't thank me enough as they wandered off. I could tell from their hands and their bobbing heads that they were prompting each other, the better to remember my bullshit in its entirety.

I dragged Isabel swiftly away in the opposite direction, turning up the first crooked street I could find, in case the couple returned. And after a short walk between pleasant old college buildings, which I named authoritatively – St. Catherine's, Emmanuel, Peterhouse, LSE – we ended up beside the river, which I correctly designated the Cam. I even pointed out the Bridge.

By this time I was sweating like a pig. If Isabel noticed, she was too polite to say and would have just assumed it was the Cambridge sunshine, which I have to say did show up the old place in the very best of lights. I found myself wishing for real that I had studied here – my life might have been so different. Better firm, bigger salary, smarter brain. But then I would probably never have met Isabel or her son. Makes you think, doesn't it?

Of course one of the serious recreational activities students here had gone in for over the centuries, for reasons lost in history and equally lost to me, was punting. I'd seen footage on TV of those narrow, flat-bottomed boats, the ones with a guy standing at one square end holding a huge pole that he sticks right down through the water to the river-bed to propel the whole business along, while his passengers sit as far away as possible and just laugh and act superior, watching the old colleges drift by. It looked bloody silly but I supposed it was probably quite pleasant, provided you weren't the bloke with the pole.

Isabel was fascinated. "You did this as a student, yes?"

"Mm hmm," I said. "In fact – I punted against Oxford. Got myself a punting blue."

In for a penny. Yet as I looked at her face, which I did as often as I could, because it was more breathtaking than any Cambridge college, even King's, I realised that I could almost hear her brain working and could see exactly where her mind was going. I had to stop it – fast. So I checked my watch.

"Look at the time! Do you fancy a nice pub lunch, Isabel, beside the river? It's what people do here."

"Si. But first, Richard…"

Remember that word I say quite a lot?

FORTY

It was around this time that the whole day began to go pear-shaped.

Isabel was reclining with an effortless languor in the punt we had been assigned, her pretty skirt splayed over the thinly-cushioned, wooden seat. I marvelled yet again, through my panic, how she always looked like she was modelling whatever she wore. The great art-director in the sky was cooking with gas that day and the fine old buildings didn't hurt. But my sultry client could make an Argentinian slum look like the last word in chic. I dearly hoped it would never come to that.

I, of course, was standing like a dick at the other end of the boat with a bloody great pole in my hand and humiliation waving at me from five minutes into the future. I felt things simply couldn't get any worse. And then they did.

"Rick, I know you do not lie to me now." She actually said it. "I could not bear this. Not any more."

Why now?

I had to tell her, didn't I? But I couldn't tell her, not after all this time. Why did these things happen to me? We knew bloody well why.

"So, I ask you only this one thing."

Come on – get it over with. Did you *really* go to Cambridge? I found I wasn't breathing.

"Do I waste my time? With this case?"

I nearly dropped the pole. I remember I felt it slide but I'm not sure what else I felt. Relief? Or just a dreadful sadness. We never feel just one thing do we, I'm beginning to realise this now.

"Oh! OH!!" is what I actually said, which wasn't really that helpful. But I swiftly rallied and continued more articulately. "Well, Isabel, gotta be totally honest with you. I mean you wouldn't expect anything less." I heaved a worldly sigh. "I'm afraid the odds still aren't exactly—"

"You can go, guys." The man who ran the punts was becoming royally pissed-off as an impatient queue backed up behind us. I stared at him as hard and as venomously as I could, praying for a sudden disqualification for bad river-courtesy, but clearly all I was going to get was an irritated shunt into oblivion.

There was absolutely no Plan B. So, with sad reluctance, I raised my wretched pole, drew it back and was just about to dig myself a watery grave when we heard a familiar voice.

"Mr Davenport?"

I twisted around in shock. This time the pole did slip from my hands, just missing Isabel's head before it fell into the river. She wasn't brained, thankfully, but she was soaked.

Quentin Shaw was reclining on the grass, reading a book. He rose politely when he realised it was indeed us. His client and her young solicitor, a hundred miles from home, punting.

"Jesus!" I said.

"No," he smiled, "that's down the road."

Cocky bastard. He brushed imaginary grass from his expensive, linen suit (I was quite surprised not to see a straw-boater or a cravat) and helped us to stabilise our craft, casting Isabel his most charming, boarding-school smile. "Good morning, Ms Velazco."

As she greeted him I seized my moment and swiftly yanked her out of the punt.

"What are you doing here?" I asked him, before he could ask me.

"I supervise a group of postgraduate students," he explained, happily watching Isabel trying to dry off. "Legal ethics." I could certainly give them a practical. "And you?"

"Mr Davenport shows me where he make his studies," said Isabel.

Quentin looked surprised, but not unpleasantly so, as he insisted on helping me to steer our radiant client onto more solid ground. I could see he was staring at me quizzically.

"Er... King's College," I told him, as we already knew the place. Okay, now let's move on, shall we?

"Ah... Was old Mickey Bowen still Director of Studies?"

Was this a trap? Surely not.

I just nodded with what I hoped would pass as happy nostalgia. Good old Mickey. It wasn't like Quentin was going to ask me to reel off the guy's inside-leg measurements. I hoped.

"You weren't one of the rogues who'd turn up to supervision with an inflatable woman?"

Who does that?

I laughed, which seemed safest. The old inflatable woman jape.

"Poor Mickey was almost blind, Ms Velazco." Ah. " Students can be very cruel... Won't you please both join me for some lunch?"

I would rather have eaten my missing punt-pole. "Oh, I don't think we—"

"Si. This would be very nice."

***

We went to an old pub that Quentin knew and which of course I remembered from many drunken hours spent within its thick, wattle and daub-stuffed walls. Happy days.

It was heaving with tourists and uncomfortably warm. The low, authentically-beamed ceilings didn't help with the air-flow. Or the noise levels. Quentin of course, with his formidable restaurant presence, found a table instantly, so I volunteered to 'get them in'. But as I waited vainly at ye olde Elizabethan bar to attract some sort of attention, I could see that Isabel was paying a great deal more attention to whatever Quentin was telling her. Nodding intently, head lightly resting on her hands, eyes never leaving his animated face.

What the hell were they talking about?

I was almost at the bar, where Milton probably bought his Scotch eggs, when my mobile rang. I didn't recognise the number but decided I had better take it in case it was something to do with our cosy group.

It wasn't. It was Mrs Armitage to tell me she had just received an unexpected promotion at work and was worried that this might affect her settlement. I found myself genuinely pleased, so I reassured her that this certainly wouldn't compromise her position. Naturally, I had absolutely no idea if I was correct, but what I did have was a vague determination to make things work out for this lady, which had to be half the battle, hadn't it?

By the time I returned to our table Isabel and Quentin were practically in each other's faces. Admittedly the noise-level was such that you could hardly hear yourself lie, but I felt that somehow I was intruding. They did swiftly pull apart, however, when I arrived, almost as if I had caught them out.

The meal was actually quite pleasant, given the circumstances and degree of threat, although it was an effort to keep him from asking me too much about my Tripos. I thought at first that this was something to do with photography, but quickly realised it was Cambridge for exams. They had a different word for bloody everything here, it was a bit pathetic actually.

What we didn't talk about was the case. I imagine Quentin felt it was inappropriate or perhaps, not having the file with him, he couldn't actually remember the details. Although I had the strongest feeling that Isabel was one client he wouldn't be forgetting in a hurry.

At least he paid for the lunch, which was great because I doubted Barney would have signed off on it. Especially on a day when I was meant to be throwing-up my breakfast.

"That was a welcome change from my lonely old Ploughman's" said our counsel with a smile, like we were meant to feel sorry for him. Then he turned to me. "You might enjoy my *ethics* class, Mr Davenport."

I didn't like where he put the emphasis but maybe that was me. Although he had just caught me on the brink of punting my client.

"Now see that you don't go without showing Ms Velazco our Great Court. Cheerio, Isabel." With that he strolled off, back to bumps or Tit Hall or the JCR or wherever.

Isabel? Great Court?

I was frantically trying to recall from my researches what and where Great Court was, when luckily Isabel spotted a bookshop on the opposite corner of the street. She began to walk towards it, seeming quite refreshed after her shepherd's pie. She had a healthy appetite for a dancer.

"I must find book for Sebastian," she enthused. "About the funny boat we nearly go on." I heard her sigh, even from half-way across the narrow road. "Perhaps this will make him like me better."

I caught up with her inside the bookshop. There was something I had to ask her, but I tried to make it casual. "So, what were you and Quentin talking about? The case, I suppose."

She picked up a glossy coffee-table book about Cambridge,

with King's College Chapel on the cover. "This and that. Children."

"Oh, he's married," I said and for some reason my spirits rose. Although gay would have been better.

"He has been."

Oh.

She flicked through another book. I was reminded of the prints on our conference room wall and mused that we had come such a long way from that first, angry meeting just a few weeks ago. Isabel and I were now only a couple more weeks from the end – although I feared more than I would have ever thought possible what that end might mean.

I watched her as she became increasingly absorbed in the books. I didn't often have the chance to look at her when she wasn't looking right back and I was struck once more by her gentle strength and her beguiling, unexpected beauty. A beauty that was no longer revealed to me simply in what my eyes could see.

Perhaps I had finally found myself, like a punter on the Cam, discovering her hidden depths as well as her alluring surfaces. There seemed no question now that I was in love with her and even less doubt that it would lead absolutely nowhere. How could it? But maybe, I thought resignedly, although not without real physical pain, this was as it should be. We came from different worlds.

As she casually flicked a strand of hair away from her eye, half-mouthing the words she was reading, the feeling almost overwhelmed me. I thanked God we had at least managed to get through this terrifying day unscathed.

"After this we see the Great Court, yes?" she enthused. The visit had clearly worked for her. She seemed invigorated. But I had to steer that vigour elsewhere.

I leaned over, as nonchalantly as possible, wondering if we might chance across this marvel in one of the books and it would inform me where the hell it was. It didn't.

"You know, Isabel," I said, with casual authority, "it's just a big old court. It is great, granted, really great in fact, but there won't be any trials going on or anything. Not since King Edward the Confess—"

"Where *did* you go to university?"

Her eyes never left the book.

I felt myself reeling, as if someone had kicked me hard in the gut and all the air had rushed out of me along with my recent lunch. I could almost hear my bowels churning. For a second I seriously thought of protesting, giving it one final, innocent shot, but there really was no point. Game over.

"Watford," I admitted. "It's in Hertfordshire." Like this helped.

I tried desperately to replay the day in my mind and work out where I had come unstuck. King's? The river? Quentin? As if it mattered. Her tiger-eyes were cold and narrow as they stared up at me. Her face was more stern than I had ever seen it and seemed, quite suddenly, deeply threatening. I should have been scared, but all I could feel was this overwhelming sadness.

And then she smiled.

More than smiled.

She glowed and giggled as she watched me crumble. The beam in her eyes instantly switched itself back on as a slim hand moved swiftly up to her quivering mouth. For a few seconds I had no words. It was as if my blood had decided to stop flowing anywhere except down to my feet. Finally, I managed to speak.

"*You've been bloody playing with me!*"

"Playing with you?" she echoed, forcing her smile back home. "No! Okay, si, a little. Yes. I have. Absolutely." She tapped my hand lightly. "Rick, you help me. You help me to get here to where we are – wherever this is. You are on the side with me. This is what matters. Is all that matters."

Her warming smile didn't make me feel any less mortified. Nor did it thrill me that she had needed this, her little joke, as some sort of light relief. I had no idea how long she had known,

208

but guessed it must have been some while. I only knew that I had to explain. "I just – wanted to impress you."

It sounded so pathetic. But the words I yearned to say would sound even more pathetic. Yet I decided at that moment, in that busy Cambridge bookshop, that I could wait no longer and was going to say them anyway.

"Isabel, I know that what I'm about to tell you is dangerous and stupid and probably wrong – no, *definitely* wrong, but—"

I didn't have time to finish. She just grabbed me. My heart was soaring – this was more than I ever expected, more than I had ever thought possible. *My Isabel!* But then she twisted my body round, so that I could see what she had just spotted. The elderly Japanese couple, to whom I had given those rubbish directions, had entered the shop. Looking even more lost than when we first met them.

"Oh crap bugger," I whispered, in subconscious homage to Gerald, "they're coming this way."

This time it was me who did the grabbing, as I yanked Isabel into a tiny corridor between two massive bookshelves. *Cambridge From the Air* fell earthwards from her hand.

We stood very close together, in a tight nonfiction huddle, trying not to breathe, although I sensed that both our hearts could form a marching band.

"Their coach must have left them," I said softly.

"They have been walking for hours," she added.

"Looking for Christ!"

I could feel the explosion coming. I tried tightening my lips together but it was no use. As one, we blurted out my blasphemy.

"WITH THE BIG CRUCIFIX!!"

On that thunderous note we fell into each other's helpless bodies, careering in a single, shuddering, hysterical blob towards one of the towering bookcases, unsettling it just enough to send the top few rows of unattainable books clattering down on top of us and onto the floor.

In a painful hail of too much information we clutched at each other, hardly able to gain our breath, tears of laughter making sloppy tracks down our evil faces.

And suddenly, as the waves of hysteria began to subside, we both knew.

"Shall we go back to the car?" whispered Isabel, looking at me in a way she had never looked at me before, yet still somehow so familiar, so right.

Despite that look, exquisitely honest in its hunger, and notwithstanding the surge of similar fervour building inside my own astonished frame, I felt something major holding me back. But it wasn't exactly scruples.

"I can't remember where I left it," I confessed.

She stared at me, trying to absorb this sad impediment to our bliss, before we both collapsed in a pathetic, quivering, snorting heap onto the carpet. Clamping onto each other for a modicum of support, we instantly expelled glossy residents from the lower shelves to join their companion volumes. I don't think I had ever felt such pure, ecstatic abandon in my life.

But something quite subtle must have nudged our senses, as we lay there writhing and whimpering with barely-constrained laughter, because we both turned at the same time from the literary rubble and glanced slowly upwards.

To see the old Japanese couple gazing sadly down.

FORTY-ONE

"What are you thinking, 'our' Mr Davenport?"

We lay very close together, not that we could do much else on that single, sub-IKEA bed. Outside, the evening traffic was trying to get through and out of the area as fast as possible. A delicate breeze teased the bright but cheap curtains Isabel had made and fitted.

"Was it better?" I asked. "You know, this time."

She didn't say anything but I could tell that it was. How could it compare with that earlier, botched invasion? And this time round I didn't feel the need to tell the world. Only her.

"Isabel, you must know that I love you."

I appreciate that it wasn't a real question but I desperately needed a real response. I don't think I had ever said those words in the way I'd just breathed them. In fact I know I hadn't. I had said similar words during the act itself, as you do, or in its immediate aftermath, and I'd mumbled them when I'd been quitting a flat, a house, a car, a phone call, where they had meant little more than goodbye and see you soon. I had of course uttered them in not-so-quiet desperation to Sophie, in what seemed like another age. But never like this, never from the soul. A soul I hardly knew I possessed.

Isabel simply stroked my cheek and rose from the bed.

I watched her walk towards the window, totally unfazed by her own nakedness, in a way I realised I had never quite been since my mum would bathe me. I couldn't take my eyes off her. Her body seemed to shine and glow, adding its own lustre to the dimness of the tiny room and making it anything but bland.

This may sound banal but for the first time I could truly understand why artists, like those I had diligently ignored in the Courtauld, have been forever obsessed with the female form. Even setting aside the turn-on factor – a pretty huge set-aside, if you ask me – there was a simple, shocking rightness of shape and texture that could take your breath away.

Yet beneath these feelings of almost total contentment ('total' would have been Isabel reciprocating my recent declaration), I could sense a pain growing deep inside myself. I wasn't certain exactly where it arose or even how badly it was hurting. But I wondered if this is always the case, that you can't have one without the other.

She stood at the window, just looking out. If she saw a car in the street with someone sitting inside, she certainly didn't mention it.

FORTY-TWO

You can understand why, when I rolled happily into work the next day, I was wrong-footed by Dimpy's concerned enquiry.

"How're you feeling, Rick?"

"Terrific thanks, Dimpy," I replied. Because I was. "Why?"

"'Cos you was vomiting yesterday."

"Er… still a bit dicky, actually," I swiftly amended. "Had a dodgy Indian on Saturday."

She threw me the sort of look Miss Collins would hurl on a bad day, to which I could only shrug apologetically, especially as the patent-holder for the look was approaching with a thick document in her hand.

"Mr Cracknell wants this read and advised upon for Mr Sandford by Friday – am," she warned, as she dumped it into my hand.

"What? More stuff? *Jesus!*" But she was already walking off to ruin someone else's day. "And the food-poisoning has cleared up. Thanks, Joan," I remarked to her departing form. "Can you believe this, Dimpy?"

"Yeah," she said. "And it's going to get worse."

She nodded to the door and right on cue, the angry Irishman arrived. Which shouldn't have been a total surprise, as he had an appointment for 9am that morning. I had apparently booked him in myself.

His first words were totally chilling. "I am watching you, Mr Davenport. I am watching you like a bloody hawk."

What could I say? In fact I couldn't say anything, because Dimpy was there first. "You're top of his pile, Mr Ryan."

I looked at her. The face was a picture of innocence.

***

I could troll through the events of those final weeks, day by day, but if I didn't find them that interesting, I doubt anyone else would.

During office hours I worked on the stuff Barney had just dumped on me, which was still a lot less stimulating than I might have wished but far more time-consuming. It didn't help that he was forever coming into my office, or rather occupying the narrow doorway and blocking most of my light, to check out whether I was on the case.

I suppose I should have been grateful, his giving me the break for which I had been lobbying since I arrived, but it was his persistently telling me how grateful I should be that somehow stole away the gloss. I recall it being quite confusing.

I also tried to make inroads into the backlog of Family work I had allowed to accumulate. Curiously this proved more involving than I'd expected. I'm not saying I had suddenly seen the light, but perhaps Leila was right, perhaps my clients *were* people, even if they weren't people with whom I would normally choose to spend any time.

Or maybe it was simply that anticipation over who would be there after dark, in a tiny flat a few miles to the south, made the hours preceding just about bearable and my disposition that bit sunnier.

I would wait patiently for Isabel each weekday evening outside the restaurant and drive her home. (Naturally, I didn't stay over when Sebastian was in residence, which was probably healthy for both of us.)

Isabel was always tired and achy after a night's work and in need of a massage with optional foot-rub, waitressing being apparently even more challenging to the body than dancing. I did notice, however, from my regular MiG vantage point, that she occasionally combined both skills, as she glided or rumba-d between the tables, a steaming bowl of pasta in either hand and a permanent, customer-friendly smile on that striking yet strained face. It was like she was hardwired for grace and there wasn't a wasted movement in anything she did.

This was true in bed too. I can't say my experience in that department was as comprehensive as her own (and sadly I had affidavits to prove it) but I doubted that I would ever make contact – that word again – with anyone as fine-tuned to both her own body and her partner's. I also doubted I would ever wish to, which was something that disturbed me almost as much as it thrilled me.

We did, of course, work on her case too. I wasn't some sort of legal predator. Okay, I probably was, but by this time I also cared about the outcome more than I would ever have believed possible. Not just cared – worried. Lost sleep over. Agonised – and there's a word I never thought I would find myself writing.

The funny thing was that little Sebastian Jorge Menzies (or 'S', as he was judiciously referred to in all the legal documents), had become almost as important to me as Isabel herself. She and that sad, curious child were joined in my mind the way they were in her own – well, not exactly the same way, obviously, but let's say I determined not to leave the slightest thing to chance. Not with the hearing less than two weeks away.

It was time to introduce my favourite client to my favourite lawyer.

FORTY-THREE

I had invited Oliver to meet me at an 'amazing' Italian restaurant I had found, in a part of London with which neither of us was familiar. I provided no other information.

I was waiting there when he arrived. I predicted confusion and a certain amount of innocent pleasure. What I hadn't anticipated was that Oliver had planned to use the occasion to surprise me too.

The enormous grin on my old friend's face, when he glimpsed me from the doorway, couldn't simply be explained by our friendship. I hadn't just been released from prison or returned from a posting in Papua New Guinea. It didn't take me long to realise that he wasn't alone. Accompanying him, and looking even more fetching than when I had last seen her, was the young woman from the Vortext. Clearly I wasn't the only lawyer in Casa Mia that night who had resolved to bring his work home with him.

"Rick, I'd like you to meet Eirwen," he announced. " I'm conveying her new flat. She's a dental hygienist. She's Welsh."

"What sort of an introduction is that, Ollie?" laughed the young woman, in the softest of accents, with the cleanest of teeth. "Sounded more like a warning."

I had indeed moaned about Evan Griffiths several times, but

this seemed more like my old pal's irrepressible gaucheness. A quality which, to my genuine delight, someone rather lovely had at last found more appealing than frustrating. I had high hopes for the spaghetti vongole that would inevitably be on the menu and soon after on his rather smart, new shirt.

"I was just explaining your weird name," continued Oliver helpfully, as he pulled out a chair for his new lady. "Eirwen isn't Jewish," he added, which seemed totally unnecessary, unless he was expecting me to shake a disapproving finger at her choice of pork or seafood.

"Oliver tells me you're also having a thing with a client," said Eirwen.

There was a God! My best friend had finally met the one person as tactless and inappropriate as himself.

The weirdly well-matched couple had hardly sat down before our waitress brought the menus and offered my guests an excessively friendly smile. Oliver's eyes lost their ability to blink. Eirwen noticed and caught my own eye and we both enjoyed the moment. When his head swivelled round about one hundred and eighty degrees to follow the speciality of the casa, Eirwen gave him a dig that clearly caused him some physical pain.

"Sorry," he said. "I was just…"

"I know what you were just," she said. "And just don't."

"She was very beautiful," he explained, which didn't help.

What also didn't help was when the same waitress returned and pulled up a chair next to Oliver. His face went the colour of ketchup and I think he put his breathing on hold.

"I just want to thank you," said the waitress, "for all you have done for me."

For a moment Oliver was totally bewildered. I could see his mind working – what had he done other than sat down and accepted the offer of a menu with rather excessive gratitude? But finally the peso dropped.

"*Isabel?* Er, Ms Velaszco?"

Of course Eirwen was still in murky waters, but fair play to her, she drifted back in fairly swiftly. Her knowing 'Ah!' was pretty bloody loud actually. She had clearly been briefed.

"I cannot stay," said Isabel, "or my boss, he will—"

Oliver nodded, but not without giving me a surreptitious yet totally transparent look, eyes wide, eyebrows up, mouth open, as if to say 'I see what you mean now'. Which of course I expected, although I didn't expect it to be so accurately mirrored by his new friend. It was like watching a mime-troupe in action.

"You're very lucky you have two such brilliant lawyers on your case," said the young woman, which was kind of her.

"You don't have to do that now, Eirwen," said one of the brilliant lawyers. "Ms. Velazco knows about Rick."

Oh thanks, Oliver. I had kept my old friend up to speed after Cambridge, but clearly Eirwen was only just processing the details. "Ah," she said again, with a serious nod.

Isabel caught her boss' quizzical eye and swiftly rose. As did Oliver, which was polite but unnecessary. Eirwen pulled him back down again.

"Poor lady," she said sweetly. "What do you think of her chances, Rick?"

Oliver answered before I could speak. "Better but still negligible," he said. "Single mother. Foreigner. Dodgy past. Fish out of water. And all that time apart." He was reeling them off. "How's her relationship with the kid these days?"

I shrugged. Isabel and I both suspected that S's brain was being clinically washed on a daily basis back home, unravelling much of what I had been helping Isabel to do. "A lot can happen in two weeks," I said, like I knew.

Oliver and Eirwen just stared at me.

"Perhaps you should keep some distance, Rick," said my pal.

At first I assumed he was thinking about Sebastian, but later on, as I drove Isabel home, I realised that it was me he was looking out for. With a clarity that almost felled me, I began to appreciate that for the first time in my life I was no longer the most important person in it.

Which was quite unsettling.

FORTY-FOUR

Some time ago, at one of their Friday-night-dinners, Cyril Rosen had chosen to expound on his philosophy of GALMI. He told Sophie and myself that it was one to which many of his race adhered, so I had assumed it might be something like the Kabbalah, that curious, mystical business with the wristbands that celebs such as Madonna were into.

It wasn't.

"You only practise it," he continued, with one of his mischievous, face-crinkling smiles, "when a DIY task or something on the domestic front, involving strength or physical dexterity, either needs doing or has been attempted and gone terribly wrong."

It stood for Get A Little Man In.

Apparently Jewish people compete amongst themselves as to who is the most crap at anything handy and each of them knows, at the very most, one person who isn't. (And is thereby jokingly regarded as a throwback or adopted or something.)

I hadn't thought of it again, until a weekend close to the hearing, when my car needed a good clean. And I knew just the little man to get in.

For such a small chap Sebastian was a maestro with the chammy. He needed some encouragement to cover those places the dilettante car-cleaner might miss, but all things considered, he did himself proud.

Isabel performed the honours with tea/lemonade and biscuits, trotting out with her little tray into the quiet Sunday street. "Here is food for workers," she said. "But I see only one guy who works."

Her tone was patently cheery but perhaps I had become more adept at reading the signs. I could sense the overarching strain beneath the jollity, pick up on spikes of fear that tightened her weary smile like a surgeon's stitches. We had survived CAFCASS lady (although she was due to return one final time) and, of course, the case of the dingy flat. But I wondered how much more rejection she could actually take.

I knew that she had attempted more than once to explain to a confused Sebastian what was actually happening with all the lawyers and the courts, and what might transpire thereafter, but whenever she broached it, he simply shook his head fiercely, drew his bony knees up to his chest and closed up, like it was all too much for his tiny frame. And how could it not be, when it was ripping the adults apart?

"Rick is the boss," piped Sebastian, scrubbing with a vigour that threatened to sear the paint off the car. I could tell that it was almost like therapy for him (which feels a more comfortable description than child-labour.)

"Yeah, get real Isabel," I said, pointing out a spec of dust that my lackey had missed. I took a photo of him on my Nokia, for no better reason than I really wanted a photo of him. How weird is that?

"After this we go for a drive, yes Rick?" said Sebastian.

I nodded, hoping he'd keep his trim-picking hands in check, then caught the disappointment dropping like a winter blind over Isabel's face, even though she tried her best to remain unruffled.

"Ah. You and Rick... Si, this is nice," she enthused,

unconvincingly. "I make you both some tortilla. It is meaning 'little cake.' For when you come back." She turned away and I knew she was doing her best not to cry.

"Don't be silly, mami," said Sebastian, matter-of-factly. "You are coming too."

These may be the simplest of words to write. And to read. But I can only say that when Isabel heard them, the tears began to flow so freely that Sebastian and I didn't know quite where to look. The poor woman was mouthing the tiny sound to herself, over and over again, like it was the most beautiful thing she had ever heard. And perhaps it was.

Sebastian – who hadn't a clue as to the import of what he had said – just turned to me and shrugged. I shrugged back. *Women!*

By the time we lads were on the road, our passenger, crumpled once more into the tiny back-seat, had cheered up considerably. So much so that she decided to share an anecdote from her childhood. We didn't appear to have a lot of choice in the matter.

"I will tell you the wonderful story. You would like to hear this? Never mind. You are hearing this."

Isabel had to lean forward. She explained that it was so that her guys upfront could hear the entire saga above the noise of the engine and the big world outside. But I knew it was so that she could be closer to one little guy, whom she couldn't stop touching as she spoke.

I'll tell the story as she did, because it came from the soul of this extraordinary woman whom I had begun, against all odds, to adore beyond reason. (Even if I still had little idea of what she truly thought of me.)

And, in its own way, it offered me my first, real-time introduction to their true relationship. Isabel and her son. If I had been troubled by doubts before, I knew now that the only one who'd been telling lies over the past extraordinary weeks had been me.

"When I am little girl," she began, "there is a gentleman in my street who has a nice blue car. A blue Ford, I think. Red? No, blue. Never mind, it is big car. He is proud of this car. So, so proud. And every Saturday morning he polish it. He love to do this, until it is very shiny. Oh and…"

"Ever notice that women can't tell stories?" I asked my smallest passenger. He nodded but I could see that he was listening to every word.

"I ignore this," continued our storyteller. "Anyway, it is in this street, my street, that your mami and her cousins would play the football." Sebastian and I exchanged a look. Yeah, right.

"I had the good feet!" she protested, laughing. I could certainly vouch for that. "Okay. One Saturday, just after this guy he wash his special, precious car, I kick the ball – and it go bounce, bounce on the top. It make a tiny bit of dust, so tiny tiny you hardly see it. So what? But you know what he does…?"

"Takes your ball away," I said. "Obviously."

"So you know what we do, Mr Clever?"

Sebastian was in there like a Spurs centre-forward. "You kick him! No, you smash up his door and you rob up his house!"

Isabel seemed happily outraged. "No, *mi querido*! We do not do these things!"

She spoke more slowly now, building up the picture in her mind, the better to share it with us. "We wait all the week until this next Saturday. And, in the morning – very, very early, while it is still the darkness – we climb out of our bedrooms. So, so quietly. So our mamis and dads, they do not hear us. And we go across the road to the blue Ford car. Now what do we do?"

"You break it and you bash and smash it." Sebastian was really getting into it. And, of course, taking it out on the trim of my dashboard, yet somehow it didn't bother me quite so much. I still smacked his hand away.

"No," said his mum, in a deeply portentous tone. "Worse. We do much, much worse."

223

"*WORSE?*" we boys cried as one. What could be worse? It was Argentina, maybe they kidnapped it.

Isabel came back with her clincher. You could almost taste the triumph in her voice. "*We clean it and we shine it and we polish it!*"

No, she'd lost us.

From the rear of the MIG came sounds of volcanic frustration. "It is the thing he like most to do in the whole week! To clean his beautiful car. So, because he take away our big pleasure, we take away his! Is wonderful, yes?"

She whooped as she said this, aloud and alone. Sebastian simply turned round to look at her. Leaning his chin into her folded arms, as they lay on the back of his seat, he spoke the words that set her right off again.

"*Sos muy tonta, mami!*"

Who would have thought that four little words in another language, piped out by one skinny little boy and referencing his own mother's imbecility, could have proved as incandescent as the Writing on the Wall?

Isabel was crying so much by this point that I don't think she even noticed the town sign as we approached.

Welcoming us at last to my old alma mater. Watford.

FORTY-FIVE

It was the week of the court hearing.

I had submitted all I was going to submit and ascertained all I was ever going to know. The world's most important decision now lay in the hands of barristers, witnesses, CAFCASS once again, God on high (possibly) and – most of all – our judge.

And I was fast asleep at my desk.

"Buy, sell, BUY! SELL!!"

Leila thought it was hilarious to slam into my office and wake me up. But I suppose she was only protecting me from Barney, who would probably do it with a loaded P45.

"Eh? Oh sorry, Leila," I said and nodded towards the huge Sandford file on my desk. "Big boy's law is hurting this little boy's head."

Leila looked confused. "Isn't this what you always craved, Rick?"

Before I could compose an adequate response, because I admit she had thrown me, she was moving on. "Anyway, talking of little boys, you can have a nice break from it all when mum comes in again today."

It was probably lack of sleep or a surfeit of what else we were doing in that cramped, little bed, or maybe just the sheer stress of the moment, but I lost it with the person who least deserved to be at the receiving end.

"*For fuck's sake, Leila,*" I yelled. "I could lose everything here! The case, my job, my-And she does *not* come in every day!"

My point was slightly undercut by the door opening and Isabel sweeping in.

"*Richard!*" She seemed unusually excited, as if she had won her case already. Then she noticed Leila. "Oh, I am sorry."

"It's okay," I said. "It's only Leila."

"Hi. I'm only Leila," said Leila. She seemed a bit miffed, but left with a gentle smile for my client. "Good luck on Thursday."

"*Gracias.* Thank you."

The door closed but Isabel didn't sit down. "You forgive me, Rick, to bust in like this. I am with Quentin." She saw by my face that this was not something over which I could totally share her excitement. "A practise! You know, for the court."

She seemed to want to gloss over this little nugget – along with the fact that I wasn't party to a meeting I should have attended. I noticed that there were tears in her eyes, yet she seemed anything but sad.

"Rick, is most wonderful news!" Even for her she was speaking fast, the words tumbling over themselves like rocks down an Ande. "I have the phone call from Laurence. Tonight is concert at Sebastian's school – and my little boy say he does not do it *if I am not there!*"

She was clearly waiting for a response but I must have been a bit slow. I would like to think it was just fatigue, only now I'm not so sure. "This is good, yes?" she persisted.

"Of course," I said swiftly. "About as good as it gets, Isabel." Which it was, actually.

"I have this night off, from my work. Especial for concert. You must write this." She tapped the file on my desk, which was actually Hugo Sandford's, but the point was well made.

"I can still see you tonight?" I said. "You know..."

"Yes, yes," she dismissed. "Afterward. Perhaps. I go now. I must buy Sebastian a nice concert present."

She left at the same velocity as she had entered and I could hear her giving Dimpy a cheery, personalised goodbye on her way out. I couldn't understand why I wasn't totally sharing her elation, but I wasn't big on self-searching back then.

Anyway, I had work to do.

***

I was still doing the work at ten o'clock that night when I heard my dad trudge slowly up the stairs. But I didn't hear any china clinking. Even if he wasn't making his usual drop-off at Rick's Place, London E8, I thought it might be prudent to slip the coke, to which I was about to treat myself, right back where it came from. Well, not quite Bolivia, but my desk drawer, where it would be safe from prying eyes. Sadly, at that distance, it wasn't going to keep me as buzzed as I needed for the job – Barney's job – in hand.

I was doubly surprised when my dad finally did come in. He had my mum in tow – a parental convoy on a mission into choppy waters. They looked more concerned than I had seen them in a long while – probably not since my gran died – but I had no idea what was bothering them. I soon found out.

"Not going out tonight?" asked my father.

Was that what they were worried about? Or was it that they were desperate to know who the lucky lady was (and why I was so equally invested in not telling them)?

"Big court case, Thursday. Really big. Royal Courts in the Strand big. I might pop out later, you know, for a bit of fresh air."

I thought they would perk up at the mention of their lad in that genuinely great court, but they seemed even more perturbed. "For the night?" asked my dad. I just shrugged. "You know your mum, Ricky – she gets…"

He didn't tell me how my mum got, although I could guess, because she stepped right in there while my dad was still finding the words.

"If you just told us where you were going, love," she said.

"You two got married when you were twenty-three!" I protested. "Did you ring your mums?"

"Well, why don't you bring the girl here some time?" tried my dad, changing tack. "You'd bring little Sophie."

There he went again with the 'little'. "That was different," I protested, which of course laid me wide open. "Isabel's—"

"Got a husband." Mum again, slipping in between breaths.

"No!" I said, quite affronted. "She's divorced… Twice… With a nine-year-old kid. Anyway…"

"*No, not 'anyway'!*" Suddenly my dad was yelling. I felt myself jolt back in my chair. The wheels began to move, so that I had to dig my feet into the floor just to stay still. "I'm your father." His face was growing red. It was quite disconcerting. "JESUS, Rick! What the hell is going on with you!" My mum touched his arm, trying to calm him down, but you try placating an angry cabbie. "You treat your poor mum and me like we was strangers, the house as if it's a bloody hotel. You've gone and dumped little Sophie for some – I dunno what – and you look like you've had too much bed and not enough ruddy sleep!"

He stopped suddenly and I was convinced he had unleashed his bolts. But then I realised he had spotted the framed photo in my open briefcase. I really should have given it back. There was a pause while he took it in, with my mum on tiptoes behind him, leaning over his shoulder and looking like she wondered if the smiling, continental-looking woman needed a child-minder.

"*She's* your ruddy case, innit?" said my dad, as the penny dropped. "Bugger me! Even I know that's not kosher. So what is she – a merger or an acquisition?"

Nice one, Dad. I wanted to respond, but the words wouldn't come. What would I say to him anyway? What do you say to someone you love, to whom you've lied with such abandon? It shouldn't have been that difficult– I'd had enough practice those past few weeks – but I plumped for simply looking sheepish and waiting until he ran out of breath.

He had more.

"Well, you won't think you're too good for us when you don't have a job no longer, eh?" He lowered his voice. "*And there's no one else around who'll bloody listen!*"

I stared at him, perhaps waiting for him to give me the most direct route to redemption, but this time he just stared right back. I was too shocked by the onslaught to compute what he was actually telling me, but I can see it all too clearly now. Your parents aren't just the people who talk you into the ground – they're also the ones who will always hear you out.

"Come on, love" he muttered to my poor, saddened mum, frustration finally overwhelming him. He forced out a wheezy, red-faced cough, as if the speech had taken all he had to give. I waited for him to slam the door but he didn't. He had made that too.

I sat there for a while, frozen into my thoughts. Then I opened the drawer again.

FORTY-SIX

I should have learned from that conversation with my dad.

Do you ever learn from a row where you're totally in the wrong and are being told you've disappointed everyone, including the cat? In my experience it only makes you even more bullheaded. And further convinced, against all reason, that you weren't nearly as bad as you'd been painted.

Or perhaps that's only when your head is full of the Bolivian cocaine you bought from a barrister's junior clerk in a pub off Fleet Street. Come to think of it, as I did whilst driving across London at my own distinctive speed, I may never have been to South America, but it had certainly been to me. I really thought I should mention that to Isabel.

I reckoned she must have heard the MiG screech to its usual stuttering halt on the pavement outside her block. As it turned out, she was a bit pre-occupied.

The second she opened her door, I was holding her. Usually, for just the briefest of moments in these early clinches, I found myself looking at us as a stranger might, wondering how such a pair ever got together – the young, unrefined Englishman and that elegant, clearly continental, older lady – how odd and unsuited we must have seemed. And deciding that the young man on the doorstep most probably couldn't believe his luck.

This was nowhere near my perspective that evening. I was totally focussed. So I was more than a little surprised when she pulled away from me, like I was some sort of stranger.

"*Rick*," she warned, speaking very softly. "Not now."

I stepped into the tiny hallway. She was looking behind her towards the closed kitchen door. When she spoke, there was an excitement seeping through the muted tones, a quiet elation that I realised had absolutely nothing to do with me.

"After the concert he ask to come home with me. *To stay this night!*" She was clearly waiting for a response. I realised I had forgotten the concert entirely.

"Yeah? Well – great. That's great," I said. "I'll put it in the notes."

"His father he is so nice about this."

Even in my coked-up state that sounded odd. But maybe Laurence was just feeling magnanimous. (Which is not a word I could have got my mouth around right then.) What I did say, however, wasn't a major contributor to my finest hour.

"So – what exactly am I supposed to do, Isabel?"

Isabel looked at me like it wasn't her problem. Which it probably wasn't

"*Mami, donde esta mi chocolate caliente?*"

I didn't know the Spanish for sod off but that seemed to be the subtext of the chirpy words coming from behind the closed kitchen door. I knew when I wasn't wanted. At least I did when Isabel pushed me out of the flat.

***

It was an hour later, in the over-lit café of a 24/7 Tesco, that I had my epiphany.

This wasn't when I was tearing into the late-night-special of egg and chips or chugging back the foul-tasting coffee. (No slight on Tesco – it probably just didn't go with Bolivian cocaine.)

The moment came when I was flicking back through the photos on my phone. I can't tell you how many hours I wasted on that bloody machine back then. But this time I locked onto a photo I'd visited several times before but which, that evening, made me suddenly catch my breath, a Tesco chip paused halfway towards my mouth (something that rarely happens, even today.)

It was the shot of Sebastian cleaning my car. It wasn't that he looked almost appealing, which in itself was a tad revelatory. It was the small and hitherto unnoticed figure in the background. Isabel, tea-tray in hand, was bestowing upon her oblivious son such a lovingly lopsided look. Which, even without benefit of the sort of amplification we're so used to today, instantly melted my…

"Rick…? *RICK!*"

I hadn't heard Sophie until she was almost touching my table. You don't expect to see the girl with whom you'd once intended to spend your life approaching you in an all-night supermarket. With a trolleyful of shopping and a not totally hostile smile.

"*Sophie*? Hi!"

I had no idea what to say. Unless she was stalking me, it was pretty obvious what she was doing here, so that was one avenue closed.

"Looking good," I tried, which was actually true. She looked lovely, smart even in her nocturnal-shopping togs. "Are you still talking to me?" Also obvious, but safe.

"Are you still lying to me?"

She sat down, so the question wasn't as rhetorical as I had thought.

"All lied out," I said, truthfully. "Soph, I'm so sorry. Really. I did try to…"

"I know. It's okay, Rick. It's cool." I didn't think it was, but good of her to say so. "How's that little boy doing? Sebastian?" In case I thought she meant Gerald, who she's probably still discussing in therapy. "Or is he not the one you're thinking about?"

I offered an inappropriate shrug. Sophie just rolled her eyes and took one of my chips. Then she noticed the photo on my phone.

"GALMI," I said, pointing to my little car-cleaner. She sort of nodded. Perhaps shared memories weren't the best way to go.

She was playing it light but I had known her a long time. The anger and hurt were described in spades on her lovely face and it was all my own work.

"I won't stay," she said, "my coupons are going to run out. Oh and before you say it – yes, I'm sure we can be friends, Ricko. I'll call you just as soon as one of my old ones dies." I imagine I looked suitably stunned, but she hadn't finished. "Meantime, any more on what you want to be when you grow up?"

She must have been waiting for ages to do this. I found myself hoping it truly hit the spot for her, even as I absorbed the blow, which had to speak something for my maturity, didn't it?

She was up and out of the café before I could think of a good word to say. "*Sophie...*" I called, a bit weakly. I knew she wouldn't turn back.

I gave her time to quit the car-park and then, leaving my chips unfinished – another first for me – I walked determinedly out through the shoppers of the night, some of whom I'm sure were in their pyjamas. I stopped, on the way, at a late-night Shell station and bought a Twix and the type of lurid flowers you seem only to find outside garages. They must thrive on diesel.

When Isabel eventually came to the door, scrutinising me through sleepy eyes, I offered her the wilting blooms and my most apologetic Spanish. "*Lo siento.*"

"You must be Ronnie Davenport's little boy," she chided.

"Yeah. So people tell me... Maybe I'm a work-in-progress." No reaction. "Hey, I'm really glad, Isabel. Truly. About the concert."

She smiled. "He has his papa's ear for music. But it was very special."

"I know it was," I said. "And hey, it was *your* achievement. All your own work. Go to bed now." I turned to go but she took my arm. And gave me the softest smile.

"Early bird," I assured her. "He won't even see me."

I was true to my word. But he wasn't the one who was looking.

FORTY-SEVEN

There were probably more people crammed into my tiny office that Tuesday morning than in its entire history, unless one of my predecessors had been acting for quads. In fact there were probably more than anyone would deem either safe or hygienic. Even Evan had insinuated himself through the narrow doorway to check out what Leila, Dimpy et al could possibly be looking at.

What was attracting their intention was my wall-chart, with which I was attempting to take them through the process of Menzies v. Velazco. A process that Quentin Shaw had unfolded in some detail for Isabel and myself the previous week (with eyes only for my client) and which would come to its final realisation just two days from now. Courts and all, as Oliver had said quite wittily, when I had spoken to him earlier that morning.

He had also thrown in 'Ignorance of the lawyer is no excuse', which he clearly didn't just make up on the spot and to which I hadn't taken quite so kindly. Love seemed to have turned him into Stephen Fry. Mind you, with my mum and dad hardly talking to me and Barney still piling on the work, it was good to have somebody in my corner. Even someone as deeply sceptical as Oliver Rosen.

"Okay. So their side will call in people to say what a great time Sebastian is having here with his lovely dad," I explained, "and we'll call in people to say that living here with his even lovelier mum would be so much…"

"They've got more people," interrupted Dimpy, tapping my chart with her morning croissant.

"It's *quality*, Dimpy," I explained, over-enthusiastically. "And we've got some ace stuff from Argentina." I hope I'm not getting too technical. Funnily, I've never been totally comfortable with lawyer-speak, or any sort of jargon. Maybe I should have been. "Y'know, stuff that says Isab— Ms Velazco – is really good news on the mum front."

At this Dimpy gave the most enormous snort. We all looked at her.

"What?" I asked, with just the faintest gallon of annoyance.

"All those boyfriends? The abortion? Working nights? The one-way ticket? Duh? *And five months, Rick?*" We all looked at her even harder. "Got to have something to read when the phone's not ringing," she muttered.

I was about to take them through the latest and rather positive CAFCASS report – the woman had bravely returned to see Isabel and Sebastian (and the new flat, unfortunately) – when Miss Collins loomed at the door. We all instinctively pressed ourselves into the nearest available wall, save for Evan of course, as though to avoid the rays.

"Going hang-gliding again this weekend, Joan?" I said cheerily. You have to make conversation.

She even smiled at this. "Of course!" And then she smiled again, which was unprecedented and vaguely unsettling. "Oh Rick, Mr Cracknell wants a little word." I sighed and picked up the Sandford file. But she hadn't finished. "And I don't think it's 'partner.'"

***

236

Barney could have just handed the photos to me.

Ever the showman, he chose instead to lay them out slowly, one by one, like a creepy game of solitaire, across his otherwise pristine desk. His face suggested that the gleaming wood beneath was forever soiled, along with his firm's reputation and my legal career.

I didn't need to inspect them to know what they were. It was as if I had managed to become a target of the paparazzi without going through the tiresome rigmarole of actually becoming famous. The final monochrome image was of her young legal adviser leaving Isabel's flat the morning after the concert, running a swift hand through his hair.

"Breakfast meeting?" I suggested, a bit pathetically.

There were other shots of me with Isabel and Sebastian. In one I even had my arm around him, which I didn't recall but rather liked. I wondered momentarily if I might get to keep them afterwards, as we did all look so great together.

"*While the kid was kipping in the next room!*" said Barney, waving a photo and raising his voice to a pitch I had never heard him use before. And probably never would again. I said nothing. What was there left to say – 'They caught my worst side'?

"You're off the case, sunshine," he growled. "As of now. If there even is a sodding case."

Looking back, there wasn't much else he could do, in the circumstances. But it didn't mean I had to go along with it, now that I was no longer fighting for myself.

I was like one of those old knights, with my lady's favour – sheer, red and lacy – dangling from my downturned lance. Okay, I was probably nothing like that, but I don't think I had ever – or will ever – fight for anything with more vigour and less hope of success than I did in that instantly chilled room on that terrible morning.

"There *is* a case. Barney. Please," I pleaded, "and I'm the only one who knows…"

"You've done enough *knowing*, matey." It's a biblical term apparently, but I didn't know that then, although obviously I got his drift. "You are on such dodgy ground," he persisted, a bit unnecessarily. "I've asked Evan to take over."

Evan? He had just been in my office, the duplicitous turd! At this my lance rose again, primed for battle.

"NO! No way, Barney. He's… Welsh." Was that really the best I could do? "If there's anyone who should take over, it's Oliver Rosen,"

Barney just stared at me like I had lost the last marble.

"He's sort of… familiar with the case," I explained, with a bit less confidence. "And you're linked up with his firm anyway. His dad's firm. *And* he knows Isab— my client. I don't mean like…"

"Jesus wept! You've screwed her from here to Christmas and now you're dictating terms? PISS OFF. Go on." He began to bundle up the photos with what I thought was a tawdry lack of respect.

But I didn't piss off. I stayed where I was, looking down at the evidence and then straight into his pudgy face.

Because suddenly I knew.

"Reckon the Law Society would like it?" I said. He just looked at me, like he had no idea what I was on about. But I could see it in his piggy eyes. "You taking on one of Laurence Menzies' cronies on some phoney corporate bollocks? Just so's you could 'overwhelm' me?" I stared him out. "What wee bit of 'holding' did oor Mr Menzies promise ye for that?"

Barney didn't say anything, not even about the crap Scottish accent that I had segued into for no apparent reason. But his eyes didn't leave my face. I had gone way too far and we both knew it. I could feel my legs begin to shake and that sphincter thing again.

"I hope she was sodding worth it," said Barney, and stuffed the photos unkindly into a folder. At least he didn't frame them for his walls.

I just had time to make it past Miss Collins' desk and into the clients' loo, before I vomited up the past eight weeks.

FORTY-EIGHT

"Wearing the same wigs and robes they've worn for centuries. Well not *literally* the same!"

I had no idea whether seeing that chirpy tourist guide outside the Royal Courts of Justice, a young woman whom I had chatted-up in what seemed another life, was a good omen or simply one of those everyday coincidences that only madmen relish. But it pointed up to me yet again how much had happened in just a few, densely-packed weeks. Of course she didn't recognise me. But then I hardly recognised myself.

"*They wear the wigs and the robes?*" gasped Isabel, suddenly squeezing my hand.

I had thought I'd told her that they didn't actually do this in the Family Division. You can't remember everything. And I had spent the past twenty-four hours either talking through the case with her and Oliver – with the occasional, deeply uncomfortable visit to Quentin Shaw – or else holding her shaking body in my arms. We both realised that this was it. Judgment day – or judgment couple-of-days, as we wouldn't get through it all in one session.

I removed my hand from hers, although – as I was no longer officially her lawyer – this perhaps had ceased to be such a problem. Quentin Shaw, however, had assured us that it was indeed such a problem. When we had told him about Barney and the photos, he had just shaken his head. He could hardly reprimand our client but the look he gave me is still etched on my brain. I had wanted to say, 'Oh, like you've never shacked up with one of your attractive, foreign clients while you were handling her custody case', but of course he probably hadn't. Wishing isn't doing.

I had already strolled down the Strand several times in the course of my brief legal career, and passed jauntily through those elaborately carved porches into the cathedralesque Great Hall. As I said, buildings don't do it for me. But I wondered that morning how it must feel for Isabel, all the pomp and stone and splendour, this forbidding Gothic edifice with its soaring arches and stained-glass windows. As if the intention was purely to scare the shit out of anyone who dared to have business inside.

"I think I am going to be sick," is what she actually said, so I wasn't far wrong.

I knew how she felt.

Okay, let's say I knew how I myself felt that day and just tried multiplying that by at least a thousand.

Sebastian wasn't here, of course, yet he was everywhere. Wiry, little frame and glistening eyes (sometimes from tears, yet lately also with laughter) dominating our thoughts, our words, the pores of the massive building itself. Just as I supposed the poor victim must haunt a murder trial. Only this time the subject of our case had his whole life ahead of him. And I had rashly been entrusted with responsibility as to how he would spend that life.

This is what I would have to live with. But not as surely as one scared, confused little boy.

We met Oliver outside the courtroom. He looked rather smart in his as-yet-unstained court suit – and extremely angry.

"You shouldn't be here, Rick." This wasn't his first warning and I imagined it wouldn't be his last.

"I want him here," said Isabel.

"I'm her McKenzie friend," I explained, a touch grandly.

Oliver just stared at me. As did Isabel. "How the hell do *you* know about McKenzie friends?" demanded my incredulous pal.

"I'm a lawyer," I protested, which I suppose was a bit rich, considering I hadn't exactly displayed mastery of my chosen field to date.

"O-kay," allowed Oliver. "Well normally, so far as I know, you bring a 'McKenzie friend' to hold your hand in court, when you don't actually have a lawyer. But I suppose when it comes to hand-holding…"

Yes, alright Oliver. But I did prise myself from Isabel's clasp. For the time being.

"As long as you keep your mouth shut, okay?" I didn't say anything. "*Rick?*"

I wanted to remind Oliver that he also was exchanging more than contracts with a client, but that would have seemed a bit petty in the circumstances. His point was well-made and I wasn't going to do more damage than I had already done. At least I hoped I wasn't.

I suddenly felt Isabel's hand groping for mine again and squeezing it like she wanted to crack a few small bones.

Laurence had just walked in with Rebecca.

My first thought was, *Who's looking after Sebastian?* But they're hardly likely to have left him by the pool, with only Jack Daniels for company. I imagine this story would have been a lot easier to write had Laurence been all bad and Isabel Velazco a saint. But that wasn't how things were. I don't think anybody is all bad. Except maybe Barney. And Miss Collins. And Evan.

Then it clicked. As I watched the not-all-bad plaintiff put a protective arm around his demure young wife's back and nod courteously to us, before sitting on a bench at the other side of the hall.

"No wonder he was so cool about Sebastian staying over after the concert," I grumbled. "The bastard set us up!"

I felt stunned by this deduction but Isabel just nodded, as if she had been ahead of me for some while. "We are grown-ups, Rick. We fire the bullet ourselves."

I caught her looking up and followed her eyes higher and higher until they reached the rarified heights of Quentin Shaw. He managed to smile down at Isabel and raise an eyebrow towards me in one gesture, which was neatly done.

"All right, Ms Velazco?" he inquired.

"I have been better."

"Well, we're all here," I added, simply by way of conversation and because I felt distinctly uncomfortable. But even in such an assumedly unchallengeable assumption, I was wrong.

Glancing towards the entrance, I saw two familiar figures moving slowly along the nave, or whatever you want to call it, dwarfed by the grandeur and seeming slightly lost. The last people in the world I might have expected to meet there. As if by employing some special radar that only kicks in with parenthood, they found me within seconds.

"*What are you doing here?*" I asked them, as the others turned to stare.

"It's your big day, isn't it?" said my dad, as if this explained it. "First proper case."

"Hello, Ollie!" said my mum, in delighted surprise. My old friend kissed her, bless him. He was probably hoping she would invite him back home afterwards for tea.

"Mum, Dad – it's a closed court," I explained, as Quentin Shaw looked on quizzically.

"Oh," said my disappointed father. My mum was smiling gently at Isabel, who returned it with some warmth and not a little bemusement.

"We'll be here if you need us," they reassured me. Which was sweet, even if it didn't bear close examination.

The doors to the court room opened.

All rise.

FORTY-NINE

It wasn't as if the courtroom itself was so terrifying.

It purposefully failed to reflect the solemnity of the Great Hall just beyond its doors. Relatively small and quite modern, it could even have been classed as comfortable. But think of it this way – the consulting-room of a cancer specialist may be cosy and welcoming, with soothing pictures on the walls. It doesn't mean you won't feel even sicker on the way out.

I was sitting with Isabel, who had immediately begun to shiver uncontrollably and swivel her head in every direction. If there had been a jury watching, they would probably have found her guilty on the spot. I can still recall the feel of her hand, sweaty yet ice-cold, which was curiously disconcerting. Next to her were Quentin Shaw and Oliver, huddled and talking. I felt both out of it and right at its quivering heart.

As far away from us as they could manage were Laurence and Rebecca, their hands clasped in front of them, in what I thought was a bit of a showy gesture for the benefit of the judge, the Honourable Mr Justice Greenslade.

The Honourable was a stocky, balding, two-pudding Yorkshireman in his late fifties – not too posh, which was sort of reassuring, and a drinker's nose which wasn't – who managed to look both stern and benevolent at the same time. Which isn't easy. Perhaps he and his mates practised looking judge-like in front of a mirror before they went on.

Quentin Shaw had told us that this wasn't the worst judge we could have been allocated but neither was he the best. Which of course meant nothing to either of us. It's not like the old days when they talked about hanging judges. You knew where you were back then.

Laurence's barrister was Ms Olivia Harris, a small but striking Afro-Caribbean woman in her mid-thirties, with the reputation of someone considerably older. I would have congratulated Laurence Menzies on his choice, had circumstances been different.

If Isabel found the room intimidating and the judge an unknown quantity, I was genuinely fearful to think what she would make of the opposing counsel. And what the redoubtable Ms Harris would make of her. (Quentin had warned me privately that this lady was not good news, although he was very fond of her on a personal level. I just bet he was. I wondered if they swapped shirts at the end of a hard fixture.)

I won't go through all the formalities, because I honestly don't remember them the way I recall the more important stuff. And, naturally, aside from attempting to maintain circulation in my hand, I was far too preoccupied in telling my ex-client that everything was going to be all right, although I knew that it almost certainly wasn't.

I had tried as best I could to avoid going to that forlorn place where Isabel had finally lost it all. End of story. They talk so much these days about staying in the moment. I realised even then that if I looked any further than the next word coming out of someone's mouth, I would probably lose the ability to breathe, stand-up or utter a single, intelligible sound.

As expected, what followed over the next couple of days was mostly talk, so I'll put it down as I remember it. There'll be the odd aside thrown in – to give a sense of the stuff that wasn't spoken or recorded and some measure at least of how I was feeling. I can only guess about the others, because however close you are to someone, and of course Isabel and I were pretty close by then (there were photos to prove it), you can't put yourself totally in their shoes. I know people try, but we're only guessing.

I thought I had seen Joanne rolling up through the main doors as we were going into the courtroom, so I imagined that she would be outside right now, working on her script and scaring my parents. She had wanted to accompany Isabel but she wouldn't have been allowed into court, except to give her evidence. Isabel had suggested that she might be needing her old friend a whole lot more when it was over.

I could string this out with all the well-meaning souls on either side, each one majorly bigging-up the parenting skills of whoever they were there to support, but they just did what everyone expected them to do. As for Joanne, she did it really loud and with colourful language that she was finally asked by the judge to tone down.

I suspect Mr Justice Greenslade wasn't overly swayed by any of this. Or even by the tree-loads of reports, witness statements (some of which I'd had translated from Spanish, at Barney's expense) and assorted documents he had assumedly read.

I could sense, however, that he was quite taken with Rebecca Menzies, who unfortunately came across as the pleasant if unimaginative woman I believe she probably was, and not the sadistic, poison-apple-wielding stepmother some of us might have wished. But the supporting cast were all going to say or write nice things, weren't they? It wasn't them to whom two-puddings was going to award custody.

Laurence and Isabel were the ones who mattered on those extraordinary days. Father and Mother of 'S'. The others were just warm-up bouts before the big fight.

Ms Harris began by questioning Laurence.

Naturally she was being warm and friendly, because she was

one hundred per cent on his side. I couldn't help thinking we were in such a weird business. If it was us who had hired Ms Harris, she would have been sweetness itself to Isabel, because she would have convinced herself that her client totally deserved to win back her child. She would be the one giving poor Laurence one of her celebrated hard-times. The only difference between her and Quentin Shaw would be that she probably wouldn't be staring into Isabel's eyes quite so much, unless there was something I didn't know about Ms Olivia Harris.

She approached Laurence like she was meeting up with an old friend at a function he had already told her he was attending. He looked straight back like she was the person he most wanted to see there.

MS HARRIS: *Mr Menzies, will you please guide the court through the events of three years ago – leading to your ex-wife's decision to return with your son to Buenos Aires?*

LAURENCE: *I shall certainly try, Ms Harris. Well, firstly of course, the marriage went awry. To my deep regret. And I'm afraid I have to shoulder much of the blame here – I was so immersed in my work. My, you know, companies, interests. Anyway, poor Isabel found it hard to make a life here. She isn't exactly a big fan of England. The people, the weather. So, as you say, three years ago – with my consent – she returned to her home country. To Argentina, with wee Sebastian. It was probably the hardest decision of my life.*

MS HARRIS: *I'm sure it was, Mr Menzies. How difficult for you.* (Oh please!) *And you went over there to visit?*

LAURENCE: *Of course. Regularly. He's my son.*

He threw the tiniest of looks to the judge at this point, in case he might be in some doubt as to the paternity of the boy in question. Laurence was wearing the most beautifully-tailored linen suit, which I imagined was hugely expensive. It was exactly the wardrobe I had been expecting (and which, to be honest, I wouldn't be averse to wearing myself, only in a slimmer size).

Rebecca looked equally well turned-out, as if there were a store that dealt exclusively in conscientious-stepmother outfits and she had steamed in on the first day of their new season. Isabel couldn't match either of them where exclusivity was concerned and had insisted on wearing that orange outfit in which I had first seen her. Personally, I considered it a bit fiery for WC2, but she was clearly comfortable. Or as comfortable as anyone could be in quite so uncomfortable a situation.

MS HARRIS: Between then and now, Mr Menzies, did circumstances change for you?

LAURENCE: Immeasurably, Ms Harris. I met and married my dear wife Rebecca. And – thankfully – she gave me some perspective. On my work and on my responsibilities as a father.

We all turned to look at his dear wife Rebecca, who was giving him perspective even as he spoke. It wasn't an act, I believe she did genuinely adore the man. I'm certain she was fond of Sebastian too, in her own way. Sorry if anyone was expecting Cruella de Vil.

LAURENCE: Nobody wants on their gravestone 'I wish I'd spent more time in the office'.

The judge smiled at this, as if he had never heard it before and maybe he hadn't. They lead very sheltered lives. The others nodded sagely. Isabel wasn't nodding. She had gone rigid.

LAURENCE: I think we've heard from other people today – and you've no doubt read, Ms Harris, in so very many sworn statements – how content my son is here with us. I have to say that it can only get better. For all three of us.

QUENTIN: My Lord, with respect. Unless Mr Menzies is blessed with the gift of prescience, this can only be the purest speculation.

I was with him there. I could feel Isabel bristling beside me as I recalled Sebastian's tiny, bitten nails. And his quiet yearning for a pal. Happily the judge was on it, politely but firmly.

JUDGE: Please confine your answers, Mr Menzies, to what you know objectively to be true at this moment.

Right on, pal. Obviously I didn't say this out loud. I'm sure I didn't.

LAURENCE: I apologise, Your Lordship. But I do know that Sebastian will have a wee sibling joining him here quite soon. As for the gender, well this is indeed speculative.

Whoa! Where did that come from?

It wasn't just Isabel who seemed shocked – we were all reeling. I checked out Laurence, who couldn't help looking at us with that little smile. If he could have licked his fingertip and wiggled it up in the air, without pissing off His Lordship, I'm sure this would have been his suck-on-that gesture of choice. Splitting a family – I think not. Ms Harris beamed, like it was the best news she had heard all year.

MS HARRIS: Congratulations to you both, Mr and Mrs Menzies. And, of course, I imagine Mrs Menzies will now be staying at home for some years to come.

Oh, of course she will. No latch-key kids for our Rebecca. Well played, Ms Harris.

MS HARRIS: Now could you please tell the court what happened around the end of last year?

LAURENCE: Well, in early December I received a phone call from my ex-wife. From Isabel. Asking me if I would have Sebastian to stay.

MS HARRIS: Did you understand that this was for a holiday or for something more permanent?

LAURENCE: Initially, for an extended holiday. But then, in subsequent conversations, it became patently clear that she was thinking of something far more long-term.

I caught Isabel whispering urgently to Quentin, who was shaking his head. Oliver looked over to me, for the first time since the hearing began. I wasn't sure why now, although I could guess, but I smiled, glad to make contact with my oldest friend. That word again. The one that started it all.

MS HARRIS: Were you surprised by this?

LAURENCE: Indeed I was, Ms Harris. Very. But, in truth, I can't say unpleasantly so. Of course the circumstances were sad – Isabel's late mother was gravely ill, poor woman – and my ex-wife was her only child. But I also gathered that Isabel's career – she's a choreographer and a dance-teacher – was taking off in a way it sadly never had in this country. She needed her 'artistic freedom'.

QUENTIN: Your Lordship...

JUDGE: Perhaps we can just stick to the facts, Mr Menzies?

Laurence nodded 'contritely'. 'It just slipped out, Your Honour'. *Bollocks.*

MS HARRIS: Could you explain to us the travel arrangements last Christmas?

Here we go.

LAURENCE: It was a one-way ticket. I offered to pay, but Isabel refused the offer. As she has refused so much from me. She's very proud. And equally determined to make her own way.

MS HARRIS: So your understanding, if I'm correct, is that Señora Velazco intended Sebastian should come and live with you and Mrs Menzies. On a permanent basis?

LAURENCE: That has been the understanding, for the past... well, it must be a good six months now. And we've all adjusted to this quite happily. But I do appreciate that a lady is entitled to change her mind.

This time Quentin and I both instinctively stretched out a hand to calm Isabel – or perhaps to restrain her. I think we mild-mannered Anglo-Saxons knew we needed to make every effort at this point to prevent her from doing something South American. Not sure how Oliver felt but I'm pretty certain he was on board with us.

Meantime, Ms Harris was almost packing up to go home.

MS HARRIS: No further questions, My Lord.

Laurence took the opportunity to gulp down some water. He looked satisfied with how things had gone but was bright enough to realise that the next phase was going to be a good deal less comfortable. I was betting he would love to have his hand around that tumbler of fine Scotch I had met on our first encounter.

Quentin rose and walked towards the man with deliberate slowness, blond hair gently stirring, using height and haughtiness to their best advantage. Isabel leaned forward, as if she didn't want to miss a thing.

QUENTIN: *Mr Menzies – is it possible that you may have misunderstood your ex-wife's intentions? When she sent Sebastian over to you for Christmas?*

LAURENCE: *It's always possible that one person can misunderstand another, Mr Shaw. But rarely three.*

QUENTIN: *Three?*

Oh come on, Quentin. Keep up.

LAURENCE: *Rebecca – my wife – felt as I did. And my son soon realised that his vacation was to be a permanent one.*

QUENTIN (*with a disbelieving laugh*): *Are you honestly telling this court, Mr Menzies, that you had no – shall we say – influence on your little boy's perceptions in this matter?*

LAURENCE: *Mr Shaw, are you suggesting that I brainwashed him? (Laughing at the very notion.) Children aren't stupid. They know what they feel. And poor Sebastian was devastated.*

QUENTIN: *Doesn't this suggest he wished to be with his mother?*

LAURENCE: *It suggested his mother didn't wish to be with him.*

QUENTIN: *But even you concede that she has now 'changed her mind'.*

LAURENCE: *Aye. But it's not her interests we're discussing, is it?*

Isabel turned to me and whispered just loud enough for Quentin Shaw to hear. "Laurence, he is running the ring around this man."

I just shook my head, although I wasn't so sure that she was wrong. But good barristers play the long game, so even I realised that we might have to wait a while. At least I hoped to God that was what was in play.

QUENTIN: *You're right, Mr Menzies. This is not about your ex-wife's best interests. Nor indeed your own. It's all about Sebastian.*

He walked away from Laurence at this point, long fingers stroking a firm English chin, as if thinking to himself.

QUENTIN: *So, would you agree it is in Sebastian's best interests that Ms Velazco has made arrangements to settle permanently in London? Renting a flat very near to his school, taking a job to help support them both.*

Way to go, Quent!

LAURENCE: *I think it... can be good for a child, to have his mother nearby.*

I nodded to Isabel. We were back. She just shrugged.

QUENTIN: *Well then, how much better for a little nine year old to have his mummy right there – in the very same home?*

Laurence just looked at Quentin seriously, then across to Isabel, then finally back to the court at large.

LAURENCE: *That would rather depend on who the 'mummy' is, wouldn't it, Mr Shaw?*

The remark hung in the air like last night's fish supper. And here was the smile again. He was setting us up for something. Perhaps Quentin was already there, when he shrugged, conceding just a little.

That was when we broke for lunch, although at least two of us didn't have much appetite.

FIFTY

My mum and dad were still there, as we shuffled out of the courtroom. They were munching chunky, wholemeal sandwiches which I recognised as home-grown. Dad leaped up when he saw us, out of courtesy I think to Isabel, but I could see he was almost bursting to know what had gone on behind closed doors.

"Guys, you really didn't have to stay," I protested.

I'm not sure whether I was embarrassed or touched. It's hard to recall events in single emotions, when the truth is that at least a good half-dozen from your repertoire are usually roiling around inside of you, each one fighting for space.

My mother ignored me and went straight over to my client. She immediately stroked Isabel's hand, which was very un-Mum. Perhaps some of the continental flavour of the day had rubbed off.

"This must be so hard for you, dear," she said. "If someone took our Ricky away, I don't – well, I don't think I could withstand it."

I just stared at her. I don't believe I had ever seen this person overtaken by such heartfelt emotion. Until this moment I had barely given a thought to the notion that I was actually quite lucky to have come from a home that wasn't fractured or at war.

Why would I? But I was realising that aggravation, however intense, hardly compares.

"Thank you, Mrs Davenport," replied Isabel, managing to summon up a grateful smile. "You are very kind."

My dad waved to Oliver, who was in deep discussion with Quentin Shaw. They didn't look too happy and I think Dad picked that up. I'm pretty sure Isabel did too.

"What happens this afternoon then?" he asked.

"I fight for my life," said Isabel, reaching out and clutching my hand.

I noticed my parents register this intimacy and glance swiftly at each other. Isabel also caught it, but what could she say?

"I think you two could do with a bit of fresh air," suggested my dad.

My mum smiled at us both, with a warmth that was totally accepting and to which, despite the fear, I could only respond in kind. I don't think I had ever loved them more. Not entirely accurate. I don't reckon, until that moment, I had even thought about whether I loved them at all.

***

It was Isabel's turn to take the stand.

I watched her rise slowly and move towards the judge, who appraised her over the top of his thick glasses, probably notching-up the impressions: Hispanic, volatile, trouble. (It surely can't have escaped his notice that she was beautiful – or do their Lordships park that stuff in their chambers along with the morning paper?)

Even with the huge rocks that I knew were sitting in the pit of her stomach, she walked with her usual grace, poised and dignified, past Quentin Shaw, who nodded reassuringly.

Isabel glanced at me as she settled herself on the chair, repeatedly sweeping away a strand of hair that hadn't actually slipped down, in a gesture I recognised as a tell of just how troubled she was. I tried to send hearty waves of confidence her way but Oliver's face was projecting a very different story, one that I wished I could subtly deflect without giving him a kick.

QUENTIN: *Ms Velazco.*

I have to say it, the tall guy gave off warmth like a three-bar heater when the occasion demanded it. Isabel seemed to relax instantly.

ISABEL: *Hello, Mr Shaw.*

QUENTIN: *Ms Velazco, we've heard today – and I'm sure Your Lordship has also read – the many statements praising your competence and devotion as a parent. And indeed the CAFCASS reports have been highly favourable in this regard. Especially the most recent. So, can I ask you, Ms Velazco – why should you have custody of your son?*

Isabel's voice was soft but confident. She was on home ground.

ISABEL: *Because I am his mami, Mr Shaw... His mother. Because he is just nine years old. And my little boy, he needs me.*

She turned and stared directly at Laurence, who clearly wasn't expecting it. Her voice lost its hitherto gentle notes.

ISABEL: *And because the parent who is the best for a child IS NOT THE ONE WHO BLOODY KIDNAPS HIM!*

Ms Harris was up from her seat like it had a spike bursting through it.

MS HARRIS: *My Lord!*

Isabel turned her gaze away from Laurence, who was shaking his head, to find me doing exactly the same. I could hear Quentin Shaw sigh in frustration.

JUDGE: *Ms Velazco, the court will not tolerate...*

ISABEL: *I am sorry, Your Honour. I try to be English.*

QUENTIN: *We have our moments, Ms Velazco.*

Nice one, Quent. He had lightened the mood and I was pleased to see Isabel relax again into an apologetic smile.

QUENTIN: So – Ms Velazco – can you please tell this court what sacrifices you have recently made, out of love for your little boy?

I could see Ms Harris roll her eyes theatrically at this, like she had just wandered into a Forties weepie.

ISABEL: Sacrifice? I do not use this word, Mr Shaw. My little boy he is everything to me. No sacrifice. But if you ask me what do I give up, then I am having to say – a whole life. A life in a city I love, that is on the other side of this world… where I have the friends – and the family – and the reputation. In England I am, at this moment, a waitress. I am very good waitress. I do the choreography with plates.

The judge smiled at this. I noticed that even stern Ms Harris did too. It was a lovely smile. She may have been acting for the other side but it didn't mean she had to hate everyone who wasn't on it. I actually don't think I ever hated Laurence. I just thought he was a bit of a tosser and not the dad I personally would have wanted. In fact, I was beginning to think I had the dad I would have wanted.

ISABEL: This is not what I am born to do. But so what? Being a mami – this I am born to do.

QUENTIN: And should you be awarded custody of Sebastian, would you still be away from home at nights working?

Smart move. Shoot this one out there, before they do.

ISABEL: I try not to. I enjoy to be with my son. But I am single-mother, I admit this. There are many single-mothers in UK, I think. And most of these, they are doing the best for their children.

QUENTIN: Indeed they are. Finally Ms Velazco, what do you think you can offer your child that your ex-husband and his new wife – and swimming-pool and puppy and air-miles – and indeed conveniently imminent half-sibling – cannot?

Isabel appeared to think for a moment.

ISABEL: Me, Mr Shaw. His mami. I can offer me.

QUENTIN: *Thank you, Ms Velazco.*

Isabel just had time for a swift exhalation of breath and a gulp of water before Ms Harris moved towards her with a deceptively casual warmth that fooled none of us. Least of all my hitherto defiant client, who had been warned to fear the worst. You could almost hear the theme from *Jaws*.

Yet how can you truly prepare for an attack that can come from any direction? I was reminded of that chilling threat my dad talked about, from the days of the IRA campaign. They only have to be lucky once.

No wonder my proud friend and lover looked so terrified. And so alone.

MS HARRIS: *'Me'?... This is what you said, isn't it? You can offer yourself, Señora Velazco. So, might we briefly examine who that 'me', that self, that 'señora' really is?*

QUENTIN: *Your Lordship, if this is a question, it's a trifle all-embracing.*

Personally, I wouldn't have objected at that point but I realise now that our man was just trying to break her momentum. If so, it didn't work. Mind you, straws like these were probably all we had to clutch at. Not sure I liked the '*Señora* business.

MS HARRIS: *I'll be more specific, My Lord. You had an abortion a year ago, Señora Velazco, while Sebastian was living with you. A procedure which is, I believe, illegal under Argentinian law.*

QUENTIN: *Could someone please explain to my learned friend that this is not a criminal trial in Buenos Aires.*

JUDGE: *Ms Velazco brought up the issue of her own character, Mr Shaw. I will allow some exploration.*

MS HARRIS: *Please answer the question, Señora Velazco.*

ISABEL: *Is not a question. But if you ask me did I get pregnant and did I stop myself to be pregnant? Yes. I did.*

MS HARRIS: *Can I ask why you chose to terminate your pregnancy?*

ISABEL: *Because my – my partner and I, we were not any more together. And…*

MS HARRIS: *And you felt the child deserved better than a single parent.*

Isabel looked shocked at being so neatly routed. She shook her head, swirling that strong, beautiful hair around her face almost manically.

And up he went.

QUENTIN: *My Lord!*

The judge simply waved nifty Ms Harris on.

MS HARRIS: *You don't have much luck with relationships, do you, Ms Velazco? I gather there have been quite a few 'partners' over the past three years.*

ISABEL: *I would be a nun but nuns don't have children. Or dance.*

Oh God! Don't get snarky, please Isabel. It wasn't just the judge who was looking at her with disapproval. Quentin was doing a Tango with his eyebrows and Oliver sunk back into his seat with a weary sigh.

MS HARRIS: *Would you say that an apartment with hot and cold running men was the ideal environment for…?*

Quentin didn't even need to leap up this time. Or shout 'Objection!' (Which, unfortunately, we don't actually do here, except on TV shows.)

JUDGE: *I'm sure you could phrase this less judgmentally, Ms Harris.*

MS HARRIS: *I'm sure I could, Your Lordship. Ms Velazco – what is the exact nature of the relationship between yourself and your solicitor?*

And there it was.

I'd be lying if I said we had never expected it to come up. But the speed with which exposure happened – and the state of shock we were still in – had prevented us from composing a fully-finessed response. Actually, there *was* no appropriate response. Finessed or rough-hewn. Even Quentin Shaw had thrown his well-manicured hands up in the air.

Isabel flashed me a look of pure terror, but I noticed that the judge was focussing all his disapproval directly onto Oliver. My best and oldest friend immediately did everything except point a giant cardboard-hand in my direction. But all credit to Quentin Shaw – the poor guy did his best.

QUENTIN: *With the greatest respect, My Lord. This line of questioning is totally irrelevant and scurrilous.*

I really don't think so, Quent, but nice try.

MS HARRIS: *It goes directly to character your honour. And, by the way, I should have said 'trainee-solicitor'.*

JUDGE: *I'll allow it. Is the gentleman we're talking about...?*

I was already pointing at myself. The McKenzie more-than-just-a-friend. Our judge refocussed his judgmental glare in my direction.

MS HARRIS: *Can you answer the question please, Señora Velazco? What is the exact nature of your relationship with this young man?*

Isabel stared at me again, in total panic. I think I just looked blank. I had absolutely nothing to offer. Ms Harris instantly picked this up and ran with it.

MS HARRIS: *Would you like some photographic assistance, Señora?*

There it was.

I had blown it.

What had started out as a bit of a game, the chance of a lifetime for a lying, Hackney wide-boy to get a grubby leg-over with a gorgeously defenceless woman way outside his league – without damaging anything else he might have had going for him (including long-sought job and long-term girlfriend) – had turned into the single-handed destruction of a decent woman's reputation and the future of a totally innocent little boy. Way to go, Ricardo.

So, with nothing more to lose, I stood up – and accidentally knocked over my water-glass. *Shitttt!!!*

ME: *I'll answer it. My Lordship... Your—*

Quentin spun round to me, shaking his flaxen head violently and looking furious. Oliver tugged wildly at my jacket, whilst at the same time mopping his sodden papers. Neither attempt was going to work.

I suddenly thought of Cyril Rosen's old Perry Mason videos, the ones Ollie and I used to watch for a laugh. They were forever having people leap up from the body of the court and confess like mad. Rarely the lawyer though. And rarely with water seeping into their trousers.

JUDGE: *Young man...*

I'm still not sure whether I did it deliberately, or if it was simply the real me finally cracking through the dodgy 'City whiz-kid' veneer. Whatever – it was the East End lad in the sharp whistle'n flute who addressed the court.

ME: *She was a seriously vulnerable client, Your Honour! A desperate mum fighting for her kid? On her own, out of her depth – thousands of miles from home? On a plate! So yeah, okay, I took advantage. Told a few porkies. Whatever worked. I mean excuse me, but it was a piece of cake. Or maybe tortilla...*

I didn't dare look at anyone other than the judge. I couldn't be distracted, even though I knew that the dialogue spouting from my mouth was definitely hokey.

JUDGE: *(Checking his notes) Mr... Davenport? I would advise you to sit down, before you jeopardise an entire career. Which you may very well already have...*

I could feel Oliver and Quentin nodding madly. I was about to ignore them just as madly and carry on – in for a penny, guv – but I didn't get the chance. Somebody was there before me.

ISABEL: *Stop this! Is MY question. I will tell the lady what she is wanting to know, Your Lordship. The truthful story. About this 'relationship'.*

Oh Jesus. No, Isabel!

This was the one time when she surely should have remained shtum. Held her peace. But Isabel was looking straight at me, yet paying no attention to the full-on warning glares I was aiming her way. Even after I sat back down into my damp chair, on the judge's orders.

ISABEL: *Mr Davenport, he did not 'take the advantage'. Not for one second. I am a grown-up woman. Is obvious, yes? And a mother. I know exactly what it is I am doing and what I must do. From the very first moment when I see him, when I see what he is thinking, when I see where he is looking, I know what it is I must do.*

I just stared at her. As it all became so painfully clear.

ISABEL: *My child – he came first.*

It was that simple.

MS HARRIS: *So you are telling this court, Señora Velazco, that you actively, deliberately and calculatedly seduced a young trainee-solicitor, a man at least twelve years your junior, with his whole career ahead of him, simply in order to make sure he worked a little bit harder on your case?*

Isabel nodded. She bloody nodded.

My client admitted this – under oath!

Worst of all, it had the ring of total truth, which made me wonder exactly how stupid and gullible I had been these past few tumultuous weeks. Me who was 'calling all the shots'. *Me –* unscrupulous, ever-so-ruthless, Double-first Davenport!

All those days together, those nights!

But I could also hear, growing louder in my dorkish brain, the warning bells of imminent disaster. I caught the satisfied nod of opposing counsel, echoed at the other side's table. Did my scheming, manipulative, frantic client have to resolve, at this critical juncture, to add insanely-honest to her list?

Then of course she threw me all over again.

ISABEL: *This is how it start. But is not how it finish.*

I'm sorry?

I watched Ms Harris stumble at this. Join the club. She looked at Isabel and then at the judge, totally wrong-footed. Suddenly it wasn't going quite the way she had planned.

MS HARRIS: I think 'started' is quite enough. So, Señora Vel—

JUDGE: I'd like to hear Señora Velazco's response, Ms Harris. Please go on, madam.

I wanted to hear it too. It was like discovering that the favourite song you thought you knew by heart didn't have quite the words you'd been singing.

And now the sound in that small courtroom changed again. As Isabel began to sob.

JUDGE: Ms Velazco? Señora... are you all right?

Ms Harris, predictably, did a reprise of her eye-rolling, head-shaking schtick, but she was hardly the focus of the court's attention.

ISABEL: Si. I am sorry, Your Lordship. Thank you... As I say, it begin as... una estrategia. A – a 'strategy'. Yes? To make sure this guy, he work only on my case and on not anything else. That he do all that is important and is necessary for me. I hear about the lawyers and their piles.

The people in the court found themselves smiling at this. Bad move.

ISABEL: Why do you smile? I say something funny? This is NOT funny! I am sorry that I shout. This is not easy for me... I am telling you that it did work, this – strategy. Si. He do all of this for me, the 'lawyer-ing' he call it, twenty-four hours seven. What lawyer he does this? I am always the very top of his pile.

Now her voice became softer. As the flame in her eyes died down. I could feel the entire court lean forward.

ISABEL: But something it happen here – something I do not ever plan. I do not ever expect. This man, he become not just a lawyer – excuse me, a 'training' lawyer – doing what is his job, for a lot of my money. And not just a person who I can 'use' – as a woman she uses a man – to do everything that I am needing him to do. No. He become a friend. A real friend. Vero. To me, but more especial to my little boy. To Sebastian." She smiled softly then, as she said, *"A McKenzie friend."*

After a moment's pause she spoke again, but so quietly that even in this small, intensely quiet room we struggled to hear her.

ISABEL: And I fall in love with him.

JUDGE: I'm sorry, Ms…?

ISABEL: I FALL IN LOVE WITH HIM!

Oh shit!

ISABEL: Not just for this day, not just for these weeks, that I have the need of him. But – I think – no, I do not think, because I am very sure of this. For the longest time.

I had waited so long to hear her say exactly this. These words. But not now. Not here. With so much at stake. I found myself on my feet again, despite His Lordship's warning.

ME: NO! Now she's taking the blame for me, Your Lordship. She's a nice, kind lady and she wants to save my 'career'. But you've got to believe me, I made all the running." Then I went and sealed both our fates. *C'mon, why the hell would a woman like this – on any normal day – go for me?*

Ms Harris was in there like a Sidewinder.

MS HARRIS: 'A woman like this'. I leave Your Lordship to ponder the very same thing. Thank you, Señora Velazco. No further questions.

No further anything. We were done.

FIFTY-ONE

If being married is lying in bed with your partner, without wanting or needing to have sex, and knowing there would be absolutely no chance even if you did want to, then Isabel and I were as good as wed.

Making love that evening was the farthest thing from our minds. Yet I do believe we were closer to each other, as we lay huddled in silence in that rickety bed, than we had been at any time in our relatively brief encounter.

In just a few hours everything would change. We had no way of knowing in which direction, although we had a pretty good idea after that afternoon's train-crash.

"You were playing me the whole time, weren't you?" I said, as she tucked herself under my outstretched arm.

"Not all of the time," she corrected, then paused. "Si, most of the time."

"So I had you exactly where you wanted me."

She looked puzzled and I realised this was far too complex a construction for someone in the state she was in.

"And I thought I was holding all the cards," I said, which was a bit easier for her.

She just turned to me and smiled. But it wasn't a smile full of mischief or satisfaction. It was almost apologetic, as if she hadn't wanted to take advantage of me the way I had clearly set out to take advantage of her.

And it was telling me that those days were over.

"I was so young last month, wasn't I?" I said.

I was still too young to realise that you can live a relationship without constantly unscrolling it for examination or holding it too close to the light. Yet Isabel soon made it clear that it wasn't 'us' she needed to talk about right then.

"Do you think he still makes up his mind?"

"The judge? He's probably waiting for you to pop round and make it up for him." She looked at me. "What with this thing you have for lawyers."

"You English and the jokes."

I shrugged. She wasn't wrong. It must be how some of us make sense of the world. But she suddenly looked very concerned.

"Richard, do you think you are still a lawyer?" I didn't say anything. This time it was me who didn't want to examine stuff too closely. Or lighten things up. "Just answer the question, Mr Davenport."

***

At first glance the only element that had changed, as we filed into the courtroom the following morning, was the wardrobe of the players. Everything else, from the royal crest to the water jugs, the unheeding sunlight spilling onto the bench, the professional smiles of the ushers, was the same. Yet you could almost taste the difference in the air, as if expectation had a tang and a texture and fear was curling in from every duct in the walls.

We nodded to the opposing side, checking each other out for smugness as we attempted to conceal our feelings behind a ridiculous mask of cool. Making out that it was only a game as opposed to life or death.

The moment the judge walked in, Isabel's powerful fingers found their usual place on the inside of my wrist, right at the pressure-point they apparently recommend to cure sea-sickness. It seemed to be having quite the reverse effect on me.

The judge didn't take long to settle himself, which I took as a gesture of kindness, as he must have known how urgently we awaited whatever he had to say. He spoke in a deliberate but gentle tone, evidently wanting to let us know that he was a thoughtful human being, sensitive to our concerns, and not just the mouthpiece for a process to which circumstance had sadly led us.

It wouldn't have made any difference if he was a robot or a screamer. All we wanted was the result. Forget the edited bloody highlights. So here's what he said, to the best of my recollection.

JUDGE: *A decision like this is never a simple one. When there are two parents who both clearly love their child and wish only the best for him. A father who has weighed priorities and recalibrated his life accordingly. A mother who has sacrificed a homeland, a family and a successful career in order to remain close to her son and to further disrupt his life as little as possible.*

I remember I had stopped breathing. Isabel apparently had too. We would probably keel over before he reached the end.

JUDGE: *On the evidence I have heard, I am not convinced that the mother sent her son to England to live here on a permanent basis.*

This time I squeezed Isabel's hand. Far too soon.

JUDGE: *Perhaps the father misinterpreted. Or indeed chose to. But blame is not the issue. The child is here now – in the country of his birth and early childhood – and has for some months been physically settled here with his father and stepmother. Who – from what I saw and heard yesterday – appear genuinely to be fond of him.*

I couldn't resist a look towards Laurence et al and wished that I hadn't.

JUDGE: As for the unfortunate – and some might say unseemly – manipulation between the mother and her young legal adviser, I suspect that this was more evenly balanced than either of them might care to admit. But matters, in an emotional sense, have clearly – and perhaps even fortuitously – moved on. There has been no suggestion that Sebastian himself suffered unduly because of this situation. In fact, quite possibly, the reverse.

He looked at Isabel and myself at this point, eyes widening above his glasses, almost as if he was sanctioning the relationship. Or, at least, not totally condemning it out of hand. Oliver and Quentin Shaw both shook their heads, like they weren't so sure. *Thanks, guys.* But I could feel Isabel beside me, nodding in time to his words.

I stroked her hand tenderly, wanting to show the judge that he was indeed an astute observer of human nature, which probably went for nothing as he was too busy looking down at his notes. But Isabel did take my own hand in hers, not for the court but for me.

JUDGE: Yet above and beyond all this, the decision I make has to be in the best interests of the child – of Sebastian.

And here it comes. Suddenly I wanted that infuriating little boy right here with us, the curious child who had, against all expectations, become such a part of my life. To see his face, to hear his sweet – albeit occasionally grating – voice, to feel his glow. It seemed so wrong to be in this place without him.

JUDGE: I believe there has always been a very strong bond between mother and son. And I am inclined to reflect that this bond – whilst having been subjected to the most rigorous and unfortunate of tests – has proved itself to be more than resilient.

It is for this reason I have determined that Sebastian – still only nine years of age – should be returned as soon as possible to his mother's care. I would like to think that she and the father, as reasonable, loving parents, will regularly come together – by whatever means – to make important decisions concerning their son. And so…

We didn't hear the rest. The legal bit. We didn't need to. That was the moment when Isabel lost it. With a tiny yelp that perhaps only I caught, closely followed by one enormous sigh which most of the City of London would have picked up, she sank right back into her chair. I thought for a moment that she had passed out. It was almost as if the pressure of all that instantly expelled air, held in for so long, had forced her downwards as her centre of gravity suddenly plummeted.

I sneaked another look towards Laurence, trying extremely hard not to appear triumphant. I expected to see him sad and totally gutted, as his dear wife tried bravely but vainly to console him. Yet if I had to describe in a word how he came across at that moment, it was 'thwarted'. Which made me feel that Mr Justice Greenfield had played an absolute blinder and deserved however many puddings were set in front of him.

Oliver and Quentin Shaw were shaking hands with each other and with Isabel, doing their level best with the respectful dignity stuff. I had known Oliver since we were seven – he was exultant.

I kissed Isabel very gently on the lips, while she held me close. That familiar glow was returning to her face, like one of those magic colouring-books that kids have, only the water here was coming from her tears. It was over. After these few tempestuous, life-changing weeks and to no-one's greater surprise than my own, we had done it. All credit to Quentin, who was now smiling gently down on us both from above. He had been masterly.

I couldn't wait to tell my mum and dad.

FIFTY-TWO

I could, of course, have travelled home with my parents after the hearing. Or accompanied a thoroughly drained but wholly contented Isabel, as indeed she had implored me to do, perhaps even stopping for a weepy, celebratory lunch on what little funds I had left. But there would be time for all that. I was a lawyer, my day was less than half over. And I had work to do.

Dimpy almost leapt on me as I walked into reception. Her phone was ringing but she knew they would call back. They always do.

"*Well?*"

"Darcy, Cracknell *and* Davenport," I said, which of course was bollocks, but I was on a roll. She screamed then gave me her hugest, sloppiest kiss, because words wouldn't do for the genuine delight I could feel surging through her. Then she burst into tears. The clients sitting all around us looked a bit bemused. But they had to feel encouraged – it's always good to be associated with winners. Especially winners who seem to care so much.

I pointed towards Barney's office and she squeezed my arm. So he was clearly there and on his own.

I didn't even bother with the wrong Joan Collins. I was too preoccupied to trade barbs or even pointedly to ignore her, so I just ignored her in an unpointed way and strolled in to see the boss.

Naturally he didn't look up. I suppose anyone who popped in without an appointment was, by definition, one of his inferiors, so they could stand and wait. I stood and waited. Then I thought sod it.

"Dunno whether you heard. The 'hot tamale' won. Despite you and your little pals."

He looked up at this, but he didn't look happy. He certainly didn't look like the boss of a firm that had just won a major case. "Bully for you," he grunted. "Now go bill your girlfriend – and that isn't a new sexual practice."

I didn't say anything. I just stared at him. Because I had finally worked something out. Something that suddenly seemed so obvious.

"Christ, I'm a dick!" I said. "You didn't just try to overload me with work. You *wanted* me to have a… a thing with her. From the get-go. It suited your new 'associates'. And what was good for them was gonna be *so* good for Darcy, Cracknell." He just looked at me, all definable expression erased from his pasty face. *"You told them where to send the sodding cameras!"*

Barney smiled a familiar smile. He must have been practising with his new homeys, Laurence and Hugo. Maybe there's a club they all go to.

"Nothing wrong with a suspicious mind, matey." His eyes narrowed. I believe he genuinely hated me. "Even good lawyers have those."

I realised I had nothing more to lose. "There's an old legal expression they taught us at 'Watford Tech'. Go fuck yourself."

I couldn't very well hang around after that, could I? If ever there was an exit line. Exit office, exit firm. Exit career.

As I left the room, I knew that he had simply gone back to work.

***

The industrial-strength bravado, that was lighting me up like a flare, powered me past an evil-eyed Miss Collins and as far as reception. Dimpy was chatting to Leila and Evan. Suddenly that same bravado took the express lift down to my bowels and I felt myself shaking inside. I knew I had gone pale and even the waiting clients were wondering what the hell was wrong. I must have looked like a victorious athlete whose dope-test had just come up positive.

Like a scene from one of the crap sit-coms my mum and dad love, the angry Irishman chose this exact moment to storm into the practice, one enormous hand pointing straight out, the other hidden behind his back. He stared ruddily at me and I only saw the concealed mitt as it swung round towards my face.

I recoiled with a yelp, instinctively closing my eyes. Which rather upset poor Mr Ryan, as he had assumed I would appreciate a bottle of Jameson's, tied with a ribbon, after the way I had helped him finally to screw his wife 'like she screwed him'.

Of course I accepted it gratefully. Nodded to my former colleagues. And quietly left the building forever.

I knew a bench by the river, in the heart of legal London, which wasn't the Queens Bench but would do for what I had in mind.

It had been that sort of a day.

FIFTY-THREE

"Your car's fucked."

Guess who?

I had decided to drive over to Isabel's flat, on the first day of Sebastian's tenure, with a very special type of welcome gift. That potty-mouthed, scrotum-scratching feature no family home should be without.

"I *know* it's fucked!" I told him, as we rattled to an asthmatic halt. "And don't say fucked."

"If it was a baby rabbit, I'd drown it," he said, which gave me a delightful glimpse of what nurture was doing to nature in his neck of the Hackney woods.

Isabel was standing outside the block when we arrived that Sunday. She would probably have heard the MiG from half a mile away. Or smelled its occupant. We walked up the stairs together, (ex-)lawyer and ex-client, hand clutching hand, manoeuvring around the impressive cluster of small suitcases and toy-filled cardboard-boxes that filled her narrow hallway. Joanne was there too, helping out, but when she saw Gerald she swiftly shrank back into the kitchen.

Sebastian launched himself out of his bedroom. "Wanker!" he cried.

"Fuckwit!" responded his new best amigo. (I thanked God

the other side had never found out about Gerald.)

Joanne shouted back into the kitchen, where I realised her own kids were cowering. "Guys, meet your first real delinquent."

"*Sos un bolodo!*" said the victorious S, who was now apparently on a bilingual roll.

Isabel was smiling with the simple joy I felt I had been waiting on forever. The glow that says I've got my little boy back and all's right with the world, even if he is now putting his own hand down his trousers.

The boys ran off to demolish Sebastian's bedroom, while Joanne closed the kitchen door. I had no idea whether this was out of uncharacteristic sensitivity or simply for her own protection. Isabel grabbed hold of my arms and giggled with pure excitement. Clearly there was something she couldn't wait to tell me.

"Tomorrow morning I will take my little boy to his school," she gushed. "As I was used to. Tomorrow and every morning. Like a normal mother! But you will stay, yes – for the coffee?" I shook my head and she laughed that wonderfully earthy, dirty laugh. "Is all right now," she smiled, cheekily. "You and the old client. Is legitimate." She chuckled with delight at her correct usage of an unexpected word.

"Yeah, I'm not a bastard any more." Right over her head. "You just do your settling in. I've got to try to fix old MiG before it's too late. And... a couple of other things."

I didn't want to lumber her with my career plans right then. Why spoil her day? But I could tell from the lines creasing her brow that she was ahead of me and a long way from unconcerned. I gave her an appreciative kiss on the lips and turned to go.

"Gerald's uncle said he'd pick him up later," I assured her. "Just tell our friend not to play Strip Cluedo with Joanne's kids. It's his new favourite game at my mum's."

I was almost at the door when she grabbed me.

She held onto me so tightly I could barely breathe. A tad

unexpected but I can't say I wasn't pleased. Jesus, I really did love this woman, I had absolutely no doubt on that score. But this didn't amaze me half as much as the Ripley Believe it or Not, *Guinness Book of Records*, Hold the Front Page fact that she patently felt the same. It was right there in the court records. And in those gleaming, tiger eyes. What were the chances?

Now all I needed was a career to go with it.

FIFTY-FOUR

Of course the following day the car didn't start at all.

If I'd had a gun I would have just shot the poor old girl there and then and put us both out of our misery. A gun going off in Hackney wouldn't have caused that much of a stir. It wasn't like it was a car backfiring.

Not that I needed a car, what with having no job to go to. It was still too early to be totally sure that no law-firm would ever employ me – but I was pretty sure. Once good old Barney spread the word.

Yet that early Monday morning I still felt reasonably optimistic. And I really did need to get somewhere in a hurry. With the new mood of goodwill-to-all pervading the household, I knew just the man. I would even pay him.

"You bloody won't, lad," was what my dad said, as I knew he would. "Get your skates on. I know a ruddy marvellous new route. Fact."

It was so easy I was almost ashamed of myself. But I had been ashamed of myself with such regularity over the preceding few weeks that this seemed like a minor infraction. And at least this time I didn't have to lie to anyone.

"I really want to see her face when she comes out of that school."

My mum melted at this. She didn't read all those paperback romances without knowing love when she saw it.

"I still like to see your mum's face," said my dad, smiling at her. "Well maybe not first thing in the morning."

My mum just gave us one of her affectionate 'what will I do with you both' shakes of the head, a gesture that until very recently had figured in my catalogue of the crucifyingly annoying, but suddenly made me realise, to my shame, that I had made way too much of those unfavourable comparisons with Ollie's family. As my best pal himself once said – the grass is always Golders Greener…

She waved us off down the road.

Naturally, I sat in the back of the cab. Aside from making it obvious to flaggers that he wasn't picking up, it was also the way Dad liked to chat. Looking straight at you in his mirror. I was just waiting for him to ask me if I was Ronnie Davenport's son. Which I would have been proud to say I was.

I was especially proud that his talk of hitherto undiscovered routes wasn't just talk. The man was as good as his paragraphs. We were outside that little South London school just as the final stragglers were being dragged in by their mums or au pairs. (It was indeed a private school – thank you, Laurence Menzies.)

The caretaker was observing us carefully from inside the school gates.

"They don't like grown men watching schools," said my dad, who had probably waited outside a few schools in his time.

After we had been sitting there for about fifteen minutes and the playground was totally deserted, the man ambled over. My father explained that we were waiting for someone, but that we had begun to realise we'd missed her. I suspected that, in her excitement, Isabel had over-anticipated how long it would take, without courtesy of a BMW, to ensure that her little boy wasn't accused of some sort of *mañana* complex on his first day of the new regime.

"What now?" he asked.

"I'll walk, Dad. It's okay." I opened the door. "You're way out of your 'hood'."

"Shut that door and just tell me where I'm going."

Isabel's flat wasn't far from the school. Someone had done her homework. But she was taking a while to answer the door, after my dad had puffed up all the stairs. I wondered for the first time if he was getting old. I hadn't thought of it before and I didn't want to think about it now.

"*Isabel*," I called, when she hadn't responded to several hearty knocks. "Hi…? We just went to the school."

"Perhaps she's gone to the shops," said my dad, still catching his breath. "Women do that."

I shrugged. I really couldn't expect to surprise someone and then be surprised that they weren't expecting me. I knelt down and found the key under the mat.

My dad laughed almost embarrassedly, as if this was an aspect of his son's life to which he shouldn't be party. Like condoms falling out of a wallet.

I let him into the tiny flat. He tiptoed into the hallway, clearly discomforted to be intruding. But there was nothing much for him to see – the place was deserted.

Deserted doesn't quite sum it up. Vacated. Packed-up. Abandoned. Except, of course, for some boxes of toys and games in the second bedroom. But no tatty giraffe.

I just stared at my dad but he was already wandering into the kitchen. He laid his hand on the kettle, as if he was somehow expecting a cup of tea. Beside it was an envelope, on which was scrawled just my name. The shortened version.

"They've not been gone long," said my dad.

I grabbed the letter. I could read it on the way.

FIFTY-FIVE

I never saw it coming.

I admit it.

Perhaps somebody else might have caught on quicker. Somebody with a double-first in deception.

I don't think I stopped gasping and shaking my stupid head all the way to the airport. Aside, of course, from when I was verbally whipping my poor dad, like a trusty but knackered steed, to go just that bit faster. Bless him, he was already doing the best he could this side of prison, revealing hitherto uncharted 'corridors' with every turn of the wheel.

I kept up the conversation from the back, but I was really just talking to myself.

"She didn't expect me to find the note so fast, did she?" No response – it didn't need one. "Well, she thinks she's the only one who does fucking surprises."

"Traffic's touch and go this time of day." My poor dad. He had no idea what to say and when in doubt, traffic fills the gaps.

"Can't you go just a bit faster?" I urged. "*Please,* Dad! I'll tell you if I see a camera."

***

I was still talking and cursing as we approached Heathrow, which was bloody miles from where we had started. But I was a lot closer to working out what had been going on.

My dad just kept looking at me in the mirror, his old heart breaking at the same time as mine was trying to burst its way out of my chest.

"It wasn't love," I said, mostly to myself, but loud enough for him to hear every word. Especially without his taxi-drivers' news station blaring. "Oh no. It wasn't love," I repeated. "She *played* me, Dad. She played me like a pro. Right to the very end. And all the time I thought I was playing her. No – that I was trusting her."

"I'm sure she didn't—" attempted my dad, with total futility.

"*Brilliant!*" I almost enthused. Because I had to admire it. I truly did. "She managed to convince everyone. Laurence, his people, even the bloody judge." My dad looked confused; I had forgotten he hadn't actually been in court. "That she was here and she was staying! Here, in good old London, for keeps. And what made it so fucking credible? The icing on the tortilla? *Because she had me!*"

I paused for effect. My dad was concentrating on which line looked the shortest. Somewhere I wondered – and I still do – if he had been waiting for a breathless dash to the airport all his working life. Who knew that it would be in the gift of his own son?

"Me!" I persisted, flagellating myself with every word. "Her little Hackney toy-boy. *'Che! I fall in lurve weeth heem!'* Bullshit!"

We were en route to short-term parking. Together we had worked out which terminal while we drove. At least I hoped we had.

"And, of course, Laurence had to give her back the kid's passport, didn't he?" I told the universe. "Along with his other worldly goods."

"Son," was all my dad said. This was killing him. I don't think the bad language helped. He began to weave in and out of the traffic. Cars were hooting him – he was being everything we hate about cabbies and I loved him for it.

But I knew it was too late.

FIFTY-SIX

As soon as we were inside the terminal, I grabbed someone in a uniform. "How do I find out if a person's on a flight?"

The man extricated himself with a sigh, like there's always one. "Security, sir. You don't."

We wandered around, looking totally lost and I imagine quite suspicious. Unless they were a championship basketball-player wearing lifts, I didn't imagine there was a chance in hell of one person spotting another on a crowded, September-morning forecourt in the world's busiest airport. Especially if they were probably not there in the first place.

So I wasn't expecting the over-demonstrative thump my father landed me on my chest. Painfully, I followed his gaze towards the departure gate. Of course I had to see those legs again, didn't I, as they bent so effortlessly to fix a little boy's new SpiderMan satchel.

"ISABEL!!!"

A load of people turned, who can't all have been called Isabel. But the one person who was didn't turn. She swiftly stood up and, pausing only to grab satchel-boy, scampered at full-pelt to the gate.

I was too late.

Or I would have been, had Sebastian not broken away at that moment and turned back.

"*Rick!*"

The little boy ran towards me and leaped onto my leg, almost the way dogs do but without the humping. He had never done it before – no child had, or at least no child I liked – but he had a grip of steel and it felt like he would be holding on forever. And it felt like I wouldn't have minded if he did.

Isabel seemed torn. Yet, of course, she had no alternative but to follow. After all, he was why she came, wasn't he? If not entirely why she was leaving.

"Going somewhere nice?" I asked her.

I could feel my father shuffling around, like he wanted to be on the exit-lane to anywhere-else.

"Please, Richard…"

"No! Not '*Richard*', Isabel. Not now. How could you do this?" I left 'to me' unspoken.

"You see the note?" she murmured. "I write this note."

I grabbed the crumpled note from my pocket, waved it at her then threw it onto the ground. All very dramatic and I hoped nobody official would ask me to pick it up.

Sebastian was still on my leg. Without thinking I began to swing him around, which he seemed to love. But I was starting to cry and I didn't want him to see this.

"Sometimes, Isabel, 'sorry' doesn't quite cut it. Or *lo siento*."

She nodded a greeting to my dad, who was making inordinately silly faces at Sebastian. The boy seemed to respond. He certainly wasn't listening to the grown-up talk, which I reckon was the purpose of Dad's bizarre distraction.

"We must go home, Rick," she said. "If I tell you this before today – I think perhaps I will not be going. And then I make both of us, you and me, so unhappy."

I looked down at the little boy. She read this as the question I had intended.

"He say to me he will like this also. I do not force…" She saw my face. "*Ask* him, Rick! *Por favor!* I know I am not the saint, but I am not kidnapper. And Laurence, he will visit. Whenever he want. With his new family."

Sebastian was smiling. I looked across to my dad who, for some mysterious reason, was setting free the various blades on the huge Swiss Army Knife he always kept in his pocket. What was he going to do – sever the boy's clinging arms at the wrist?

"Ever seen one of these, son?" he asked him.

Sebastian clearly hadn't. The boy gave me back my leg and went across to take a look.

It was then that I must have made a lucky throw of the mental dice, because I suddenly felt myself shimmying up a ladder and looking down on the whole, hitherto slithery picture.

"*QUENTIN SHAW!*" I almost yelled it. In fact I think I did. "He *told* you to do a runner! 'Convince the court you're all for staying in London, Isabel heart. Ooh I know, even tell them you're properly in love with the little Cockney geezer and that he's a keeper. That'll swing it. But, oh by jingo, once we've won – *hasta la vista, baby*.'"

I had no idea who was writing my script – and if I did I would have sacked them – but the words just came tumbling out like rupees hurled to Indian beggar-children.

"So, how *was* your boarding-school chum?" I continued. "Did you take it up the…?"

"NO!" She stopped me. Probably just as well. "Okay, we do talk. About this," she sighed. "Quent – Mr Shaw and me. But is my idea."

I wasn't totally convinced.

That was when she touched me.

And something which, until this moment, had been so beautiful was now the most exquisitely painful thing a person could do. She might as well have begun cutting me with my dad's knife, something I still worried, with a corner of my frenzied mind, that Sebastian was going to do to himself any minute. He had moved with my father just stabbing distance away.

Isabel was looking anxiously back at the departure gate. "Please Rick – I must… I have to…"

What more could I do – call the police? It did cross my mind but, of course, I just nodded. And looked back at the 'lads'. My father understood, disarmed the Swiss Army knife and handed it over to Sebastian.

"*Dad?*" I shook my head and turned to the little boy. "Sebastian, mate, I'm so sorry. They're not going to allow you to take that thing through." I knelt down to his eye-level and held both his bony little shoulders. He was staring straight into my teary face, with an openness that engulfed me like a sudden, intense pain. Those conker-brown eyes, once so shuttered and angry, now moist and bright and drawing me straight in. I found it hard to speak.

How had it come to this? That a stroppy, scrawny kid, from half-way across the world, had wormed his way through years of prickly undergrowth and managed to find my heart. Or at least show me that I had one. "I'll – I'll send you something better. I promise." I told him, croakily. "Lots of things. All the time."

The boy nodded and passed the knife back to my dad. "Please give it to Gerald," he said.

Isabel and I caught each other's eye and immediately shared a shudder. For that brief, sweet second we were as close as we had ever been. Or were ever going to be. And I suddenly knew without question that what she had said about us in court last week, despite today, despite everything, she truly meant.

Yes, I'm sure she did.

They walked away. Mother and son, hand-in-hand. Going back. Going home.

And I watched. Because it was all I could do.

I felt my dad's arm around my shoulder, something I didn't recall his ever having done before. We're not a touchy family. Yet I folded back into it as if we had been doing this for as long as I could remember.

"Until you become a parent, son, you just don't…" He shook his head, in wonder. "You'd do ruddy anything for them. Fact. You would. Ruddy anything."

"Screw anyone?" I mumbled into his shoulder.

He didn't respond, but just led me back towards the cab.

"You did good, son," he said.

"Then why does it feel so bad?"

I think he was already onto discovering the new North-West London passage, but perhaps the extra squeeze he gave me was sufficient.

I hoped she didn't sit behind someone fat on the plane.

12 YEARS AND
A FEW MONTHS LATER

Ex postcard facto

There's a world of difference between a life-story and a story that changes your life.

I reached thirty-five this year. Hardly a pivotal age, you might say, now that three-score-and-ten has ceased to be our accepted span. But it was Isabel's age when I met her. And I suddenly began to wonder if I would be the person I am right now, the parent I am right now, had Isabel Velazco not walked into my office. (Okay, into Barney's office.)

I have a bigger office these days. Not huge but sufficient for me – and for my clients. People who want to move house, dissolve their marriage gently, make a will. The stuff Oliver used to do. And still does, bless him, in the room next door to mine.

Cyril Rosen retired last year, so he can enjoy more time with his wife and their lovely grandchildren, the ones with the impenetrable Welsh names. Courtesy of Ollie and former client Eirwen. Law Society, take note.

If I mention that I had another postcard from Buenos Aires just last week, you'll only think 'How convenient'. Fine, but I'm gazing at it, right next to the framed picture of my wife and twins. (No, I didn't marry Sophie. I know from Oliver that somebody did, and I can only wish her joy.)

I hope I'm a good parent. How can you ever know? What I

do know is that I had the best teachers and a summer of quite intensive tuition.

The photo is also nudging the pile of cases I should be attending to, rather than finishing this, my first and hopefully sole confession.

Yes, I still have the pile, only no one is kicking it around these days. (Yet, inevitably, there's still always someone on top.)

The postcard is of the current Argentinian soccer team and the message scrawled on the back reads 'England Are Wankers!' Apparently my young friend – a law graduate now (mea culpa!) – is not far wrong. I was certainly wrong about him – he's well-built, sporty and rather handsome. I have a framed photo of him also, behind me on my wall. He's sitting in a lush garden with a quite lovely, middle-aged woman of a certain elegance, whom I used to know and to whom I hope life is being kind. Perhaps kinder than I was, at least at the start.

I realise now that there's someone who needs to see the postcard. He's out there in reception, expertly putting up some new pine shelves above the desk. I can spy him through the doorway, a broad-shouldered, twenty-two year-old man, builder's crack just peeking out above his paint-stained jeans. And a well-used Swiss Army knife dangling from his leather belt.

ACKNOWLEDGMENTS

I'd like to thank Alan Mahar, for his incisive editing and generous encouragement and The Literary Consultancy for making the match. Thanks also to my dear friend Karol Griffiths, doyenne of script-editors, for her acuity, kindness and support.

Muchas gracias to Elena Pollard, for the authentically colloquial Argentinian.

Finally, thanks to Chiara and her lovely staff at Costa Coffee, Pinner. If there's a best-novel-written-almost-entirely-in-Costa award, I would willingly share the podium with them.

ABOUT THE AUTHOR

PAUL A. MENDELSON graduated from Cambridge with a first in Law, which did him little good as he very swiftly left legal practice to create award-winning advertising campaigns. He then moved from 30-seconds to 30-minutes to create several hit BBC comedy series, including BAFTA-nominated 'May to December', 'So Haunt Me' and 'My Hero', then back to ITV for the much-acclaimed Martin Clunes cancer drama 'Losing It'. He co-created 'Neighbors From Hell' for DreamWorks Animation and writes regularly for BBC Radio 4 Drama. He has several feature films in development.

Paul's first novel for children, *Losing Arthur*, is being published by The Book Guild. Paul is married with two daughters and lives in North London.